Supreme Truth

W. Mace Brady

ISBN: 1494904497
ISBN 13: 9781494904494
Library of Congress Control Number: 2014900196
CreateSpace Independent Publishing Platform
North Charleston, South Carolina

Dedicated to my wife, Janet

PREFACE

This is a work of fiction. Although some real-world names, characters, organizations, places, and situations are used to enhance the authenticity of the story, any similarities to real-world persons, units, places, or situations are coincidental and all portrayals are purely the product of the author's imagination.

PROLOGUE

JAPAN

1985

No sooner had he entered the simple, one-story wooden structure, to observe another new-wave religion in action, than he noticed the guru's flock begin to rouse. Kiyohide Haruka followed the gaze of a couple of followers, who were the first to glance up from their meditative trance, to see what caused them to stir. Haruka surmised that from their vantage point, the guru appeared to be slowly rising while in his lotus pose. His followers looked on in awe as they watched the guru levitate before their eyes. *God was lifting their spiritual leader toward the heavens in this, their house of worship.* During this short episode, much of the congregation was able to see what was occurring before the guru settled back down on the platform.

From Haruka's vantage point, he saw something different. A slight smile crossed his face. *Well, I'll be damned,* he thought, *the illustrious guru is a fraud.*

Having just entered, Haruka was the only one standing, observing from a height that allowed him to see what the guru was doing. His audience had been purposefully seated at the ground level. From their viewpoint, they couldn't see how the guru was using his leg strength to slowly raise his body, giving the illusion that he was capable of drawing power from the almighty during their religious ritual.

One of the guru's assistants noticed Haruka standing and quickly walked to his side, hoping to divert his attention, but he was too late. Haruka had already seen what he wanted. *The incapacitated blind man had a pretty good gig going for himself.*

The man offered to find him space to sit on the carpeted floor.

But Haruka simply held up his hand to ward off his approach, then said, "I'm here to speak with your spiritual leader."

"May I ask the purpose of your visit?"

"Tell him," he nodded toward the guru, "I've come to make him an offer."

"Sir, could you be more specific?"

Haruka looked him straight in the eye, ignored his question, and said, "I'll return with a few of my associates at the conclusion of these services, and then I can discuss this with him. Make sure he's prepared to meet with me. We shouldn't have any interruptions."

The guru's assistant nodded. He could respond no differently than the way a guru's assistant was expected to react. He knew what the visitor had witnessed and knew this man should be taken seriously.

Haruka returned and saw the same assistant, now among four others. These others had been strategically located throughout the congregation earlier. The assistant had his forearm partially extended for the legally blind guru to use in guiding him down from the stand.

Haruka approached, to place himself before the guru. The guru's assistant saw him and whispered something into his master's ear. Haruka could see the master nod.

Haruka gave the assistant a kindly smile, looked to the guru, and said, "I see that you can use my assistance."

The guru responded, showing a rather benign smile. "I appreciate that, but I wasn't aware that I needed any additional help beyond those who already are here to assist me."

"Oh, but you do, for I would not have allowed you to make a mistake, as you just did."

"And what mistake would that be?" The guru replied innocently.

"No one should be allowed to enter during your service, yet alone stand during your ceremony."

Playing along, the guru responded, "Yes, that would seem rude. I'll take that under advisement. I appreciate you providing suggestions, but you seem to have me at a disadvantage. I don't know who you are or why you are here."

"My name is Kiyohide Haruka. I can provide a service for you. I've made some inquiries into your activities and organization, and I believe we can work well together."

"Meaning?"

"Our working together can be of mutual benefit."

"And how might that be?"

"It seems in the legal arena, you've made a number of enemies who seem unhappy with you."

"As much as we try to please everyone, there is always someone who may be unhappy."

"Yes, but I understand that some are willing to take you to court to regain what they have lost to the church. Some, it seems, have donated great portions of their personal wealth. Now that they are having misgivings about what the church represents, they want their money back."

"A minor misunderstanding. Once someone donates, it's difficult to rationalize why it would be appropriate to return that money. Besides, all of our money is tied up in a number of honorable causes. I'm sure the courts will see it my way."

"You speak too lightly of your problems. I'm not just talking about your legal issues, or even the money it will cost you. You should not allow these people to leave your church, let alone speak negatively in public."

"You speak as if I could stop it."

"No, *you* may not be able to stop it, but my associates and I can. We can even manage your recruiting and financial situation in such a way that I can guarantee you'll expand beyond your greatest dreams. At your current rate, you're doomed to failure in a very short time period."

"You intrigue me, Mr. Haruka. I'm willing to listen to your offer."

"I thought you would be."

"I have a private room behind the stage. Please join me." Haruka stood back to allow the guru's assistant to lead them into the adjoining back room where they sat around a simple, rectangular table with folding chairs.

The guru spoke more openly, now that they were in a private room. "I have a feeling you're talking about more unorthodox methods of keeping my followers in line, so to speak. What makes you think I might condone your methods?"

"Your exhibition today was quite remarkable. You seem to show exceptional leg strength."

"My assistant has informed me about what you witnessed."

"As well he should. But I wasn't criticizing what you did. I commend you on your, let's say, creativity. You see, I have experience in these matters."

"Tell me."

"Until a few months ago, I was associated with the Unification Church, in Seoul."

"I see. You chose to leave?"

"Let's just say they did not approve of my methods, as effective as they might have been."

"I see, and what did they most disapprove of?"

"Ah, good. Now I see that we can talk more openly about your greatest need. My methods of keeping members true to the church were where we excelled. We, too, had members who began to have doubts about the church. That's when I began a process to allow them the choice to leave the church, with the church's blessing. But that would only occur if they successfully completed the process. It required them to explore, in depth, their true religious beliefs and values."

"You were successful in convincing them they should stay?"

"One hundred percent. Yes," Haruka added with a sly grin.

"Remarkable."

"By the time they completed this procedure, the fear of God was so ingrained in them that they always chose to stay, fearing God's reprisal, or ours, if they left."

"I see. But why would I want you to join me?"

"Because beyond that, I can also recruit the followers and profits that will make you the most renowned spiritual leader in the land."

The guru's eyebrows lifted in interest, with Haruka's last statement. "How would you go about this?" he inquired.

"For starters, I will organize and monitor your organization to guarantee you success, and, to show you how serious I am, I will invest eight million of my own funds."

"While I'm impressed with your demonstration of commitment, it feels to me more like a corporate takeover."

"Maybe so, but you'll be well compensated. You'll have more power than you've ever experienced before. My investment of people and money will ensure you succeed. I wouldn't be able to do this without you. Besides, you really don't have any other alternative…you see, your downfall will occur if your followers discovered you are a fraud."

"It seems you have left me with few options."

"Let me be very clear about your options. You can either succeed as the icon of the church, with me taking the lead, or you can suffer your own downfall, without me."

Chapter 1

EASTERN RUSSIA

DECEMBER 1992

B odhisattva, otherwise known as "boss," drained his martini glass with a smug look of satisfaction. He placed the empty crystal flute on the club car's table and gazed out at a spectacular view of Russia's open tundra, highlighted by a deep blue sky. He had plenty to feel good about. He had come a long way since leaving, rather being banished by, the Unification Church's Reverend Sun Myung Moon eight years earlier.

"Thanks for having faith in me, boss," his associate stated.

"Well, you've certainly earned the opportunity to be part of this meeting," the boss responded. "Besides, it's important for them to see who'll oversee your part of the operation. I just want to know if you can handle it. Can you?"

"Yes, I can. Do you have any doubts?"

"I'm not the one who needs to be convinced. Don't leave them with any uncertainties. You do understand the importance of your role, correct?"

The associate, Hideo Mori, could only hope that he wasn't showing the nervousness that was beginning to stir in his stomach. "I understand," he said softly, avoiding eye contact with the bodhisattva.

The boss watched him carefully. *Not making eye contact is a giveaway. At least I didn't see a discernible change in his expression*, the boss thought. *I need to put him at ease now that I've given him another little test.*

"We've come a long way together, you and I. Like I've said, you've earned the right to be here. It's easy for me to want to reward those who have been loyal over the years, and of the thirty of you who have been with me since leaving the Unification Church, your performance has been most outstanding, especially what you've done with our weapons program. I see that I made the right choice making you our minister of science and technology. Even greater things may be in store for you under our new government."

Haruka could see Mori begin to relax after the last comment.

With regained composure and calm, Mori replied, "Thanks to your recruiting our latest group member from the IV Kurchatov Institute of Energy, we can consider our nuclear weapons team complete." He was referring to Russia's oldest nuclear weapons laboratory.

"It's because of the progress you all have made that I was able to go forward and reestablish contact with an old acquaintance of ours to the north. I even sent him a sample to demonstrate what we're capable of. He, in turn, gave it to another 'man of influence' within the inner circle of their government who had expressed an interest in what our army of scientists could provide. He wouldn't say who the man was, but obviously we now know someone close to the Dear Leader is interested, at least enough to have their ambassador to Russia meet with us. He made it clear though that no one must know about this 'unofficial meeting.' You do understand that, don't you?"

"Of course," Mori responded.

"I believe that's why he scheduled this meeting for when he was making the trip back, by rail, rather than by flying," the boss clarified. "Remember, I'll do the talking. You're just here for added assurance."

Mori nodded. "Care for another drink?"

"No. I don't want to lose my edge."

The boss's new partner drained the last of his own drink and turned to wave the waitress over. Instead, he decided to stand and approach her himself.

Haruka glanced over. Her attractiveness didn't go unnoticed, or the fact that the luxury VIP railcar was empty, except for two other patrons for her to attend to.

"Our company should be here any minute," the boss warned.

"I'll just be a moment," Mori responded. "Just going to warm her up a bit," he added with a sly grin.

Mori's actions brought back thoughts of his earlier days. He remembered how he worked to make contacts and recruit, as well as send out the cult's missionaries—people he had personally trained—throughout the country to establish new branches. At first, that had been sort of fun, even exciting. Even then, he enjoyed his journeys by train, winding through the countryside in luxurious style. On the railroad, it was perfectly acceptable for rich foreigners, like him, to also travel in such a manner. It didn't hurt that he was operating under the cover of the Ukraine Ministry of Industry and Trade, using credentials that he had acquired with the help of a KGB official, Vitaly Masenko. Mingling with the rich allowed him the opportunity to draw in those who would most benefit his cause financially, usually those he'd targeted prior to the train trip. The long ride helped him capture their attention. He remembered, too, that his powers of persuasion also worked well on the ladies.

Haruka recollected how he had to make adjustments, following a series of back-to-back recruiting trips to Russia. Some of those who he traveled with were so devoted to the guru's religious façade that they complained about his travels and extravagant spending. They had grumbled, "Kiyohide Haruka's too busy chasing Russian women." *I'll have to remember to caution Hideo,* Kiyohide thought. *That little episode caused me to pay penance to show that I was, in fact, dedicated to the church's ways. Now, at least, I know to buffer myself with my trusted associates—those thirty members of the cult who stayed with me after being banished in South Korea. While I didn't meet the guru until arriving in Japan, at least we both recognize that we need each other.*

Haruka watched Mori try to impress the cocktail waitress. His ability to make an impression was improving. She smiled and didn't seem to be in any hurry to move on.

Ah, the possibilities, Haruka thought. *With what we can achieve as a result of today's meeting there can be no end to our power. We'll no longer just have to maintain a covert existence behind high-walled compounds located around the world. We'll be able to live as a sovereign nation. I'm good, really good, not just as a negotiator, but a master manipulator who can get others to do my bidding. Even Mori's beginning to get excited. If he only knew what other plans I have in store for him, as well as the others."*

Haruka stood and moved to the railcar's furthest window. Its walls were inlaid with richly stained wood panels, a plush red carpet stretched from wall to wall, and it was furnished with a series of black leather lounge chairs, strategically clustered about the room. The décor matched Haruka's polished demeanor. He moved in a fluid, graceful manner that belied his simmering arrogance. At the window he stopped and took in the view of the mountains.

He was separating himself from any distractions in order to ponder the issues he would need to discuss in just moments. It was important for him to perform at his peak, as he would be negotiating with the government dignitaries. They needed to accept his terms if he was to be successful in this proceeding.

From the far end of the luxury railcar, Haruka heard the click of the door and turned to watch, as it swung open. He stood near the car's rear window, observing, as three husky men stepped through. He could see that they were government officials. They just had *that look.* Each scanned the lounge car as they entered. One stayed next to the door, and the other two approached the center of the compartment. One of the pair spoke to the two gentlemen sitting in lounge chairs near the center of the open bar. There was a short discussion before the two gentlemen rose and exited the rear of the car. One of the three men, flipped the placard over to show the car was no longer available, and locked the rear door before standing at his new post.

One of the other men spoke first with the associate and then with the cocktail waitress. Mori responded to a question by gesturing toward his boss. He then turned back to the waitress while the official walked toward Haruka.

The official approached and with a slight bow asked, "You are Mr. Haruka?"

Haruka also bowed and answered, "I am."

The official introduced himself as the ambassador's assistant and interpreter and invited Haruka to join him in the center of the railcar where the chairs were grouped.

Mori excused himself from the waitress, who had just handed him a note before quickly exiting the railcar. When Mori joined Haruka, they both began to sit, but stopped and waited when they heard the door open again. The North Korean emissaries entered. The ambassador entered first, followed by an assistant. As the two approached and introduced themselves to Haruka and Mori, another man discreetly stepped through the entry and sat not far from the door and the nearby guard.

There was something strongly familiar about the younger man who was carefully keeping his distance, Haruka thought. He had seen him, or perhaps a picture of him, somewhere before. He had a boyish face, and a rotund frame, one that would seem odd even among the elite in North Korea.

Perhaps he was the minister's political or legal advisor, Haruka thought.

Understanding the importance of maintaining proper protocols, Haruka stayed focused on the ambassador. With the completion of the introductions, the group took their seats. The ambassador was quick to dismiss the invitation for a drink and made it clear that he was here only to discuss business.

"You can assume by our meeting here today that we've been able to validate your capabilities from our people in Japan. We've been able to confirm that our working together can be of mutual benefit," the ambassador started.

"I'm pleased to hear you say that," Haruka said.

The emissary nodded his head. "We do have a few issues we'd like to discuss, however."

"That is to be expected," Haruka responded.

"You say you can help us reunite with our southern brethren, and you boast of being able to make us a nuclear power," the ambassador stated. "We're ready to listen to more of your plan."

Haruka watched as the overweight young man moved closer to sit just behind the ambassador. Though no introductions were made,

Haruka and the young man acknowledged one another with subtle nods.

An accepted signal and show of respect, Haruka noticed.

The ambassador looked at Haruka and simply stated, "My advisor. Please begin."

The interpreter moved to sit next to the rotund man. The ambassador didn't seem to need one. His Japanese was fluent.

Haruka began to share his strategy. At times the ambassador would stop him and ask a question while the interpreter spoke exclusively to the overweight young man.

He first emphasized their ability to train the scientists, while helping to stockpile weapons-grade uranium. Then he addressed the reciprocal benefits and overall strategy.

After forty-five minutes, Haruka had concluded his comments. "So as you can see, the manner in which we implement this operation will not allow anyone to determine who is behind these actions. The United States and UN forces would not be able to provide any type of affective response."

"Although this involves a great risk, you seem to have the advantage of operating with some immunity from your government's eyes. Is that true?"

"In a manner of speaking, yes," Haruka said.

"I find that intriguing. And what do you wish of us?" the ambassador stated.

"We need some special trade considerations, once we succeeded in taking control of our government, and also financial support to help us develop our product," Haruka answered.

"I see no problems with those requests. I assume you have some numbers for us to consider?"

Haruka turned to Mori, who handed him a sheaf of papers. The boss slid them across the table, so the ambassador could carefully review them.

"These have the same schematics you sent to us earlier I see."

"Yes, but as you can see, it also contains itemized costs, with related timelines."

"I see that you're very thorough. So, you're asking us to pay for most of the final product?"

"Yes."

"Since we're mutually sharing in the outcome, why not equally share the cost?" the ambassador inquired.

"We are taking most of the initial risk, both in conducting operations in our country and in transporting the stockpiles across the border to you. You have seen the samples?"

"Yes. Our scientists were quite pleased with the initial test shipment and are anxious to receive an ongoing supply. Can you provide all of our immediate stockpile needs until our own plant is completed?"

"Mr. Mori, here, can answer that."

"We have no doubt whatsoever, Mr. Ambassador," Mori responded. "I give you my personal assurance that our methods of operation and supply base are sound."

"Very well," the young rotund man stated. Then he looked Mori directly in the eyes and continued. "In any event, we will hold you personally responsible, Mr. Hideo Mori."

Mori swallowed and bowed his head, hoping it would be seen as a sign of respect rather than what he really felt, insecurity. "Very well," he said softly.

The rotund man gestured to the ambassador and the two moved off to the side.

That's when Haruka realized who the young man was and thought, *I'm not the only boss in this room.*

A short time later, the two returned. "While we're interested in what you have to offer, be aware that we've already held up negotiations elsewhere until we learned what your plans were. So as you can see, we too are taking a risk. We'll pay one-third prior to action and a total of fifty percent after the mission is completed."

The boss nodded his head. "We are in agreement. If it is all right with you, Mr. Mori will coordinate the trips to North Korea as well as Russia."

"Very well," the ambassador said. "We'll let our interpreter stay with Mr. Mori to coordinate the details. Payment will be made through our supporters in your country."

With that completed, everyone stood, exchanged pleasantries, and then all the emissaries, less the interpreter, who moved over and sat with Mori, exited the railcar.

Haruka leaned back in his chair and smiled, considering the deal's potential. *Now it would become just a matter of time before we become a new power to be reckoned with, but we will need to expand our financial base. It's going to be expensive, but well worth it. An investment in our securing a country of our own.*

Chapter 2

THE WHITE HOUSE, WASHINGTON, DC

MAY 1993

They worked their way through a variety of intelligence matters for some forty minutes. Particular attention was paid to terrorist groups of various kinds and the new menace poised by the possible expansion of terrorist activities in those countries with ties to North Korea. The discussion seemed inordinately long until you considered that President Bill Clinton was inaugurated just two and a half months earlier. Congress was still approving cabinet members, and the new administration had a great deal to learn before making any decisions in the foreign affairs arena.

President Clinton knew he had only a few minutes to bring closure to his involvement in this meeting. There were a number of issues his chief of staff would want to brief him on shortly in the adjacent oval office. In the cabinet room, the concerns of the National Security Council, which serves as the president's national security and foreign policy staff within the White House, was chaired by the president. Its members were the vice president, secretaries of state and defense, the chairman of the Joint Chiefs of Staff and the director of the Central Intelligence Agency.

Having discussed a multitude of issues surrounding US and North Korean relations, the president finally said, "Thank you all for being so candid. Since most of us are new to this council, it's important that we remember to consider all the information at hand before determining a course of action. Let's review what we believe are the main points before moving forward."

Turning to his new secretary of state, Warren Christopher, he said, "Warren, let's start with you. What's your take on the situation?"

The secretary of state hesitated just long enough to put his thoughts in order before beginning. "Sir, just four months ago Pyongyang agreed to inspections of seven nuclear sites. We were making progress until we discovered, through our satellite photos, that two unannounced sites showed increased activities. When we insisted on extending our inspection rights to those undeclared facilities, they refused to permit us to conduct inspections. That was on February tenth. When we pressed further, they announced their intention to withdraw from the Non-Proliferation Treaty altogether, so we declared North Korea to be in noncompliance and referred the situation to the United Nations. Two days ago the UN Security Council passed a resolution asking North Korea to allow IAEA inspections under the NPT. Yesterday they rejected the request and have basically refused us access to any of their sites. Sir," he paused long enough to allow the group to absorb what he had said before making his recommendation, "by announcing our knowledge of these sites, we believe we've caused them to pause their production of a nuclear arsenal. But in doing so, we've also placed them in an embarrassing situation. They probably feel they can do nothing else but act tough. I'm not so sure we should press them any further. Perhaps we need time to allow things to cool off."

General Colin Powell, having had experience in this area, first as the president's national security advisor, and now as the chairman of the Joint Chiefs of Staff, chose to interject. "Mr. President, it seems that we have caught them with their pants down, so to speak, when we discovered new activity at these two sites they didn't declare earlier. If we press them further, I don't know what we can expect. While it seems obvious that they have something to hide, their refusal to allow us access could be just to allow them time to clean up these sites, or it could be their way of testing our new administration. What advantage do we have to continue pressing them? We may have more to lose than gain."

"While I have the same concern as everyone else here, that we don't want to be seen as weak by not taking any action at all, we do need to know what they may be up to," the president responded.

It was the secretary of defense, Les Aspin, who responded to the president's comment. "Sir, perhaps if we look at what they've already done, we can determine what further actions are possible."

"Okay, Les. What do you have in mind?"

"Well, what type of actions have they conducted so far?"

The president said, "James…Colin…what can you tell us?"

James Woolsey, the new director of the CIA, began. "On three different occasions they've tried to assassinate South Korea's presidents, and they did down a South Korean airliner, killing a hundred and fifteen passengers and crew, when it strayed into their airspace."

"What have we been seeing along the military lines, Colin?" the president inquired.

"Many of their military and operations for the past forty years have caused a number of armed clashes in and near the Demilitarized Zone," the chairman of the Joint Chiefs began. "The worst one being the 'tree-cutting' incident that led to Operation 'Paul Bunyan.' We believe that was their response to our first Team Spirit Exercise in 1976."

Realizing that he had just broken the unwritten rule of speaking jargon that some present might not understand, General Powell quickly recovered by clarifying, "In the 'tree-cutting' incident, we lost two of our officers when approximately thirty North Korean soldiers beat them to death using axe handles. This followed their refusal to stop trimming a tree to improve visibility along the DMZ. We later responded by cutting it to the ground in operation 'Paul Bunyan.' The 'Team Spirit Exercise' is one that we've been conducting annually, to test our ship-mobilization capabilities, primarily from Ft. Lewis and the Port of Tacoma in Washington State to Pusan, Korea. While we've discovered minor incursions since then, they've primarily been for infiltration and reconnaissance."

Vice President Al Gore had been quietly absorbing much of the latter part of the conversation without participating, but now that he was able to observe a pattern of escalation worth mentioning, he spoke. "A great deal of what's already been said shows that the activities are nothing new since the armistice of 1953. They seem to want to make trouble along the DMZ and are willing to kill, but in such a way so as not to extend hostilities. Based on when we know all these events have occurred, one thing that does seem to be different is their increase in infiltration to the south and terrorizing the civilian population. I can't help but wonder if they are planning on increasing their hostilities beyond their borders."

"Good point, Al," the president said. "So they have shown an increased willingness to terrorize. We need to be cautious about how we approach them, but we also can't just sit back and do nothing. Recommendations, anyone?"

Again, it was the secretary of state who chose to take the lead. "Sir, my recommendation stands. We give the situation time to cool, but rather than not show action, we press them to meet further on the issues."

Looking about the room, the president noticed everyone giving a nod to the proposal. "That sounds reasonable. Let's see if we can get them back to the table by the end of this month. Les…let's also press to get the UN to host this. Do you have anyone in mind to lead these talks?

"Yes sir, Lynn Davis, the undersecretary of state."

"Very well, anything else before I move on?" Seeing no response, the president stood, and everyone else joined him. Turning to his national security advisor and then back to the vice president, the president said, "Al, you'll ensure the national security advisor has the opportunity to summarize everyone is supporting actions before you adjourn?"

"Yes, sir."

Before stepping out, the president moved toward General Powell and gestured for Colin to walk with him to the exit. As he began turning the knob, the Marine outside the door pulled the door open. "Colin, you've been in this game longer than anyone in this room. I hope you know I value any insights you may have."

"Thank you, sir. I appreciate the comment."

"There's more to this that we haven't discussed, isn't there?"

Always expressionless, the general paused, thinking carefully before replying. "Sir, I believe we're taking the appropriate actions... and I hope you realize I need to be very careful not to make recommendations outside my area of responsibility."

"I can appreciate your position, Colin. But I'm just asking your opinion."

"Sir, I too think that, for the moment, we have pushed them as far as we dare. To take further actions now would not give us room to maneuver later. The next step may be to propose sanctions. But for now, we should appear patient at the negotiations table, as long as we're making progress. In the meantime, we should also try and get closer to the situation."

"What do you have in mind?"

"Obviously, they are going to be doing something about those sites, while we decide what to do next. What, I don't know. But I do know that President Kim can be surprising at times."

"Go on."

"Sir, I'm proposing that we ask our intelligence experts to do what they can, and while we know the North is still not capable of delivering a nuclear threat, I'd sure like to know how they're progressing. The General Assignment Board has just published their results. We now know who the newly promoted general officers will be. I've already talked with General Luck about one particular intelligence officer. He's a good man, experienced, familiar with the culture, and is known to get results. I was thinking about assuring he gets the support he needs by giving him my personal endorsement."

"Okay, sounds good. Keep me informed," he turned to see his chief of staff approaching from the adjoining office. "Okay, Chief. What's next?"

General Powell returned to his seat in the meeting knowing now what he would be reporting to the vice president and the national security advisor. After the president left, the vice president presided over the rest of the discussion, allowing the national security advisor an opportunity to produce a summary of the actions needed to support the decisions made. The NSC staff received its direction from the president through the national security advisor.

Chapter 3

PYONGYANG, NORTH KOREA

JUNE 1993

"He doesn't have long for this world," the middle-aged medical adviser thought.

At 9:30 p.m., at Pyongyang's most exclusive private hospital in North Korea, the chief medical adviser, Dr. Yong Choung, pushed his way through the lobby and reached beneath his surgical apron for a package of cigarettes. Although this habit was contrary to his position as senior diplomatic medical adviser, he found that he, like many others in a position of prominence, took advantage of those around him who wished to gain favor by feeding his vices, a practice provided for the privileged few.

The hospital was more substantial than most. There was an ample supply of medical staff, equipment, and supplies, often at the expense of neighboring facilities. Most of the rooms were marked for exclusive use by the top diplomatic and military corp. Other facilities showed the wear brought about by lack of maintenance and years of neglect. The wall paint was peeling and bubbling, pipes rattled and clanked, and there were signs of leaks from many of the exposed pipes. These hospitals were also stretched for the medical supplies desperately needed for the outbreak of tuberculosis, dysentery, and other ailments brought on by the famine and malnutrition spreading throughout the country.

Dr. Choung was a fifty-two-year-old North Korean trained at Pyongyang and Peking. Before being assigned as the president's personal physician, he had been professor of cardiac surgery at Pyongyang's elite Kim II Sung University Hospital.

His cigarettes were bought on the black market. One of the nurses, who didn't smoke but knew the doctor did, would collect them whenever she could from other high-ranking patients. Keeping her boss well supplied didn't hurt her standing on the ward, nor did the special relationship she had with the doctor on a personal level. In fact, she was looking forward to rendezvousing with him later that same night.

He lit his cigarette. His hands were shaking; exhaling, he struggled to gain control.

It had been time to take a break, to leave the president's room and step outside into the welcome cold of the night, light a cigarette, and get a cup of coffee, if he could find one.

Though the president was still awaiting his attention, the doctor had learned that stepping out was best when others needed to meet with the Dear Leader. After so many years in this position, as the president's personal physician, what he saw and heard concerned him. The stresses endured by Kim were affecting his judgment, as well as his health.

Dr. Choung had diagnosed his patient with high blood pressure that if left untreated, would lead to congestive heart failure. Further, the president had shown all the signs of someone whose personality traits would make lowering his blood pressure difficult. His erratic behavior concerned him most.

What the doctor desperately wanted was a drink and some time to unwind with nurse Sun. But that would have to wait until later, much later. The president's advisers had just arrived and would stay who knew how long. He would probably have to wait until the early morning for that break. Then he would take several deep pulls from the neck of his bottle of rice wine before his get-together with Seungyon Sun.

He took two more puffs and pushed himself away from the stairwell railing.

"I will make a quick check on the status of the president. Once I determine how long his visitors are staying, I will do nothing for the next few minutes except smoke my cigarette and drink my coffee, if I can find any," the doctor said to Kim's guard by the stairwell.

He made his way past the same guard, who waved him through to the stairwell. Another was posted at the other end of the hall, providing protection for the president as well as his visiting dignitaries. Dr. Choung then passed three of the president's visitors—his closest friend and chief of staff, his minister of defense, and another loyal patriot, the ambassador to Russia. Surprisingly, they had only stayed a few minutes.

Getting the nod from a bodyguard, who stood just outside the adjoining conference room door, Dr. Choung entered, saw that the president had just passed through to his examination room, and quickly followed. He paused as he saw the door was partially open and peeked inside to confirm that it was a convenient time to enter.

The doctor froze in place when he heard a familiar voice say, "You dismissed them so quickly, Father. Are you so sure of what you want that you're not willing to allow their army to help us in our fight?" He knew the voice was the president's son, Kim II Jong.

"How can they help with their so-called *Soldiers of White Love Army*? They're nothing more than a group of religious fanatics. They may be growing, but how many of their twelve thousand followers have the training to perform in a military operation? I'll tell you. Very few."

"But using them would be like having an army, as small as they might be, behind enemy lines. Besides, in a way, the growth of their sect shows support for our communist way of life. They draw mainly from those who have lost faith during these uncertain economic times and have turned away from their materialistic society. Besides, they do have a group of highly trained scientists that could help us further our nuclear research capabilities," responded Jong.

"I've heard enough to know that I don't want to make this whole mess with the discovery of our nuclear facilities any more convoluted than it already is. Tensions with the US have reached a new high as a result of their discovery. Originally, I was stalling our negotiations because I knew it would take time to clean up the sites and shut them down. I really didn't know what else we could do. All our discussions about how we could transport the nuclear materials disguised as raw materials for energy research has helped me realize how to get out of this embarrassing situation. Rather than spend more time cleaning up the sites and then just plead ignorance, we can convert them to look like nothing more than nuclear waste storage facilities. We can claim that we have been exploring how to produce nuclear energy to supplement our country's electrical power output. Surely our neighbors can understand my desire to improve the living conditions of our people."

"As you wish, Father," Jong responded, knowing when not to challenge his father. However, he was bold enough to ask if he would be allowed to have Haruka and his representative continue their visit there while their own intelligence people looked into the level of expertise the scientists from their religious organization had.

Seeing the benefits of that, the president gave his blessing. His advancing years caused him to give some fatherly advice, reminding his son that some day he would be leading the country. It was important for him to understand that breaking his word with another world leader would lose international support. He would have to abide by the agreement originally established with President Bush, but Kim II Jong could see that his father was disheartened over that decision. The president had lost that glimmer of hope Jong use to see whenever he saw his father talk of a united Korea. That was something he was determined to do something about.

About this time, Dr. Choung determined that he had heard enough. His job, as personal physician, was to treat the president's physical ailments. He felt he understood the cause of the stress that resulted in Sung's poor heart condition, but he also knew he could not treat the cause of that stress. He could see that this situation was very trying for the president. His voice would quiver, and his face became flushed, causing distress for the already ailing man. The doctor realized how helpless he felt. He really needed that drink now. He walked over to the chair closest to the door he entered and loudly moved it about the floor before walking to the door where he politely knocked.

President Kim II Sung said, "Come on in, Doctor."

The good doctor completed the president's physical checkup before beginning to violate his own rule about telling his patient the truth. He didn't exactly lie though, did he? He just withheld information about what he could do about lowering the president's blood pressure. After all, Sung couldn't just step down, leaving his inexperienced son to deal with these stressful international issues. Little did the doctor know that just down the hall his favorite son was planning actions his father would not support.

This oversized young leader, with the boyish-looking face and corpulent build, left his father's side to catch up with the president's visitors, who he knew would be waiting in the hospital lobby. It was with him that North Korea's future rested. His plan, he knew, would rekindle his father's faith.

He also had an ulterior motive in wanting to authorize Haruka's travel to Pyongyang. It would hide Haruka's original intentions. His father's aim was shortsighted. Only his closest advisors knew he was ailing, and Kim II Jong was ready to show his mettle.

"Gentlemen, my father has not approved of our plan to move ahead to the extent I had hoped. However, we have enough of a commitment that we can still attain our ultimate goal. We will be able to explore with Mr. Haruka how we can further develop our nuclear capabilities outside the country, while honoring my father's wishes to convert our two facilities."

He went on to explain the details of his plan—how, in their present situation, they couldn't afford to risk developing what he needed locally. That would upset his father's plans. They could still gain the knowledge to develop fissionable material while Haruka's scientists developed and placed the devices they discussed with him earlier. They would begin the dismantling of the major parts of the two undeclared facilities. They would extract weapons-grade plutonium from the irradiated fuel to help the Soldiers of White Love Army design and build their own facility at one of the Aum sites. They would be able to finance this by diverting funds not yet sent into the country through their own underground organization in Japan, the Chosen Soren.

"In this way we gain more 'know-how' about how to build the devices, while my father keeps his promise," he concluded.

Just short of a half-bottle of rice wine later, Dr. Choung began to feel better about what he knew he could not control. With nurse Sun at his side, he tried to put all this behind him. It wasn't until he was able to share it with a sympathetic ear that he truly did begin to feel better.

Chapter 4

WESTERN AUSTRALIA

SEPTEMBER 1993

They didn't bother to conceal their activities under the cover of darkness. There was no need to. Four hundred miles from the nearest major city, Perth, this site was almost inaccessible, except for its poor quality access tracks and one entry road. The likelihood of discovery was remote. The few who did occupy this forsaken land would not stand between them and what they had to do. There was a great deal to be excited about. They were testing one of their new weapons on a local herd of merino sheep, acquired when they purchased this remote Banjawarn sheep station just months earlier.

Haruka and his assistant, Mori, were perched along the edge of Banjawarn's private airstrip, sitting on their makeshift wooden bench, a board suspended between two blocks of wood, waiting for their leader's arrival. Other than the pale green spinifex grass, which contrasted with the red and pink tones of the sand and a few mulga trees, the surrounding area was barren. A problem caused by the overpopulation of wild rabbits and feral goats and one the Australians wanted to remedy.

The morning light was just beginning to rise, not yet bringing on the unbearable heat that this area was known for, but enough to make the two men not want to don their protective suits yet. They would wait until the sheep had been herded into place, and the chemist had flown in with the package. Their illustrious guru would be accompanying him, along with his bodyguard, assigned by Haruka to keep watch over him. Although considered *legally* blind, the guru would be here to observe the demonstration and review the new timelines established for the upcoming events. Bodhisattva always made sure the guru was overseeing their activities, to ensure others saw the guru as leading them toward their religious destiny.

Haruka, the bodhisattva, had a round face and dark hair with a receding hairline. He periodically tossed red sand and dust into the air to check the wind direction. Mori, also with his back to the sun, was similar in stature and attire but had a slightly thinner face, pursed lips, and glasses. He was drinking black coffee from a cracked tan mug found at the station house. Both wore Mao-styled cotton jackets, much like the standard attire of the Chinese during Mao Zedong's reign.

Haruka looked up, after throwing another handful of sand into the air, and smiled. "The winds are consistent. Just perfect."

"Good," said Mori. "I know that our chemist has been working very hard to make this successful."

"Let us not forget, we had similar assurances when we used another biological weapon. Our biological expert botched its use on three different occasions," Haruka stated.

Mori shifted slowly, showing a little uneasiness, causing the board to rock slightly. Mori knew that Haruka would continue to closely watch him, to measure his reaction to his comments. Mori sometimes surprised even himself with how self-assured he had become.

Mori said, "That's true, but we all knew that maintaining potency once the anthrax and botulinus left the lab would be questionable. Fortunately, that little disappointment prompted us to expand our arsenal to develop chemical and even nuclear weapons. Now, thanks to finding this uranium rich ranch, we've also found the perfect place to test our other weaponry as well."

Haruka noted his associate's positive response and said, "With a little fixing up, we can also use this place as a retreat when the time is right for Armageddon."

Mori took a last sip of coffee, stood, and set his coffee mug on the bench. He adjusted his glasses and stepped forward to better see three men herding a group of sheep from the station's holding pen.

As Mori walked off a few paces, Haruka took the opportunity to be sure Mori understood his level of responsibility, "Well, it won't be long now before we see the affects. You realize of course that the deal we've struck with President Kim is really going to accelerate matters, don't you?"

"Of course. I'm ready for it," Mori said. "What better time and place for testing Armageddon?" Mori knew that Haruka had also been feeding the guru's fantasy about collapsing Japan's much-vaunted economic system. *Now he's obsessed with it, thanks to us,* Mori thought. *We've given him the dream of dominating Japan and ridding this filthy world of desires. He doesn't even suspect that he will help us achieve more than just what he has set out to accomplish.*

As if reading Mori's mind, Haruka said, "My hope now is that as we begin to conduct activities to bring about chaos and increase the number of converts, the world's attention will be diverted away from what we truly have in mind for the region. We need them to focus on the new threat of North Korea and the possibility of them unleashing nuclear devastation throughout the region. With our plan and North Korea's cooperation, Russia and the United States will be helpless if they try to intervene."

Haruka heard the sound of an airplane off in the distance. Standing to join Mori, Haruka looked at his watch and exclaimed, "It shouldn't be long now before our testing can begin. Shall we begin getting the sheep in place?"

A full thirty minutes passed before all preparations for the test were finished. A signal was given to one of the men, who walked to a metal cylinder sitting on the ground near the sheep. Carefully lifting the container, the chemist carried it to the designated location, the center point of the semicircle formally the tethered animals. The sheep pulled nervously at the tethers securing them in place, sending clouds of red dust into the air.

He began to unwrap its outer packaging but would not release its contents until the right moment, ensuring all were well protected or out of range of its devastating effects.

Chapter 5

WESTERN AUSTRALIA

M onths earlier, at Haruka's insistence, the guru had pulled his top lieutenants together to share his far-reaching plan for militarization, putting into play the formidable resources of his cult. His two top advisers convinced him that the resulting devastation would show his predictions about the future to be true, motivating others to join the cult. He was led to believe new believers would come to the understanding that they could only be saved through conversion to the group's holy cause.

Haruka saw an additional opportunity to harass and intimidate those who would dare stand up against them. It had taken time to carefully orchestrate the harassment technique of multiple phone calls. They were used to discourage those who chose to speak out against them, or stop community members who threatened legal action. Those who did drag them to court had to endure a long, drawn out set of legal battles designed to discourage even the most ardent of opposing factions. But now Haruka needed to escalate his activities. Others needed to see their organization as a great force to be reckoned with.

Some of their followers had questioned the leadership's purpose, pointing out inconsistencies between what was being preached and actual practices. So far, these few were being dealt with silently, just as he had tried to do with a member of the Unification Church in South Korea. However, some members' relatives had become more intrusive, choosing to pursue legal means to regain lost relatives.

One lawyer was able to find a few judges willing to allow a challenge to the sect's building of a new facility. For the most part, they had succeeded in misleading the community into believing that they were building a factory rather than a communal facility.

Haruka, now more than ever, needed to teach these troublemakers a lesson, one that would maintain order within their organization.

The guru considered Haruka and Mori to be his top advisors and did not know they viewed him simply as a figurehead. They certainly had paid their dues and helped to establish the foundation of his religious order. Mori's connections with the Japanese Mafia had assisted in ensuring they were able to build their secret labs while avoiding legal impediments. When Haruka cut ties with Reverend Moon, he brought his seized millions with him to help fund the new religious order and its headquarters. Further, his contacts outside the country, including the North Korean president, helped to support their new atomic research ventures.

Those the guru believed to be his greatest followers and closest lieutenants included intellectuals, like Masami, a chemist who had been recruited from Japan's top universities. Others specialized in areas such as astrophysiology, engineering, biology, and even medicine. They were given the task of bringing his predictions of doom to fruition, so "the corrupt civilization would begin its descent into apocalyptic fire."

By 1991, Japan's economy took a turn for the worse. It plummeted into its worst recession in decades. For many, this recession also focused on the evils of wealth. Dissatisfied with the changing, materialistic society, many found a more meaningful life in New Age religions that were surfacing all around. The Aum was one of the more popular of these.

Masami, like many of his cohorts, had been attracted by the group's mystical meditative practices. During yoga sessions he became aware of the group's popular Eastern and Western religious beliefs, which later led him to join their cause. He was convinced that by giving up his worldly goods he'd achieve salvation, so he did. In doing this, he gained a powerful position as one of the guru's lieutenants, but he had to prove himself faithful periodically. This is what slowly moved him to support the Aum leadership's questionable activities. As a true believer, he would join the fight to keep the nonbelievers in line. Masami chose to join "God's chosen army."

Only a select few of the guru's closest advisors knew of their army's plan to create havoc. They knew it was devised to make true believers out of the less faithful, expand their membership, test their followers, and bring in new riches. The leadership believed that only the most ardent believers would commit to violence in the name of the guru, to save the world.

Unbeknown to even the chemist Masami, a few in another more exclusive group, under Haruka's control, recognized the potential uses of the charismatic guru, Shoko Asahara. Kiyohide Haruka selected a few to infiltrate the Institute for Human Happiness, the Aum. This small cadre would expand their influence, establishing a separate military force, and plan their governmental coup. All this while they further corrupted the master by feeding his ego and lust for money.

Asahara, with his thick beard and long hair, provided just the right figure needed to create a guru-like image. He dressed in the flowing purple robes that suggested a Hindu holy man and was able to speak in a mesmerizing monotone. Asahara used a motionless, cross-legged yoga posture, moving only his lips as he imparted wisdom to his followers. He was rewarded handsomely, as believers willingly transferred their worldly possessions to attain salvation. The Aum grew, while the blind seer learned that profit and prophecy went together.

This guru's message to the world was simple. He used national pride to unite the people of Japan, while spreading the Truth. They must fight the goliaths of the world, Russia and the United States, who were corrupting morality and influencing Japan toward a materialistic society.

He warned the citizens of Japan of a terrible genocide, unleashed upon their country by an unexpected enemy, the United States. The Americans would attack them, sinking the islands into the sea and ignite a world war. Japan would be turned into a wasteland as a result of a nuclear attack.

To fight the coming battles the Aum required the most effective weapons possible. Under the direction of Bodhisattva, the sect built secret labs at Mount Fuji and at Mount Aso in central Kyushu. They ordered equipment through various front companies the cult now controlled. Many of the 1,500 devotees who lived inside Aum's communities fervently believed they were building a new Utopia, a glorious Kingdom of Aum. In reality, they were little more than cogs in what would become a massive killing machine. Masami, the chemist, would develop chemical weapons to earn favor from Haruka and the great guru.

Masami knew he'd be successful. He had experimented with other chemical agents and proven his mastery. His work on mustard gas went so well that the group had already drawn up plans to mass-produce it. By now, cult front companies had also obtained a stockpile of chemicals to create cyanide gas and at least two other nerve agents. Because of his successes, Masami knew he would be well rewarded. He worked long hours to ensure the mixes were right and that there would be no failures during this test run.

Haruka and Mori were in their protective suits now. Haruka stayed close to the airplane with the guru, his personal physician, bodyguard, and the antidote.

Chapter 6

WESTERN AUSTRALIA

SEPTEMBER 1993

M oving southwest, out of the Gibson Desert and into an area with more vegetation, Phyllis and her group bounced along the rutted dirt road in their four-wheel drive. Once there, the group could more readily forage for food. They had to be careful to stay on the access tracks. The dead, dry mulga usually fell over, exposing a radiating set of spike-like roots that could become embedded in the tires. Dense mulga scrub was impenetrable for a vehicle.

At least half of the diet of the aborigines comes from plants. Fruits, seeds, and greens are only available during certain seasons, but roots could usually be dug up all year round. The women of the Mulga Queen Aboriginal settlement usually gathered the plants, while the men hunted for kangaroos, wallaby, emus, lizards, and other small animals.

Like many of the aborigine, the people of the Mulga Queen settlement preferred to stay to themselves. However, news that there was some curious activity going on at the Banjarwarn Station traveled quickly. Whether it was curiosity or an urge to make sure these visitors treated the land with respect, Phillis, with a car full of neighboring men, drove on toward Banjarwarn Station.

A great deal of coming and going was also occurring along the station's private airfield. Phillis convinced her passengers that they might be able to catch a glimpse of one of these aircraft flying about.

They found it fascinating to see the plane swoop in low and kick up dust during its landing along the station's private runway. This time, although they were still quite a ways off, they could see a plane descending for its final approach. Curiosity got the best of them, and Phyllis headed for the ranch.

Over the last few months, the locals had heard that there was more activity at the ranch since it had changed hands. An aboriginal state park ranger friend had told Phyllis that some Japanese had acquired it. The local authorities had taken unusual measures, appointing an Australian to manage the place due to its deteriorating condition. An ecological equilibrium needed to be maintained, not to mention the need to educate this naive group of Japanese about survival in the outback.

Phillis was closer now, close enough to see that there was an airplane on the landing strip and some activity not far off.

One of Phyllis's companions called out, "There's the plane. It looks like there are some people off to the left of it."

"Strange," said Phyllis. "Look how they're dressed."

They saw five of the cult members wearing light colored protective clothing with helmets. It was obvious by their actions that they either did not know they were being watched or did not care. One seemed to be carrying a container with great care, while the others stood back.

Frightened, Phyllis said, "I have a feeling they're doing something they're not supposed to be doing. We need to keep moving, and let others know what is going on here."

Chapter 7

HALE KOA HOTEL - OAHU, HAWAII

OCTOBER 1993

"I want results."

The commanding general had made a brisk exit from the grand hall. He believed in the three "Bs": be brief, be brilliant, be gone. But his words could still be heard, murmured by many of the almost 300 attendees throughout the presentation room.

The MC quickly moved to the microphone to introduce the next speaker. "You have just heard command emphasis for the region, with special importance to matters related to our negotiations with North Korea which are intended to make the peninsula nuclear free. He paused to stress the significance of the next speaker. "Now you will hear from the man who will continue, in his new role, to 'bring it all together,' so to speak. He has not only been the collector and disseminator of intelligence for the Pacific region while stationed here in Hawaii, but he will be reporting shortly to Combined Forces Command, Korea, as the new assistant chief of staff. Ladies and gentlemen, Colonel George Byrnes."

As was the practice of formal military presentations, the room was quietly attentive as the speaker approached the podium. The trim man of fifty-three, with short-cropped brown hair, sipped from a glass of water located next to the podium, took a moment to look about the room, and began. "I'm pleased to see many familiar faces and know that many of you have crossed paths with one another before, either during your field experience or training opportunities. That's a good thing. Get to know one another as well as understand the various positions within the region. That's as important as the training and experience that have helped you learn the critical pieces of intelligence as they fit the grand, ever-changing scheme of things. Mingle and learn, that's what today is all about.

"You have all adapted your unique skills to how we do things, and you've made good use of your talents. That's why you were selected for your assignments."

He took a moment to look about the room again, this time taking his time, pausing as he recognized the most familiar of the newly assigned.

"Some of you have been in your assignments for some time. Others will report in the next few days, while still others have received orders but won't arrive at their new posting until formal training is complete. Either way, I know many of you want to stay in the field or in some cases return to the field."

His gaze rested on his twenty-seven-year-old daughter, as he finished his last statement. "It's important to personalize our discussion whenever possible when dealing with our counterparts and analyze thoroughly the intelligence we're dealing with," the colonel said.

Captain Kelly Byrnes sat with an old college friend, Major Carl Walker. He looked over at Kelly to measure her reaction to her father's acknowledgement of her presence.

Kelly sat erect, her uniform perfectly starched and form-fit to her five-foot-five-inch, toned form. Not a wrinkle could be seen as she sat poised to absorb every word of her father's presentation. Her face was lightly flushed, but her bright blue eyes were firmly fixed on the man at the podium.

Carl started to say something then decided to wait until Kelly's father had completed his briefing on the region's threat assessment.

"The commanding general covered the broader picture for the Pacific region with a special focus on Korea. Now I want to emphasize the 'hot spots' for those closer to North Korea. Once the CINCPAC commander had determined that I was going to be the J2 for Combined

Forces Command in Korea, he had a one-on-one with me to emphasize the president's concern about North Korea. That's why we've arranged for this conference today."

Colonel Byrnes swept his eyes across the room to emphasize his point, then continued, "Most of the known threats in your region are inactive. In Japan, the Chukaku-ha, or Middle Core Faction, has reduced its levels of attacks, and the Japanese Red Army remains dormant. Reports show that no international terrorist groups based outside Japan have conducted attacks there, and domestic extremist groups were less active than in recent years. Chukaku-ha, the most dangerous and active Japanese leftist group, was distracted by internal politics in the spring. It is believed to have committed only a few attacks that resulted in minimal damage and no injuries. Secret societies, such as the Yakuza, the Japanese Mafia, and religious cults, however, are factions that are more clandestine and therefore more difficult to track.

"I mentioned these groups in Japan as examples of groups I'm concerned could get additional resources from the old Soviet Union, assuming they want to become more active. While the Soviet Union is no longer a threat, that's where suppliers of military ordnance, training, and an array of weapons of mass destruction are available to the highest bidder. I would be especially concerned if a country like North Korea were to get their hands on that technology, or if they connected with any of these factions for assistance.

"For example, in Volgograde, when they suspended production of the nerve agent sarin in 1987, thousands were put out of work, including dozens of scientists with manufacturing know-how. That 'know-how' is not only for making sarin but also for the development of other weapons of mass destruction that is our new threat. There are new subversive groups beginning to crop up that are difficult to track. I want you to be aware of that and keep your eyes and ears open."

Then he went into the more classified portion of the briefing. By the time he was finished, he knew they all had a lot to think about.

Chapter 8

HALE KOA HOTEL - OAHU, HAWAII

The lunch break had come almost precisely as scheduled, 12:30 p.m.—the army way.

Major Walker and Captain Byrnes both watched as Colonel Byrnes began to make his way off stage, only to be intercepted by staff members and attendees.

"Want to wait for him here?" Carl asked Kelly.

"As good a place as any I suppose."

"I saw your dad looking straight at you when he was referring to those who longed to return to the field."

"Yeah. That *look* is all the attention I've received from him since I arrived."

"What do you mean by that?"

"I hadn't seen him for three months, and when I flew in last night, he didn't even have time for me. All I got was a note left at the front desk telling me he'd meet with me after his presentation. He apologized, of course."

"Don't be so hard on him, Kelly. He just got selected for a promotion to the senior-most intelligence officer in the region. I'm sure he's very busy."

Kelly looked hurt. "I just wish we were as close as we were before mom left."

"Looks like he's having trouble breaking away even now, but you know he cares, Kelly."

"I suppose, but sometimes I think he doesn't even notice how hard I work or what I've tried hard to accomplish."

Realizing more than a change of topic was needed, Carl said, "Want to go to the back of the room and get some water?"

"Sure, he's got to go by there on the way out anyway."

Kelly and Carl both rose from their seats and moved toward the back of the room. They followed the aisle past the last row of chairs and angled toward the row of tables that lined the back wall. All were covered with stiff table clothes, draped halfway to the floor. Across the top were trays of water pitchers interspersed with glasses formed in neat rows, like a formation of troops on a parade ground. Most of the pastry dishes had already been picked through even before the opening remarks.

Kelly stepped in front of Carl and helped herself to a pitcher of water. Carl watched while she filled her water glass. She stood with the pitcher still in one hand and flipped her brown hair back from her eyes. As a result, water splashed the front of her blouse.

"Damn," she said. "Carl, hand me one of those napkins, will you?"

"Sure." Carl began to reach for a stack of paper napkins and spotted an alternative. He lifted the pastry tray and grabbed a larger cloth napkin that was being used like a place mat and handed it to Kelly.

"Might not have happened if you'd let me be the gentleman and pour you one."

"Sorry. Not use to that." Kelly snatched the napkin from Carl and began to blot her blouse, trying to absorb as much as she could.

"You should try it some time. Let someone help you."

"Don't get me wrong, Carl. I do appreciate things like that. In fact I know Susan loves how thoughtful you are," Kelly said, referring to her college roommate and Carl's fiancée. "But I'm too use to being on my own."

"Speaking of Susan, I wanted to tell you that you're invited to our wedding. Just wanted to give you a heads up. An invitation will be coming soon."

"Oh, you set a date? Carl, that's great. Congratulations," Kelly smiled. "I'm truly happy for you."

"Hopefully I'll be happy for you as well, one of these days," Carl said.

Kelly just gave one of her tight grins and said, "You know me, Carl. Married to the army."

"Yeah, right, Kelly. When was the last time you were on a date?"

Kelly looked at Carl for a moment. "Define date."

"Never mind."

Kelly looked down at her blouse. "Oh, no. It's going to leave a mark."

"Don't worry about it. If you step outside, the wind will dry it in a short time. It'll hardly show."

Kelly, almost in desperation, continued to try to wipe it dry.

"Kelly, don't worry about it, it'll—"

"Carl, mixed with this starch, it'll leave a watermark. Look dad's coming this way now."

Looking exasperated, Carl said, "Your dad doesn't care."

Kelly gave him a stern look.

"Kelly, a lot of water has been spilled on this starched tablecloth, and I don't see any stains there."

"Just taking precautions."

"Overreacting, you mean."

"Carl, that's not true."

"If you say so. The way I see it, it's overkill. You're always trying too hard." Carl turned away, spoke more softly, and added, "You need to lighten up."

"I heard that," Kelly tossed the napkin back at Carl, turned, and smiled at her father.

"Hi, sweet pea. Am I interrupting something?"

"Hi, Dad." Kelly glanced over at Carl. "No. Major Walker here was just giving me the finer points of being a good intelligence officer."

"Oh? And what might that include?"

"Don't work so hard," Kelly said.

"I see, and since I also hear you referring to your longtime college friend by his rank, I assume you don't agree?"

Colonel Byrnes could see that Carl's face, although slightly flush, showed no expression.

"Dad, I've worked hard to get where I am."

"I don't doubt that you have. Let's see, you've graduated cum laude from Stanford, graduated with honors in every military course you've taken to date, and received excellent performance reviews. And now, as a result, you've been assigned to a posting in Asaka, Japan, following your graduating from the Defense Intelligence College. So what do you think his point is?"

"I…don't know. Ask him." Again, Kelly looked at Carl.

"I'm asking you."

"Maybe I do work too hard sometimes, but how else am I going to get ahead as a woman in this man's army?" Then she added, "Evidently I should have worked harder if I wanted to get an assignment better than a posting at Asaka."

Colonel Byrnes ignored the dig about her assignment, not wanting to comment on her placement. "Good point about this man's army… Carl?"

"Sir, I was only saying she needs to go light on the starch. And as far as Asaka goes, a posting in Japan isn't given to just anyone."

"I see. Sounds like good advice."

"What? You're taking his side?"

"Since your mother went back to the states, I'd say we both have buried ourselves in our work for far too long."

Kelly was taken aback by that comment and could only stand in silence.

"I've thought a great deal about how I got where I am today and about what would have happened if your mother hadn't had her, ah… problem."

Kelly said, "You think you would have been as successful?"

"Maybe yes, maybe no. I'm not so concerned about that. All I do know is I would have been happier."

"Dad, I always thought you wanted me to work hard…like you."

"I've always wished you success at whatever you did, but not at the expense of enjoying a balanced life. I just want you to be happy."

"What about my work?"

"You're experienced enough now. Don't work harder, work smarter. Now, let's have some lunch. Shall we go to the Koko Café?"

"Sure," Carl responded.

Kelly just nodded, her mind absorbing her father's words.

Chapter 9

KALGOORLIE, AUSTRALIA

DECEMBER 1993

It was not uncommon to hear about strange activities across the central plains of Western Australia. Many referred to this region as the "Bright Skies" area, due to reports of strange lights across the heavens as well as UFO sightings. Some even associated these with the frequent earthquakes they were experiencing. Based on the suspicion that the Russians were conducting exercises off Australia's west coast, the CIA determined that the surrounding area was worth keeping an eye on.

Vin Baker, the CIA's Western Australia station chief, heard from his predecessor that, although rare in the late 1980s, reports had increased about strange happenings in the skies. Many observers, including meteor experts and amateur astronomers, thought they were static atmospheric light emission events or massive, high-energy bursts of blue-white light that could be seen in the nighttime skies of the upper atmosphere. Personally, he thought, the locals were beginning to believe some of their own stories, particularly the UFO sightings. Baker was inclined to believe what some meteorologists had suggested. The obscure lightshows were the result of variations between the atmosphere and dry desert heat, causing a buildup of static electricity.

As interested as the CIA might be in monitoring the activities being reported in the skies of Western Australia, to permanently place a full-time CIA operative in its center would be difficult. Even Baker was reluctant to accept his new position as station chief in the major city of Perth. Although modern by any standard, he neither cared for its isolated inland location nor the inhabitants with whom he needed to conduct business. While he didn't like this assignment, he did consider the promotion to a station chief position as a move up and eventually hoped that this would advance him to a better posting later in his career.

While Perth was Baker's headquarters, it was virtually impossible to provide a cover that was plausible for his activities. So, Baker had to rely on contacts already established by his predecessor, people who had settled on these desolate plains. The few houses that did exist in the area were built with material salvaged from abandoned town buildings and mine dumps back in the early 1980s. In some places, mulga timber was cut by hand and carted from sites, sometimes as far as sixty miles away. Many of the locals used vehicles such as early model Holdens, Falcons, or Valiants, which they repaired as they traveled about the country. One such local, an aborigine with whom Baker was scheduled to meet, was Nobby Isaacs.

Nobby Isaacs, a Darmot elder, preferred the Valiant. Although it lacked horsepower, it had a dependable engine that carried him over the countryside, letting him keep an eye on the comings and goings in the area. He was paid well for providing information about outsiders' activities. Isaacs believed that preserving this land was vital to the existence of his aborigine tribe, the Darmot. That was why he kept in contact with his neighbors and park rangers, who regularly patrolled the area. Informing Baker about strange activities could lead to the departure of outsiders who were not welcome in these parts.

Those who adapted best to living in this vast wasteland were groups like the Darlot, who were part of the "Western Desert Cultural Bloc." The bloc included the Wongi, another aborigine group with whom the Darlot identified most and had much in common, including the same language and cultural beliefs. The Darlot land area fell into the boundaries of a linguistic group known as the "Koara." This group consisted of individuals who had an association with this country either through birth, marriage, or long-term habitation. They took their name from Lake Darlot. The aborigine name for the lake was Kunapulanka Nabberu.

Like much of the traditional culture, the name Kunapulanka had all but died out since the first incursions of the white man here. When the Europeans arrived in Australia in 1788, the aborigines were still living in the Stone Age, using implements of wood and stone. They lived solely by food gathering, hunting, and fishing and were always on the move, mostly in small tribes. The white settlers put them in settlements, encouraged them to adapt modern tools and culture, and discontinue their nomadic lifestyle.

As an elder of the Darlot, Nobby Isaacs was in a position to hear about events in Central Western Australia. Isaacs didn't like the way outsiders treated the land, and he wanted to do something about it.

Chapter 10

KALGOORLIE, AUSTRALIA

Vin Baker found Nobby in the Victoria Queens Hotel poolroom, at a predetermined table. The aborigine matched the description provided from Baker's files. The pool tables were old, dating from the gold rush days when the hotel had been built. This town was the closest one to the elder's settlement, Kalgoorlie.

Nobby was playing pool at the back table. An aborigine woman was watching him play.

"Aye mate, I figured you'd be here about now. Bayka, right?" Nobby said, looking up from the table when he saw Baker. He had carefully arranged balls at the lip of each of the pockets on the table. He was trying to sink as many of them as he could with one shot.

Taken aback by this greeting, Baker waited until Isaac had made his shot—sinking only two of the six balls. "How'd you know I'm Baker?" he replied coolly.

"Simple, mate. See anyone else around? You walked directly to this here table, so I assumed you came to see me. I'm here to see you…and no offense, but you look about as out of place in this town as anyone could."

Baker was a tall man who looked even taller due to his slim appearance and a lightly wrinkled sport jacket that was too short. He looked much like a modern-day Ichabod Crane. Baker was uncomfortable at having to travel in the desolate outback and wanted to complete his meeting quickly so he could get back to civilization. The sooner he got to the point, the sooner he could leave.

45

"You got anything for me?" Baker asked. Before Nobby could reply, he asked, "Who's your friend?"

"Phyllis Campbell, meet Vin Baker, the man I told you about. He's the one who replaced that other gent I used to talk with."

"How do you do, sir?" she said nervously.

"Poorly, now that you ask," Baker replied. "I don't like travelling this far inland. I'm not fond of the dust and sand in the air."

"Phyllis here is the leader of a tribe some kilometers north of a place called Banjawarn Station." Most environmental concerns were shared with the park ranger, but Nobby knew this was not an ordinary matter. He had asked Phyllis to accompany him to meet with Baker. "I brought her here 'cause I figured you'd want to hear what she has to say." Turning to his friend, he said, "Go ahead, Phyllis, tell him what you saw."

"All right," Vin said hesitantly.

Apprehensively Phyllis began, "Just north of a place called Banjawarn Station is one of our favorite campsites called Flowers Well. That's where we were headed when we saw them."

"Saw who?" Baker scowled. He felt he was wasting his time but knew it was important to establish his own contacts with the locals.

"The men in strange suits…with their heads covered," she began again.

Oh great, another UFO-alien invasion story.

"Tell them about the airplane first," the Darlot elder insisted.

"Rolly and John saw it first, the airplane that is. Snow, Willy, and Maisie were all with us, too. We were going to Flowers Well to visit Billy Hennesy and my brother Ruby. South from the campsite there is a site named Banjawarn Station."

"The rangers know it as Juri-Mi, or 'Protected Area Number Five,'" Nobby added in a slow, deliberate way, implying that Baker would have to be patient with how Phyllis's story unfolded. Then he looked at Phyllis, encouraging her to continue her story.

Phyllis began again, "We've heard so much about strange happenings in this area that we been afraid about going near there, but sometimes our curiosity gets the best of us."

Well, at least they admit they saw an airplane and not a UFO, Baker thought. "What strange happenings are you referring to?"

Nobby tried to clear things up. "Ever since a group of Japanese got that land, we've heard through a park ranger friend that there's been some odd activity going on there over the last few months. Why a religious group would pick this rangeland area is puzzling to us. They aren't very smart about survival in the outback. Since their arrival, the rangeland and rundown facilities have caused authorities to take unusual steps to make sure they don't hurt the area any further. The state appointed an Australian fellow as manager. I hear the Japanese aren't very happy about that."

A religious group, huh? I could care less about what a Japanese cult might be doing out there, especially since the state has already assigned someone to manage the land.

"Isn't this something you can report to the park ranger? Why tell me? If you're only concern is how they take care of this God-forsaken land, I can't do anything to help you."

"There's more here than how they hurt the land, Mr. Baker," Nobby persisted. "Phyllis, tell him about what you saw at the airfield."

"Right…well…there's been a great deal of coming and going along the station's airfield as well. Like I said, while heading for Flowers Well, we caught a glimpse of an aircraft flying about. Curious, we headed for the ranch. As we got closer, we saw that the plane had already landed and there was some activity not far off. We got as close as we dared, not knowing what to expect. We didn't stay long after we saw what they were doing.

"One of them carried some sort of container so careful you'd think he was afraid of it. Like he was afraid it might break. Another seemed to be directing him on where to place it, but stayed back a good distance. And there was sheep, tied up so's they couldn't get away. The man with the container set it down next to them. And the odd looking outfits they wore gave me a chill."

"Tell me about these people and their strange costumes."

"Not costumes. Suits," Phyllis said, gaining more courage despite this arrogant man's condescending manner. "We saw only a couple at first. Like I said, we knew they were up to no good so we kept moving. When we crossed the entry road, I caught a closer look at them. There were about five in all. Most were standing next to the small twin-engine plane."

"Describe the suit you say they were wearing."

"They were light colored, with helmets. They kind of looked like space suits, like we seen on television."

"Did they see you?"

"I don't think so…well, one might have. One of them seemed to look right at us."

Obviously these aborigines don't like foreigners. I can see that by how they speak to me, no respect. If they think they can use me to get rid of anyone they don't care for in the outback, they're greatly mistaken. I can't wait to get out of here and back to civilization.

"Thank you, Phyllis," Baker concluded. "I'll look into this." Turning to Nobby, Baker said, "What do you say, just you and I chat about this for a bit? Okay, Nobby?"

Nobby, seeing Phyllis's jaw begin to tighten, immediately interceded, "Sure, Mr. Baker. I was just—"

"Forget it, Nobby. He's not going to do anything. He'll just sweet talk you like all the other white folks do around here and then leave. He won't do a thing for us."

Baker glared at her as Nobby said softly, "Phyllis, I know how you feel. Just let me talk with him for a minute, okay? Why don't you go out and buy some of those supplies you were talking about? I'll meet you at the hardware store down the street when I'm through here."

Phyllis knew that any further talk would just be a waste of time, so she gave a short nod, murmured, "Yeah." As she headed out of the poolroom, she glowered at Baker.

Nobby watched Phyllis leave the room in silence before turning his attention back to Baker.

"Nobby, you've wasted my time with—"

"You and I need to come to an understanding here, Mr. Baker," Isaacs interrupted. "The way you treated Phyllis was unacceptable. You were rude and dismissive. Since you are new to this assignment, let me fill you in on a few things."

"Listen, Isaacs...you can't talk to me like—"

"I will speak to you any way I see fit, Mr. Baker, and you will not utter another word until I finish. Am I clear?"

Baker refrained from speaking.

"We aborigines are very concerned about the treatment of our lands. You may not appreciate how our culture is connected to it. We believe man is a manifestation of the spirit of Wanjina, the spirit of the earth. Our culture includes many legends regarding the formation of the mountains, lakes, streams, water holes, and much more. I, and others, have been named Custodians and Keepers. We are to look after and care for these areas. This knowledge was handed down to us from elders."

Isaacs noticed that Baker had a stunned look on his face.

"Are you surprised I know words with more than two syllables, Mr. Baker? You should know that I graduated cum laude with a degree in cultural anthropology from the Sydney University. I would have graduated magna cum laude, but I had to work two jobs to help pay for my tuition.

"If you choose not to follow up on the information you heard today, that is your decision. However, if you continue to treat aborigines as uneducated and subservient, you will find yourself without eyes and ears in the outback. Have I made myself clear?"

Baker, still stunned at what he had just heard, could only nod his head yes.

Nobby returned the pool cue to the wall rack.

As he walked past Baker on his way to find Phyllis, he added, "If you had inquired further, you would have found that this Japanese cult, calling themselves the Aum, has also been looking into uranium research under a fake name."

Baker watched Isaacs's retreating back and thought, *You little jerk. I'll pass on your information, and no one will care about or even remember it.*

Chapter 11

HEADQUARTERS, 201ST

MI GROUP, KOREA

JANUARY 1994

The most junior NCO of the intelligence analyst section looked about seventeen-years-old. He was small and slight. His light brown hair was shaved on the sides and cropped close to his skull on top, in an almost Mohawk cut. He wore government-issue plastic-framed glasses, and his loose-fitting BDUs made him look even smaller.

But he was good at his job, older and more intelligent than he looked, and had a keen eye when transcribing documents. When he logged HUMINT—human intelligence—communications, he would also note the related entries that passed by him daily.

The analyst raised a hand over his head to signal his superior. A chief warrant officer with over twenty years of service took the young NCO's printed document and separated the continuous-feed printer paper along its perforated line with practiced skill.

The lieutenant accompanying the warrant officer took the sheet of computer paper from the warrant officer and read it:

General Associate of Korean Residents in Japan (Chosen Soren),

While the number of members has declined from 290,000 in 1975 to 250,000 today, Chosen remittances in hard currencies to Pyongyang had been variously estimated at between $600 and $1.9 billion each year, with the most likely value in the lower to middle of this range.

Japanese police reported (January 10, 1994) that some $600 million had been earmarked to be sent to North Korea to date this past year; however, approximately one-third of this money had been diverted in country. The purpose of its use is unknown.

———

"What's this?" the lieutenant said.

"It's good to see they're keeping us in the loop," the chief warrant officer stated tactfully.

"It's interesting information, but what does it have to do with us?"

"North Korea's contacts with the outside world seem to have changed somewhat. There has been a significant decline in funds being supplied to North Korea from organizations outside its borders. The local law enforcement has been able to determine that not all contributions are finding their way north. That seems to suggest they're holding back funds until they're needed for a specific purpose, or perhaps they're using this money to support their causes outside the country." Turning to the young-looking NCO, the chief warrant said, "Tell the lieutenant what you know about the *Chosen Soren*."

With a short pause, the NCO adjusted his glasses and stated, "The *Chosen Soren*, the General Association of Korean Residents in Japan, is North Korea's *defacto* embassy in Tokyo. *Chosen* was the formal name of Korea when Japan ruled the peninsula. Since Japan does not have diplomatic relations with the North, Korean nationals in Japan, who do not change their nationality to South Korea, remain Chosen nationals.

The *Chosen Soren*, in Japanese, or *Chongryon*, in Korean, was founded May 25, 1955. Its organizational structure includes a headquarters in Tokyo, prefectural and regional head offices and branches with eighteen propaganda headquarters and twenty-three business enterprises.

Nearly one-third of the Japanese *pachinko,* or pinball, industry is controlled by *Chosen* affiliates or supporters."

He paused long enough to see that neither had lost interest and continued on, "*Gakushu-gum* is *Chosen's* underground organization, which is a quasi-formal body of the North Korean Workers' Party. *Gakushu-gumi,* with a membership estimated at five thousand, engages in intelligence activities and political maneuverings against South Korea."

The lieutenant, beginning to understand significance of this information, turned to his warrant and asked, "What type of activities does this group provide to the North?"

The chief warrant officer, who oversaw both the intelligence analyst and traffic analyst (COMINT and SIGINT) sections, acknowledged his NCO's contribution with a nod.

"The *Chosen Soren* supports intelligence operations in Japan, assists in the infiltration of agents into South Korea, collects open source information—information readily available to everyone—and diverts advanced technology for use by North Korea. North Korea uses several methods to acquire technology related to nuclear, biological, or chemical warfare and missiles. The *Chosen Soren* has, among other activities, tried to acquire and export advanced technology to North Korea."

"Very well," the young lieutenant replied. "Do you think we should bring this information to the new group commander's attention?"

The chief warrant said, "Absolutely. The commander's been here long enough to understand the significance of this type of information." Adding, "I believe he understands the significance of how the money, if it is not going north, could very well be used for projects that support the North."

Twenty minutes later, the commander, Major Carl Walker, had finished reading the message. He leaned back in his desk chair and looked at the lieutenant. "Seeing that we were only provided a courtesy copy and not the addressee, there's no need to respond. However, I see that our sister unit, the 200th MI Group, in Japan wasn't listed as a recipient. Let's make sure they get a copy. Go ahead and put your spin on the significance of the message, but let me review it before we send it on to the Tokyo embassy. I'll include this in my brief."

Chapter 12

HALE KOA HOTEL – HONOLULU, HAWAII

MARCH 1994

The word is surreal, Captain Kelly Byrnes decided as she took in her surroundings and viewed the letter that showed she had been nominated to an embassy position. She could anticipate a new set of orders, one more time. *The last week has been surreal,* from the moment she was told to call the office of the PERSCOM, Personnel Command, in St Louis, Missouri. *This feels like a dream.*

"Hey! Earth to Kelly! Did you hear anything I just said?" Major Carl Walker was standing in front of her, smiling. "What do you think of my outfit? Do I look like a real native Hawaiian?"

Carl was dressed in a flowered shirt and shorts, typical attire for Hawaii. His outfit, and Susan's, his fiancée, had been carefully selected by a "Hawaiian maiden." The maiden had confessed that her real name was Sergeant First Class Michelle Chou, of the 201st MI Group, but she was a real Hawaiian, born on the Big Island. Chou was a member of Walker's command and a good friend.

Captain Byrnes was also wearing typical tropical clothing, a light cotton, blue flowered shirt, white shorts, beach sandals, and a single-strand orchid lei around her neck.

"I'm afraid my ability to infiltrate the inhabitants of the island will have to wait until I have time for some sunbathing," Carl said.

Susan smiled at her future husband. "Please stand over there; the glare off your white legs is blinding me," she giggled.

When Kelly had pressed Sergeant Chou for details about what was going on, the sergeant had politely told them that, "The major will explain over dinner, which will be served at fourteen hundred hours in the Hale Koa Room."

Along one wall of the hotel's private dining room was a buffet table, on which had been arranged a selection of hors d' oeuvres, and an Asian waiter in a starched white jacket was standing behind a small bar. Brigadier General Byrnes had his back to Kelly, but she recognized his broad shoulders and trim build. He was at the bar with two other men, the father of the groom, whom she had met a number of years ago, and another gentleman who was the bride's father.

I haven't seen Dad since before he made general. He never looked more distinguished, Captain Byrnes thought.

An Asian waiter entered the room through a swinging door, carrying a huge platter of small roasted chicken, lying on a bed of sliced pineapple. An enormous Hawaiian woman from the kitchen followed and showed him where she wanted it laid on the large dining table. Then she followed him back through the swinging doors.

Spotting Kelly first was Susan's father. "Welcome. Come on over and have a drink, Kelly."

General Byrnes turned. With a broad smile, and trying not to spill his drink, he greeted her with a one-armed hug and a kiss on her forehead. He then turned back to the two men and said, "Gentlemen, I'd like you to meet my daughter, Captain Kelly Byrnes."

"Yes, of course," George Walker Sr. said. "I knew you looked familiar; I remember meeting you during Carl's Stanford days. You were in his ROTC class, weren't you?"

"Yes. But actually Carl was a class ahead of me."

Captain Byrnes turned back to her father and with a straight face said, "Do I say good evening, sir? Or, can I just say congratulations on your promotion, Dad?"

"I would say congratulations are in order for both of us, sweet pea. I understand you should be getting your orders pretty soon for your new assignment."

"As a matter of fact, I already received a phone call and a letter about my nomination to the Tokyo embassy position. I was told I'd receive the actual orders following the embassy's approval of my appointment. You didn't have anything to do with that did you?"

"According to Colonel Jackson, even that formality has been completed. And, you know I wouldn't get involved. I wanted to say something when I first saw your name on the most desired list, but chose to separate myself from the whole selection process. Would you believe that no member of my staff who reviewed the list saw the connection between our last names, or at least they chose not to say anything. Later I found out that my aide-de-camp didn't even realize I had a daughter until he heard my conversation with Colonel Jackson, and he asked how you were doing. My aide-de-camp later asked me about you."

"Oh, great. Thanks a lot. Even your own staff didn't know I existed. That shows how much you think of me," Kelly teased.

"And what do you think about your daughter now, sir?" Carl inquired, as he approached, having overheard the last few comments.

"I can now say that I'm very proud of this young lady who, on her own merits, will be joining us in the Asian theater," General Byrnes said.

"If I understand correctly, the orders she got while at the language institute showed she was going to Asaka, Japan," Carl added.

"You are mistaken, I'm afraid," Kelly's father said with a smile. "She'll be stationed at the Tokyo embassy. The individual assigned there for the last year requested a compassionate reassignment back to the states—evidently a family illness."

With a look of astonishment, Carl turned to Kelly and said, "Well, this is the first I've heard about your great news. Were you keeping it a secret from even your closest friends, Kelly?" Carl mocked.

"No," Kelly said, slightly embarrassed. "I was waiting for the right moment to announce it. It hadn't really been formally approved yet by the embassy, but now that I know it has, I guess I can make the announcement." Looking to her father, she said, "Sir, do I have your authorization?"

"You most certainly do, Captain."

"There, then I guess it's official."

"What's official?" The bride-to-be inquired, as she stepped up beside Carl and slipped an arm around his waist.

"I'll be the new foreign area officer to the Tokyo embassy as soon as I receive my orders. Since I finished my Japanese Refresher Course, I've been helping out there until they decide my reporting date."

"That's terrific," Susan exclaimed, stepping forward to give Kelly a hug.

"Well then, a toast is in order," Carl stated. Waiting until everyone had their glasses charged and raised, Carl then said, "To dreams come true."

"To dreams come true," the little group echoed.

"To the bride and groom," Kelly added.

"To the bride and groom," everyone echoed once again.

After a pause, Kelly looked at her father and asked, "Dad, were you referring to Joe Jackson? Wasn't he the one who was stationed in Japan with you when Mom was with us?"

"Yes, that's him."

"I just remember him as Uncle Joe."

"You would remember him that way. Those who were close to the family we always referred to as uncle or aunt. You were about fourteen at the time. You had a number of special nonrelatives back then."

"True, that did make it feel like one big family."

"That helped your mother cope better, too," General Byrnes confessed, diverting his eyes to gaze at his drink.

Feeling her father's discomfort talking about her mother, Kelly quickly asked, "How is Uncle Joe doing now?"

"You'll find out soon enough. You'll see him when you're in Japan. But, I suggest you not refer to him as Uncle Joe. He'll be your new boss at the embassy. He's the embassy's defense attaché."

"I'll be darned. Well, I suppose if I can't have you nearby to watch over me, it will be good to have a friend."

"Yes, and one who can keep me informed about how you're doing. You're as bad at keeping in touch with me as I am with you."

It was Kelly's turn to feel grateful, yet a little uncomfortable, so she turned to Carl and asked, "Carl, I understand originally you two were planning to marry after you completed your assignment with the 201st MI Group. What happened? Did you get too lonely?"

"Well, I confess, the logic we used for marrying after Susan completed her degree and my one-year tour didn't make sense when we considered that even though we couldn't live together, we would get benefits while being married. That would help pay for her classes. Besides, Sergeant Chou convinced me. She said she could put together a perfect Hawaiian wedding for us."

Susan joined in to add, "Once he passed that information along to me, and I had an opportunity to have a few conversations with Sergeant Chou, one of Carl's section chiefs, I thought the idea sounded great. I never liked the idea of a big wedding, but I knew that I'd disappoint family if we didn't have some sort of gathering to celebrate. Deciding on a location was difficult until I talked with Sergeant Chou. After that it was easy. I did all the planning with her by phone. I knew the Hawaiian wedding would be the ultimate."

"In other words, you got lonely," Kelly mocked.

"I got lonely," Carl admitted.

"So what now?" Kelly asked.

"You mean about the dinner, the wedding, or the honeymoon?" Carl innocently badgered.

"All the above," Kelly pressed.

"Well, first we eat. Once we get everyone settled, we'll tell you all." Seeing that everybody was now present, he steered them toward the dining table.

Of the immediate family, David and Doreen Montgomery, Susan's parents, were seated on the bride's side of the long, wide, rectangular-shaped table. The bride and groom sat at the head. David Montgomery Jr., brother of the bride, sat at the opposite end of the table with Sergeant Chou. William J. Walker Sr. and Nancy, the groom's parents, were seated across from the Montgomerys. Kelly, the maid of honor, and her father, General Byrnes, were seated alongside the Walkers.

Once the small party of ten was settled, Carl asked the waiter to ensure everyone's glass was filled with champagne before he began his announcement. "We apologize for having just a small get together like this," Carl said. "But it was either do it this way or elope without seeing any of you. So, I first want to thank Sergeant Chou for helping us make this all possible, not to mention the large phone bills." He waited for the appropriate chuckles to subside before continuing. "She convinced Susan and me that we could make this occasion seem extravagant while still keeping it simple. She used to do this sort of thing with her mother here on the islands before she joined the army. So, like I said, our wedding plans for this evening will be very simple. The services will be held on that big catamaran you see moored just off shore." Carl pointed out beyond the white sandy beach, and everyone followed his gaze. "Following the nuptials you will continue to enjoy sailing along the south shores of Oahu, while listening to Hawaiian music and drinking a beverage of your choice, as long as it can be drunk from a pineapple with a tiny umbrella. While you are all watching the sunset, Susan and I will sneak off into the night via the small outboard they pull behind the catamaran. We'll be leaving tomorrow for a Korean honeymoon, and we'd like to get an early start."

"Oh, my God!" Mrs. Walker said.

"I'll be damned!" Mr. Walker said.

"Well, well," Mr. Montgomery said, beaming.

"That's wonderful. But why is this all happening so quickly? Do you have to go back to Korea right away?"

"While I don't have to go back to work immediately, we've got reservations at Seoul's downtown Hilton for three nights and then the Dragon Hill Lodge, on South Post, Yongsan, in Seoul for another ten days," Carl clarified.

Susan joined with, "During that time I'll have an opportunity to see where he'll be working and check on housing availability for when I join him on his next assignment. Then I'll have to get back to the states for my final class term."

"That should give me plenty of time to get things ready for her return, although I need to prepare for my next assignment. There's plenty of work piling up there I understand," Carl stated.

"What is it exactly you do in your job?" Mrs. Walker inquired.

"Well, I'm about halfway through a one-year assignment with the 201st Military Intelligence Group. My job is to gather what information I can from our various sections and disseminate it to those units in the field that need it to better understand the North Korean situation.

"What kind of sections are you referring to?" Mrs. Walker continued.

"We have four sections that have the ability to conduct photo imagery, radio intercepts, and analyze traffic and intelligence. The photo imagery section analyzes ground and air photos. The intercept and traffic analysis includes electronic or radar analysis, and traffic includes communications and signal analysis. The intelligence analysis section deals with analyzing human and historical information to better project future North Korean actions."

General Byrnes chose this moment to interject hints of Carl and Kelly's next duty assignments for the benefit of all present. "His understanding of that last section is what will significantly help him in his next assignment," Byrnes went on. "Both Captain Walker and Captain Byrnes's next duty assignment will be as a foreign area officer. Both of them will be spending a great deal of time helping to ensure our military presence is not misunderstood. They will gather and assess overt intelligence—not highly secretive stuff, but off-the-street information—that can be useful to our country's defense. That's the defense attaché's primary area of responsibility, interpreting or making sense of overt intelligence. The defense attaché, in turn, consolidates this from his subordinates and reports his findings to both the ambassador and the Defense Human Intelligence Service. In other words, they'll have two bosses, the director of Defense Human Intelligence, who is interested in gathering information, and the ambassador, who's ultimately concerned with not ruffling the feathers of the people they're there to gather intelligence from."

"Does that mean he'll be working as a spy then?" Mrs. Montgomery asked.

"Not really," Carl chuckled. "Most of my duties are more like being a military diplomat. Comparing my current job with the one I'm going to, I can say that my primary focus with the 201st has been to assess both friendly and enemy military capabilities. My next job will be to understand how the people of that culture think. This, in turn, will help us to understand our best defensive posture for the region. That doesn't mean we don't deal with intelligence, it's just not spying, which is a covert operation. Is that about how you'd describe it, General Byrnes?"

"It's sometimes difficult to explain, but in layman terms, that's about as close as anyone could get. Here, let me help you with some specific examples. Sometimes information is printed openly in the newspapers. That's how we found out that the National Police Agency monitors funds being sent from an organization within Japan to North Korea. This is all open source information, readily available to the public. Anyone who wants it can get it. But we may decide to look into that further. If we found, for example, that a great deal had been siphoned back into Japan, we would then try to make sense of it."

"And what can you determine from information of that type?" Mr. Montgomery now joined in.

"This could show how much success they are having making contacts outside the country. The number of members who support them, as well as how much money they receive, is helpful information. We're still trying to track the money that stayed inside the country. We hope to find out how it could be used to support North Korea from inside Japan."

"Is that information classified?" Mr. Montgomery further asked.

"The information we receive out of the newspapers, or open source information, is not classified. As we make an interpretation about that information, we may classify it in our reports," the general clarified.

"Then he won't necessarily be dealing with classified information unless the embassy personnel classify it?" Mrs. Walker inquired, trying to absorb what her son's responsibilities would entail.

"Oh, there are times information is classified when it comes in from the field. Sometimes information walks in the front door, like an overheard conversation between the president of North Korea and his son in a hospital ward. This information I can't share with you here, but I will share it with the two of you later," General Byrnes said, looking at Carl and then Kelly. He continued, "What made me accept your gracious invitation to attend this wedding was not only the opportunity to be a part of a special occasion, but the opportunity to personally brief them on their future responsibilities. Of course, I couldn't miss the opportunity to see my one and only daughter."

Later the general briefed Kelly and Carl on the latest activities in the region, and a possible tie to the stalled talks between the United States and North Korea. He included the overheard conversation regarding President Kim's intent to recruit a religious group outside the country called the Soldiers of White Love Army. Kim's plans might also include the use of nuclear weapons. Byrnes shared how another outside connection, Japan's Chosen Soren, might be diverting funds within Japan, funds normally sent to North Korea to support their cause. This provided further evidence showing outside financial connections.

Having shared all this, General Byrnes added that while it was difficult to validate information of this sort from other more reliable sources, such as satellite photos or spies, they needed to make sure all raw intelligence was shared. Although he couldn't include this information in any formal reports yet, he stressed the importance of pursuing any avenues that might suggest the motivations behind North Korea's hardline stance at the negotiations table. He couldn't emphasize enough what General Powell had stated: "Now it would be up to those of us in the field, so to speak, to stay tuned to who was truly behind the possible expansion of terrorist activities sponsored from the North."

He just hoped that General Powell's replacement would continue to provide the same support.

Chapter 13

THE WHITE HOUSE OVAL OFFICE -

WASHINGTON DC

MARCH 1994

"Mr. President," the president's personal aide announced, "the director of the CIA is here."

"Send him in," Clinton said impatiently.

"And the secretary of state, sir."

"Him, too, for Christ's sake!" the president said.

The director entered the Oval Office, followed by the secretary of state. He looked around and saw the secretary of defense and chairman of the Joint Chiefs of Staff were also in the room.

"Good morning, Mr. President," the director said.

The president grunted.

"Good morning, sir," the secretary of state said.

The president grunted again, and waved both men onto the couch across from the coffee table. He was sitting at the end of the table, back to his desk, in one of several identical armchairs that formed a crescent around the table. The secretary of defense and JCS chairman were seated in two identical armchairs, the secretary of defense seated closest to the president.

The president slid a sheet of paper across the glass-topped coffee table to the director of the Central Intelligence Agency. "You've all seen this latest NSA report," the president stated. He knew that it was the expected practice of all members of the NSC to be briefed on all aspects of the National Security Agency's assessment, once it consolidated intelligence briefs from their sources as well as a multitude of other agencies. The area of concern this morning centered around not knowing what was impeding progress on negotiations on North Korea's nuclear program. The frustration in the room was evident.

"Those lying bastards are up to something. Why else would they first stall at the negotiations table and then test fire a ballistic missile," the president said. "I've asked you here to make it clear that I'm frustrated as hell about the situation with the North Koreans. I know that President Kim is up to something. I want to know what it is, and I want you to come up with a plan for how we can deal with them. General Shalli and Secretary Perry have already given me some military options, but I need more than that. I want better intelligence, something I can use at the negotiation's table that can put an end to this endless rhetoric."

They all nodded. Everyone knew that tensions were at a new high. The president's aide stepped into the room, accompanied by the national security adviser, and checked to see that coffee had been distributed, then he quickly exited. With the added presence of the national security advisor, they now began to pull open briefcases, and sort through their notes.

Seeing that everyone was now settled, the president began. "General Shalli has presented a military response involving deploying patriot missiles to South Korea as an immediate response to the threat posed by North Korea's ballistic missiles. Beyond that, I want to discuss Secretary Perry's options for increasing our readiness and alert posture, enhancing intelligence collection, and sharing information with South Korea and others in the area. We need to incorporate effective defense plans against a possible nuclear, chemical, or biological attack from the North. We must be prepared to take stronger measures should further efforts fail to persuade North Korea to end this situation."

Seeing that all were listening intently to what he had said, the president took the opportunity to further admit his frustration. This would be as close as he would get to an apology for a short temper and impatient attitude.

"Before General Powell retired, one of his recommendations was to consider the possible imposition of sanctions. At that time I believed that would have been an appropriate response to their rhetoric. However, now, for some unknown reason, they are taking a harder stance. Something has changed to cause this. When I think about this option, and the experience General Powell has, I can't help but reflect on how, as much as we want to be decisive and take action, it is important for us make the best, most informed decisions we can. Unfortunately, as soon as I am ready to move forward in our negotiations, gain more information, and make some headway, I have to start over again with a new staff. First, I lose General Colin Powell when he retired as our chairman, and then Les Aspin is hospitalized and resigns. Gentlemen, I want you all to get smart on the North Korean issues and start giving me options immediately."

The group knew what was at stake. They understood the importance of their mission before continuing, clarifying what was already known, and discussing options. Before ending the meeting, most had concurred with a nine-option contingency in the event North Korea did not allow implementation of the IAEA inspection. The plan included an exchange of envoys with the South to discuss the nuclear issue. The US had offered to suspend the Team Spirit '94 military exercise, which provided mobilization training.

The other options included: increase the readiness and alert posture of US and South Korean forces; deploy additional troops, fighter aircraft squadrons, Apache helicopters, and a carrier battle group to the area; enhance intelligence collection and sharing with South Korea; and address the lack of effective defenses against a chemical or biological attack from the North.

The greatest consensus came regarding the need for someone to get closer to the situation and determine possible alternative motives behind North Korea's noncompliance to inspections. Joint military training exercises and joint peacekeeping operations needed to include contingencies for dealing with nuclear, chemical, and biological hazards.

Chapter 14

TOKYO INTERNATIONAL AIRPORT -

TOKYO, JAPAN

JUNE 1994

"You are Captain Byrnes?" Masatoshi Onishi, holding a sign with Kelly's name, greeted her as she exited the international arrivals area.

"Yes, I am," she said.

Onishi gave a short bow and said, "Please, let me help you with your bags."

"Thank you." Byrnes handed him her largest bag and followed, a handbag hanging from one shoulder, and a purse strap draped over the other.

"Your ride is just outside. Please follow me."

In practiced English, Onishi said, "I am to understand we will be working together. Colonel Jackson told me you will work with the Japan Ground Self-Defense Forces."

"Yes, that's right," Kelly responded in Japanese, as they continued to walk toward the airport's passenger pickup point. "I'm to observe, if there's no position for me to participate in."

"There is a position. With me," Onishi said with a smile, realizing Kelly was practicing her Japanese while he was demonstrating his English, "We will work together, unless you only wish to observe."

As a liaison between the Japan Self-Defense Forces and the US embassy, Tokyo, Masatoshi Onishi took it upon himself to meet Captain Byrnes at the airport, since they would be working together.

Onishi looked trim and fit in the Japanese equivalent of a US army Class B uniform. His green epaulets included one gold bar next to three stars, showing his rank of captain. He was five feet eight inches tall and moved with the grace of an athletic man.

"I'd rather be a full participant than an observer," Captain Byrnes said as they exited Tokyo's International Haneda Airport.

Onishi waved at his driver. A camouflaged Ford Bronco immediately pulled forward to close the gap from where the driver had been idling his vehicle.

"Here's our ride," Onishi gestured toward the vehicle.

Rather than drive directly to Camp Zama, Onishi directed the driver to cruise by the embassy as well as a few well-known landmarks so Byrnes could see some of the local sites. Within minutes, they were on a first-name basis. Onishi, knowing Americans were less formal and had a habit of using a shortened version of their names, told Kelly to refer to him as Masa. She told him to call her Kelly.

Arriving at Camp Zama, Captain Onishi first took Captain Byrnes to the BOQ. Masa helped with her luggage as they entered. "Once you get checked in, I'll take you to the post's in-processing center. It's not far from here."

They arrived at the counter, and when Captain Byrnes told the clerk her name, the clerk immediately looked at Onishi's nametag and said, "This is for the both of you," and handed an envelope to Captain Byrnes. Kelly opened it and saw that it was addressed to both herself and Onishi and was from Colonel Jackson. Kelly read it before passing it to Onishi.

———

TO: Cpt. Byrnes & Cpt. Onishi:

I have been summoned out of country for a meeting. I need Captain Onishi, who is familiar with the embassy's role in the upcoming G-7

Summit, to represent me in an IPR (In-Process Review). I want Captain Byrnes to delay her orientation to embassy operations for a few more days. I expect to return by midday Wednesday.

Captain Byrnes, once you've completed your in-processing at Camp Zama, feel free to take a few days to become familiar with the post as well as the local area. I don't expect to see you until Wednesday afternoon, next week. At that time, Captain Onishi will be assisting you to get settled at the embassy.

———

Captain Onishi, who had been educated in New Jersey, was on loan to the embassy from the Japan Self-Defense Forces' Plans and Operations department. He would be Byrne's counterpart while performing duties in the exercises involving Japan's Ground Self-Defense Force— the main branch of the Japan Self-Defense Forces. His initial position was to assist embassy staff as a translator and help them understand the Japanese culture. Captain Byrnes's fluency in the language would relieve him of some of those responsibilities.

Onishi let her know that she was always welcome to stop by the embassy but recommended against this since it would be a busy day. During her orientation she'd be told more about her duties and meet the staff. He encouraged her to take advantage of the couple of days off before reporting on Wednesday. Colonel Joe Jackson, soon to be her new boss, wanted her oriented to the area prior to welcoming her.

Chapter 15

WEST OF TOKYO, JAPAN

THREE DAYS LATER

After a weekend shopping in Tokyo and visiting many of its well-known tourist attractions, Captain Byrnes decided to spend some time in the countryside. Reconnecting with the Japanese culture was important to her. *Mixing with the people,* as her dad would say, *is the best way to get to know the country.* The first place that came to mind was Matsumoto City, a place her mother and father had taken her when she was a child. *Those were happy times.*

Kelly decided to take the Monday morning subway to the outskirts of Tokyo and then transfer to a train that crossed Honshu Island. Her plan was to stay a couple of nights in Matsumoto City and return, hopefully refreshed, for her orientation on Wednesday. But it didn't work out as smoothly as she planned.

On Tokyo's subway system, she endured standing in the aisle, pressed between students and businessmen. By the time she found a seat, they had arrived at her stop near the train station. After transferring to the train, Kelly was only able to find an empty seat that faced the rear of the car. Kelly soon discovered that looking at the countryside while seated this way was making her woozy.

That was when she noticed a young couple sitting across from her. They reminded Kelly of Carl and his marriage to Susan, as well as her own parents. These thoughts lingered as the train crossed the plains of Japan's Honshu Island.

The big question in her mind was whether a career would interfere with family life. Would Carl's relationship with Susan survive? Her parents' had not. She remembered discussions she and Carl had that demonstrated their commitment to their individual army careers. She realized that their friendship had caused self-doubt about the career path she'd chosen. Now, when she thought about Carl, she wondered how he would be able to balance his career and family life.

Kelly recalled how much she and her parents had enjoyed being together when she was young. They travelled to neighboring countries with each of her father's new assignments. She cherished those special times together. They would go on picnics, camping, and skiing, enjoying each other as well as the surrounding countryside of the various nations.

Her mother had spoiled it by leaving them. As much as she tried to understand how her mother's depression was to blame for her behavior, Kelly was upset at her for that and had mixed emotions about her condition. She didn't understand what her mother could and could not control.

Kelly saw her mother change over time. She slowly became more somber and withdrawn. When she did overhear her parents' discussions, they often included her mother's complaint about feeling tired all the time, lonely, with an inability to stay focused. She even stopped reading, which had been a favorite pastime. Her mother felt inadequate doing those things she once loved.

Kelly could not understand how her mother could make statements like, *I find life as an army wife exciting,* and then have times when she couldn't bear to be there any longer. Kelly was in her teens when her mother first left to go back to the states, to be with her parents. The first absence was for three months. After returning, she only stayed a few months before leaving again—this time for six months. The next time she left, it was for a year.

Her father visited her mother when he could, but he soon found solace in his job and the company of his only child.

Kelly adapted to her mother's absence, as any teenager would. She became more absorbed in school, friends, and being with her father, at least as much as his busy schedule allowed. Her grades were excellent and her relationship with her father couldn't have been any better, she thought.

During her last year of high school, Kelly had a phone call from her mother. That's when she explained to Kelly, "I need to spend some time with my parents. They're having health issues."

When discussing this with her father, he admitted, "While your grandmother and grandfather aren't getting around as easily as they use to, that really isn't the issue. Your mother thought she might improve if she stayed with her parents, in familiar surroundings. I didn't want that to happen, but she needed to have a strong support structure. I knew my job wouldn't allow me to be with her as much as she needed, and being in a foreign country was hard on her."

"Did she see a doctor?" Kelly asked.

"She refused to go. She said people would think she had mental problems. She didn't like the stigma attached to that. Your mother believed she should be able to overcome the depression on her own. But she ended up isolating herself and just sat around the house. I couldn't get her interested in doing anything. I felt helpless."

Time passed and Kelly went off to college at Stanford.

Periodically, Kelly's father would talk with her about her mother, but Kelly would change the subject. She understood that her father didn't want her mother home alone, sitting around the house, while he was busy at work and Kelly was at school.

The train slowed for the next stop, bringing Kelly out of her trance.

As the train came to a halt, the young couple sitting across from her vacated their seats and made their way to the sliding doors. Kelly quickly moved across to the window seat so she could face forward. *At least the last two-hour part of the leg, climbing into the mountains, would be more comfortable,* she thought. This improved her mood considerably.

Now she could better envision her childhood memories when she and her parents traveled this same route together and trekked through the hills surrounding Matsumoto City. *Can't think of a better way to get rejuvenated before reporting to my new assignment,* Kelly thought.

Little did she know that soon she would face an unforeseen and challenging adventure.

PART 2

Terrorism is the unlawful use of force or violence against persons or property to intimidate or coerce a government, the civilian population, or any segment thereof, in furtherance of political or social objectives.

– FBI Definition

Chapter 16

MATSUMOTO CITY, JAPAN

SAME DAY

During a conversation with the conductor, shortly after boarding the train to Matsumoto City, Kelly found out that the engine on an earlier run had mechanical problems, cancelling that trip. This made traveling this day more crowded than usual. Exasperating this even more was an unusual warming trend that brought temperatures into the '80s, making the air in the train stuffy.

When the train finally reached its destination, she was glad to finally be able to stretch her legs. Kelly exited the train and stepped out onto the platform, following the crowd as they turned south along the landing. She glanced up briefly and caught a glimpse of the electronic display proudly counting the days to the 1998 Winter Olympics, which would be held in the nearby mountains. What she really wanted to do was go for a walk, see the surrounding hills and plains, and take in all the pleasures that the city had to offer.

To avoid being swept up in the movement of the crowd, Kelly stepped off to the side, away from the other passengers. There she waited for the masses to pass. She could feel the sun's rays as it beat down upon her on this unusually warm June day and appreciated this brief moment alone. Kelly could feel herself relaxing as her mind flashed back to the times she and her parents ventured out into this same district. The air was clean, reminiscent of an earlier time.

Kelly's Western clothing was similar to those around her. Much of Japan now consisted of a mix between Western-style attire and the older, more traditional clothing. It no longer seemed unusual to see a person dressed in a *kimono* walking along, talking with another person wearing American-style jeans. Her own jeans, tennis shoes, and soft, white cotton blouse blended well with those. Even her backpack was similar in style to those carried by the students she observed on the train.

Kelly made her way along the streets, recalling moments from her past. She headed toward the center of the old town, remembering a place they had stayed many years ago, not far from Matsumoto Castle.

Matsumoto Castle stood at the heart of the resort town of 200,000 people, a monument to Japan's finest feudal architecture. This great structure was composed of a five-stage, six-storied main donjon in the center. It was linked by a bridge tower to a small adjacent lookout to the north called "Inui" mini donjon and a moon watching tower to the east. Its stone base was coated with white plaster. Located in the wall were openings through which weapons could be discharged.

Originally the castle was a small fortress, called Fukashi Castle, built in 1504. By the time the fortress was completed in 1614, Japan had been united under the government of the Shogun Ieyasu Tokugawa in the city of Edo, known today as Tokyo.

Just a few blocks from the Matsumoto Castle, not far from the center of old town, Kelly found the hotel that she so fondly remembered.

After getting settled into her room, she decided to get an early dinner at a local restaurant and then take a short nap before venturing out for an evening walk.

However, Kelly's late afternoon walk became a late night stroll. Her short rest turned into a long nap. She awoke, still dressed in her traveling attire, and decided to shake off her long train trip by getting outside and stretching her legs. She looked at her watch and saw it was after 11:00 p.m. Although she knew all the stores were closed, she decided to walk around the castle before turning in for the night.

Kelly left the hotel, pulling her light jacket around herself tightly. The temperature had dropped as quickly as it had climbed, and the cooler mountain air had returned with the darkness. When she caught sight of the mountain's silhouette, her heart surged.

Reaching the castle, she followed the road around its massive walls. The glow from the castle floodlights allowed her enough light to follow the road, while enjoying the scenery provided by the brightly lit stars and moon.

Kelly didn't know how much time had passed while she gazed out over the horizon. This day's activities continued to repeat in her mind as she rounded the last section of the castle and headed back to the hotel.

The town hadn't changed too much from when she and her parents had made their trip many years ago. Of course it did seem more spacious back then, but then she was smaller. Kelly paused briefly to get her bearings. She made a choice and turned toward the old town center.

As she rounded a turn, she caught sight of something rather peculiar—movement on the outskirts of a dimly lit vacant lot. It wasn't so much the movement itself that alerted her as much as the way the two men's silhouettes drew her attention. They were separated from each other, looking out toward the city lights, away from her. When she stopped to watch, she saw what seemed to be nervous pacing with periodic glances across the lot. An engine idled in the same direction they were looking. One man bent over, lifted a handful of dirt, and tossed it into the air.

A chill ran through Kelly and she pulled her jacket closely around her. She continued her journey, but in the back of her mind remained a nagging feeling.

Kelly's father had always urged her to sharpen her instincts. He had honed his own skills while working in the counter intelligence arena. As a young girl, he taught her to pay attention to what was around her and trust her feelings. Once she had followed her instincts and helped a girlfriend escape her mother's molesting boyfriend.

Kelly continued along a pathway that took her away from the two men. She stopped near a pond that was surrounded with a few trees and brush. From her new vantage point, she remained concealed but could make out the vehicle across the lot. It was a large rig that looked like a delivery truck.

Her attention to the truck made a boy's movement nearby go almost undetected. He moved from right to left across the dimly lit streetlight. The light's amber tinge helped her distinguish his features. He carried a shopping bag, only it didn't have the look of a neat, tidy parcel. *He's taking out the garbage,* Kelly concluded. *We must be the only ones out at this late hour.*

Then she spotted another man, not far behind the boy. He was not one of the first two she had spotted earlier. He came from a different direction and seemed to be following the boy. The man was dressed in black and stayed clear of the lights, as if trying to avoid their glow. Something wasn't right. Then she saw a reflective glimmer in his hand.

He has a knife. Oh, my God. I've got to do something, Kelly thought, *but what?*

Kelly hurried to the edge of the pathway and squatted behind a bush that the boy had just passed.

The man was coming closer. Kelly grabbed the base of the shrub in front of her and gave it a quick tug. The leaves made an unsettling rustling noise.

The man stopped abruptly and stared in her direction.

At least the boy is getting away, Kelly thought.

The man approached the bush. She felt like his eyes were burning right through her.

Kelly remained frozen in place for what seemed like a long time.

Then she heard a shout.

"Help!" A man's voice. It came from another direction, past the truck.

"Sumiko, come quickly, somebody's done something to our dogs… I think we should call the police…Sumiko!"

A door slammed shut.

Kelly kept her eyes on the man dressed in black. She saw him look in the direction of the yelling. Out of the corner of her eye, she saw a single light come on just beyond where the yelling had been. Then, a second and third house lit up.

Kelly didn't move.

Chapter 17

MATSUMOTO CITY, JAPAN

SAME DAY

Hideo Mori's truck moved swiftly through his rehearsed exit route. He knew the sentry vehicle would follow in close pursuit.

With a gravel flying, the driver of that truck shot out of the lot as soon as Mori said, "Let's go, I see someone coming out of that nearest house."

The driver barely waited for the operators to finish the shutdown procedures before taking off.

The sentinels responded immediately, as well. They were to follow the truck as soon as it left, but they knew not to get too close.

Although Mori had calculated the odds of killing the three judges a hundred times, he knew the probability was not 100 percent. His original plan was to pipe the deadly serum into the district courthouse from the customized truck. But he had worked so long into the night to transfer the sarin gas into a bolted-down canister he had overslept that morning and missed his opportunity to arrive during court hours.

At first Mori was upset but then had to remind himself that his ultimate plan was to intimidate, not necessarily kill.

Mori's sleeping in had caused him to change his plans for the day, but he couldn't delay the attack. The court was due to reconvene and announce a decision on their case within the next few days, and the temperatures could not be any better than today. Releasing the deadly gas outdoors would be more difficult to control than piping it into a building. But today's inversion would keep the gas lingering longer, allowing maximum affect on their target—a dormitory where the judges stayed. It was near the courthouse and provided a place for them to stay while working on long cases.

So Mori planned his attack for this evening. Although he was careful, he didn't factor in all the delays he had encountered.

Mori had taken into account the traveling time needed to drive from their Mt. Fuji chemical plant while avoiding the cameras that recorded license plates along the expressway's route. But he didn't consider the limited speed of the aged vehicle. Fully loaded, with forty-four pounds of toxin, 1,000 pounds of batteries, a heater, fan, protective gear, an atomizer, and two other men, the old two-ton vehicle was only able to reach a top speed of thirty miles per hour. Despite all this, he knew he had to deal with the judges tonight.

His superior, Haruka, had carefully selected Mori to handle this matter. These judges were interfering with their organization's expansion plans. The judges needed to be so incapacitated they could not attend court. His actions tonight would hopefully postpone the ruling on their land dispute. If not, it would certainly cause anyone connected with this case to take pause before taking any further action against them, personally or legally.

Mori, concerned that the winds could shift at any time, felt fortunate to have been able to stay in place to disburse the gas as long as they had—about thirty minutes. Normally, the gaseous cloud would not be visible, but tonight's blend included more isopropyl chloride.

It was no wonder the team was anxious about being caught. The white mist created by the additional chloride was easy to see, even at night.

Mori could only hope that they had been there long enough to allow the gas to spread effectively.

Chapter 18

MATSUMOTO CITY, JAPAN

Reacting to the neighborhood commotion, the man in black turned and ran. Kelly watched in amazement, giving a sigh of relief, as he left. She heard a truck's engine rev loudly and its doors bang shut. As the truck exited the lot, she could see that the back of the vehicle had high-paneled sides, like a refrigeration truck. The illumination from a streetlight allowed a glimpse of smoke coming from the rear of the vehicle.

Kelly saw the man in black join others as he entered a dark-colored minivan, which began to move even before all the doors were shut. The van followed the truck. Kelly felt confused as she tried to process what she had just witnessed.

Once she realized there was nothing she could do about the men who were escaping, and not sure what they were escaping from, she turned her attention to the nearby house where the man had been yelling. Kelly hurried to the house and saw a gray mist moving just beyond its rooftop. *Just like the smoke from the truck,* Kelly thought. In that same direction, she saw more lights coming to life and heard more yelling between neighbors.

As Kelly came closer, a man ran out the front door, frantic. Still thinking about the gaseous cloud, she wondered if she might be in danger, but her urge to help overcame her fear.

He met her outside his home, his eyes wide in desperation. "Please help me; it's my wife," he yelled before running inside.

Kelly stumbled over the shoes left at the front door as she entered. Catching up, she found the man bent over a woman, lying on the living room floor. The woman was having difficulty breathing. Her gasps for air were short and irregular. Kelly helped the man lift his wife and transport her outside to fresh air.

"There's something in the air," the man said. "It affected my two dogs. I found them earlier in our yard. Dead."

As they gently laid the woman down, the man begged Kelly to check on his two children in the other bedroom, while he stayed with his wife. Kelly entered cautiously, covering her nose and mouth with a hanky she had wet under an outside faucet. She rushed down the hall to a bedroom where she saw the lights burning, the windows closed, and the room empty. Not sure how much of the gas was trapped inside, she continued down the hallway to find another bedroom. She turned on the lights and noticed two children sleeping soundly in their beds below an open window. *Well ventilated*, she thought. Kelly shook them awake, and although groggy, the children obediently walked with her, out to their parents.

The man's wife was convulsing now. She lay across her husband's lap as he rocked forward and back, not knowing what to do.

Kelly heard a siren coming up the street. *The neighbors must have called for help*, she thought.

She told the man, "Just stay here, I'll get help," and ran to greet the vehicle. She saw that it was an ambulance, waved it down, and immediately directed the medics to the man and his wife.

While the family was being attended to, she scanned her surroundings and saw people exiting their houses and apartments. Some had already gathered in groups along the street.

Some were vomiting, others reached out as if blind, still others were carried or led to the street from their homes. Many were in their pajamas and bathrobes. A series of vehicles, sirens blaring, began to arrive along the road. Even more sirens could be heard in the distance.

Police and fire trucks were arriving as well. A few deployed in an intersection where the medics could establish a triage, and the police could conduct interviews. All of Matsumoto seemed to be awakening from its deep slumber into a state of confusion.

Some greeted the police as they exited neighboring apartments and pointed saying, "It's coming from that direction." Others directed the arriving aid units to those most in need. Police radios began broadcasting bits of information and asking for more backup as they tried to sort out the situation.

Police organized into teams. Some accompanied medical groups who provided aid, others questioned bystanders, and still others were used for crowd control. The air was alive with frantic radio calls making inquiries to various hospital facilities, police precincts, and fire stations. Reporters too had arrived, setting up their satellite dishes and extending their antennas to get the word out to the populace.

Still concerned about the poisonous cloud, Kelly kept her distance from the chaos after helping the man and his family. However, with her adrenaline pumping, she knew she wouldn't get any sleep if she returned to her room. She felt compelled to stay and observe the chaos from a distance.

Periodically Kelly strayed to where the medics and police had gathered to find out what she could. Following a number of these visits, Kelly was able to determine that she was correct about where the toxic cloud had originated and was convinced that the men and vehicles she had observed caused this.

Unfortunately, the more she heard, the more she was also convinced that the police had drawn the wrong conclusion.

From what she gathered from police discussions, they believed that the toxic cloud came from the house Kelly had entered, and a man they called Kono was the cause. Based on the location of his house, they believed it couldn't have come from anywhere else. The only other thing in the vicinity was a vacant lot. And the man had chemicals stored in his home. Perhaps he had accidently mixed them together and released the toxic gas into the air, the police conjectured.

Knowing she had to say something, Kelly approached one of the officers. "Please excuse me," she began in Japanese. "I believe I have information you don't have about this incident."

The officer courteously acknowledged Kelly and asked her to continue. She did, first explaining how she had arrived by train that day and came to be out so late before getting to the point.

"I saw a big truck in the parking lot that seemed to have a number of men standing around it, like they were protecting it," Kelly said. "I believe it had something to do with the chemical that affected all these people." But as she continued, she realized that the officer's attention was wandering. He didn't follow up with questions and seemed to be gazing past her.

When she finished, the officer stood with a blank expression before seeming to realize he should say something. He cordially thanked her, then shrugged and said, "Oh, the truck you saw was probably just making a delivery to the supermarket. They often make their deliveries after hours," he added a smile. "But thank you for your information. I'll make a note of it and look into it further."

Byrnes had a feeling that she hadn't been taken serious. That she had been pegged as an outsider. She realized they probably saw her as an American who spoke Japanese but didn't understand their ways. Clearly, from what she heard in the officer's earlier conversations, they believed they had found their man, Kono.

Kelly decided not to pursue it, assuming they'd eventually confirm her information as they investigated further. The buildup of adrenaline that had kept her going throughout the night had passed, and she realized now she was exhausted. Believing that a good sleep would help her recover from the night's traumatic activities, she returned to her room to sleep.

As she walked back to the hotel, she began to question what she had witnessed. *Perhaps the policeman was correct,* Kelly wondered. It had just been a truck making a delivery.

It was well past 3:00 a.m. before Kelly finally dropped off to sleep, and even then she didn't sleep well. A slight headache had made rest difficult.

When sunlight woke her a few hours later, the slight headache she had gone to bed with was now pounding and her mouth felt dry. She lay in bed and rubbed her temples.

It was the middle of that afternoon when she decided to see a local doctor.

When Kelly arrived at the local clinic, she was amazed at the number of people there. Even after the night's events, the citizens of Kaichi Heights (the affected neighborhood) continued to arrive, many with symptoms similar to her own. As she sat in the waiting room, she heard many of the victims talking of a white mist and complaining of symptoms that ranged from nausea to throbbing headaches and even clouded vision. Some complained of having dimmed vision, while others described seeing kaleidoscopic fragments.

When she finally did see the doctor, he gave her a shot of atropine. "That should relieve the symptoms," he said, "but if they continue, come back and see me. I've already seen erratic temperatures and damage to lungs and digestive systems.

After hearing that, she felt she'd been lucky. The doctor checked her pupils, explaining that the organic phosphorous gas they had found in other patients might explain the slight contraction of her pupils.

He felt confident that Kelly's condition would eventually go away and that the shot he gave her should help move things along more rapidly. She hoped so. Being on top of her game when she reported to her new position at the embassy was important.

The events of the night would result in seven deaths. Those who died did so in agony, writhing in pain. Spasms would consume their bodies, uncontrollable vomiting would devastate their digestive system, and massive brain damage would result from damaged lungs and heart. Over 150 casualties would overwhelm the Matsumoto emergency services, but a last-minute change in wind direction meant the three judges did not receive a direct hit. One judge was hospitalized, along with his wife, while the others would suffer only mild symptoms. Kono's wife, Sumiko, would finally succumb to her ailments after being bedridden and in a coma for nineteen years.

Chapter 19

CAMP ZAMA, JAPAN

THE NEXT DAY

Standing at the BOQ counter, Colonel Jackson used the desk phone to call Captain Byrnes's room, unaware that she was just arriving at the Camp Zama subway station. He had looked forward to surprising Byrnes and was disappointed she wasn't there.

After dropping the colonel off at the front door and parking his government vehicle, Captain Onishi rejoined the colonel.

Jackson wanted to personally welcome Kelly to her new assignment and invite her to attend a briefing at the camp that related to her position with the embassy. There was no need for her to report to the embassy immediately.

Colonel Jackson had known Captain Kelly Byrnes since she was a young girl. Her father and he had been close friends for many years, and he had taken on the role as her surrogate uncle. As her new boss, he knew he would have to keep a balance between that role and being a family friend. Meeting with her away from the embassy gave him the opportunity to greet her and clarify their professional role. Their first official meeting would be with the 200ᵗʰ MI Group.

Colonel Jackson's position as the US embassy's military attaché was to advise the US ambassador on military matters and at times act as a liaison between the US Army and Japanese defense forces.

Today, those duties called for him to look into a situation that had come to their attention through local news agencies. The incident could potentially require military assistance. Jackson was responsible for gathering and disseminating intelligence that pertained to internal or external threats to Japan. This required him to periodically attend briefings with the Commander of the 200th MI Group, Major Charles "Chuck" Jaegar. Major Jaegar was the local intelligence officer Captain Byrnes would need to rely on for much of their information. It was important for her to meet him as well.

Rather than wait for Captain Byrnes to return to her BOQ room, Jackson left a note on her door explaining where she could find him and Captain Onishi, prior to the briefing. The two officers then made their way to the mess hall for a cup of coffee. Jackson tried to relax but found himself glancing at his watch.

About an hour after arriving at the BOQ, Captain Byrnes entered the mess hall.

"There she is," Colonel Jackson said. "Your timing is perfect. We were just about to head over to the Group's headquarters for our briefing."

Captain Byrnes had just completed the two-hour ride back from Matsumoto City. After getting the colonel's note, she had quickly changed into her uniform and rushed to meet them.

Greetings were made all around.

"Well then, are you ready to get started?" the colonel began, looking at Captain Byrnes.

"Yes, sir," Byrnes replied.

"I would be remiss if I didn't invite you for dinner tonight, at our home. Eighteen hundred hours?" the colonel asked.

"I'd be honored, sir," Byrnes said.

Jackson continued, "The briefing you will be attending with us will cover an incident that occurred the other day in Matsumoto City. This will give us insight into how well a city responds to a large-scale medical emergency. And it will give you the opportunity to meet Major Jaegar's team and see how they work. His 200th MI Group already has a team gathering and analyzing the situation."

Byrnes lifted her eyebrows in surprise.

Jackson, seeing this, said, "You've heard about this incident?"

"I was there," Byrnes replied. *That's an understatement,* she thought. "I got back less than an hour ago. Came back by rail this morning. I witnessed a great deal of it firsthand."

Colonel Jackson glanced at his watch and said, "I'd like to hear all about it, but for now I think I'll just ask you to share what you know following the brief. We better be getting over there. I don't want to keep them waiting."

A few of Major Jaegar's team members were still updating their charts as Jackson, Onishi and Byrnes arrived. The Major called the room to attention, and Colonel Jackson told them to carry on.

"Good to see you, sir. We're just about ready to proceed," Jaegar replied.

"Whenever you're ready, Major,"

Major Jaegar started by introducing the members of his team, beginning with the 200th MI Group, then an MP by the name of Major Northrup.

Colonel Jackson made two introductions of his own, Captain Byrnes and Captain Onishi. Once that was done, Jaegar's two warrant officers and senior NCOs worked together to present their briefing.

During the presentation, much of what Captain Byrnes heard she already knew. Most of what was reported came primarily from the morning newspaper, radio, and television broadcasts. It was no surprise that Matsumoto City's emergency services were taxed, having to cope with more than 150 casualties.

The first calls for assistance began shortly after 11:00 p.m. Doctors were clear that it was not an ordinary gas leak. Blood tests on patients revealed a shocking lack of a cholinesterase enzyme that normally assists with muscle relaxation following contraction, suggesting an organophosphate poisoning of some kind. Physicians had prescribed injections of atropine to counteract the symptoms. Kelly had heard a great deal of this information while in the hospital the morning after the incident.

Further investigation by police alleged that the fumes had originated from a local residence, where some of the earliest casualties were reported. Local authorities continued to focus their search there. An

MP relayed that they had confiscated nineteen types of chemicals from the home of a man named Yoshiyuki Kono. He may have inadvertently produced, what police chemists had identified, as a nerve agent called "sarin," while mixing a homemade herbicide in his back garden.

Reports also indicated that the number of citizens being treated was expected to rise. The current death toll was five, with three Kaichi Heights residents in a coma. The presenter described the symptoms and concluded that while some symptoms might subside in a few days or weeks, others could last a lifetime.

Personal confirmation of these findings was primarily made through base military police personnel, who normally coordinated closely with the Japanese police precincts within their various jurisdictions. Major Ted Northrup, the MP operations officer, reported these findings. He confirmed that what was being shared here today came from the news media, and had been verified by his sources as true and complete. He had very little new information to add.

"At this juncture, are there any questions?" Major Jaegar asked.

A few were asked and addressed. Major Jaegar's closing statement was, "No military support was requested for this incident. The neighboring prefectures were assisting as needed when help was requested."

Following the briefing, Colonel Jackson announced that Captain Byrnes had just come from Matsumoto City and asked if she'd share her experience, observations, and any conclusions. She was invited to take the podium.

Captain Byrnes poured herself a glass of water and made her way to the front, giving herself time to pull her thoughts together.

"As you've already heard, there were a number of casualties. I can confirm that the first responders did an excellent job of triaging casualties. The people were already gathered at major street intersections, so responders were quick to establish aid stations. The residents were quick to point out where the gas was drifting from and where it was headed, so the responders also knew what areas to avoid and where to find more victims.

"The difficulty arose first in trying to determine what was causing the symptoms so they could provide proper treatment. The gas that came from the victims' clothing also affected some of the early responders. You can imagine the problems this would create. Thank goodness the neighboring prefectures were able to provide medical assistance as well."

Kelly could see that she had the audience's attention and saw many of them nod in agreement. They seemed to appreciate hearing from someone who was actually on site.

Kelly stopped, had another sip of water, and took a deep breath before continuing.

"Unfortunately, while the police have their facts right, they've come to the wrong conclusion," Brynes said. "The man you heard about, named Kono, he's not guilty of this crime. It was an act of terror by another group of men."

The audience seemed to sit up in their seats.

Kelly continued, explaining how she came to be walking about town so late that night.

She described how the men who had fanned out from a minivan had first caught her attention. Byrnes described how the white, misty cloud could be seen drifting from the truck, and how the sentries abruptly evacuated the site in a minivan and followed the truck out of the lot.

"Even Kono and his family were affected by the gas," Captain Byrnes said. "I don't know what the motive may be, but all indications lead me to believe an organized group caused an incident designed to terrorize the local residents."

At the end of the briefing, the group commander and Colonel Jackson remained silent, allowing the experts in the room to ask the questions they were trained to pursue. Kelly was concise in answering them and reinforced each conclusion with facts.

Overall, Captain Byrnes was pleased with how she conveyed her observations, but she felt uneasy about the signals she was receiving from the group commander. Major Jaegar looked uncomfortable. He had been fidgeting, constantly moving about, repositioning himself in his chair throughout Kelly's question and answer period. His eyes seemed to be boring a hole right through her. When she had completed most of the audience's questions, Jaegar slowly rose and sat on the edge of the table. This was the signal for his people to wrap up their questions.

When all were finished, he began with, "Let me see if I'm clear on what you've said."

Why do I feel uncomfortable about this? Byrnes thought. She looked over to Colonel Jackson, who was sitting quietly while watching Major Jaeger.

The major began his questioning with, "I can't help but wonder how sure you are about what you saw, Captain Byrnes." He paused. "Are you sure you weren't affected by the gas yourself? You did say your conclusions were different from the police. Is that correct?"

"Yes sir, and I am sure about what I saw," Byrnes said. She wasn't about to share any information about her headache or having received an injection of atropine.

"The city of Matsumoto has over two thousand very competent police, many of who have collected evidence that clearly implicates Mr. Kono inadvertently mixed the poisonous gas. You even admitted that you saw the cloud near his home, yet you say he didn't do it, insinuating that the police experts have drawn the wrong conclusion. That's a pretty strong accusation, Captain Byrnes."

Byrnes was shocked. Suddenly she felt like she was in a courtroom, being cross-examined by a prosecuting attorney, but she remained calm. Perhaps the major just wanted to see how she held up to tough scrutiny.

"They drew the best conclusion they could with the information they had. I simply witnessed something they hadn't taken into account in their investigation," Byrnes said calmly.

"Why didn't you provide that information to the police?" he continued.

"I did. The officer I spoke with said he would follow up and check. Although I suspected he wouldn't."

"Did you think to follow up with more questions to the officer yourself? Perhaps you weren't so sure of what you really saw."

Kelly wasn't going to fall into his trap. "I didn't because I saw how they might view me," she said.

"Oh, and how is that?"

"As an outsider, an American who didn't belong. Perhaps as someone who didn't really understand what activities were normal for the area."

"And what draws you to that conclusion?"

"The way the officer quickly wrote off the truck as being a delivery truck."

"You chose not to push the issue?" Jaegar said.

Captain Byrnes, although frustrated, wasn't about to show the major any weakness. "I didn't pursue this because I felt the police would eventually find out the truth on their own."

"Yet, you call this an act of terror. I believe I would think that worth pursuing, don't you?"

"I have confidence that the authorities will verify the evidence I saw."

"What's stopping you from following up now?"

"I have my responsibilities here." She had just about had enough of Major Jaegar's insinuations, so Kelly made one last comment. "Listen, I don't know what the objective of those men were. All I do know is that it had to have been a planned attack."

With that, Major Jaegar chose to break off his line of questioning and said, "Captain Byrnes, hopefully you understand that this is a local matter and know enough not to get involved any further or interfere with their investigation." The only thing you said that makes sense is that 'they'll figure it out on their own.'"

I don't understand what his problems is, Byrnes thought, *but evidently he's achieved what he set out to do.* He had shown that this was his briefing, that he was in charge and didn't care for anyone presenting information contrary to his own, especially if it came from a newcomer. *Either that or he has an odd way of testing me.* Kelly wondered if she looked too confident for someone who had just arrived in country.

Following that statement, Major Jaegar looked at Colonel Jackson as he made his final statement, "Sir, I recommend we continue to monitor the situation." Glancing toward Captain Byrnes, he added, "But take no further action to interfere with their local investigation, for clearly this a local matter."

"Thank you, Major Jaegar. I believe we can assume that Captain Byrnes, as well as everyone in this room, knows better than to represent the embassy or the US Army when making inquiries." Jackson, looking about the room, then said, "Unless anyone has further questions, thank you for your efforts and insights. Major Jaegar, may I use your office to meet with Captain Byrnes and Captain Onishi?"

"Yes, sir."

All the room came to attention as Colonel Jackson stood to leave.

Surely we'll be paying close attention to what this terrorist action could be leading to, Byrnes thought as she entered Jaegar's office.

Chapter 20

PYONGYANG, NORTH KOREA

JULY 1994

The days of mourning for the country had passed. The prominent display of black armbands was no longer expected, but the president's son remained distressed by his father's loss. More than ever he was determined to make his father's dreams for the country his own. In a broadcast to the citizens of North Korea, he promised a commitment equal to his father's. Feeling secure about his political position as Dear Leader, Kim II Jong-il would expand his focus beyond his own country and the might of his military.

Turning to his top security advisor, Kim said, "We need to increase our efforts to become a nuclear power, and we're going to do it in a way nobody would expect. You are to be the one in communication with our friends in Japan regarding this."

"Yes, sir," his advisor said. "What about the dismantling of our nuclear reprocessing facilities?"

"As per my father's wishes, we need to comply with the UN inspectors. So yes, we will continue the dismantling process, but we need to slow it down as much as we can without making the inspectors suspicious. We will comply with the Non-Proliferation Treaty…at least in country, but I want our friends in Japan, Haruka and Mori, close at hand. I want them here to see as much as they can before the dismantling and reconfiguration is completed. No one is to know."

"Yes, sir," the security advisor said.

Mori had obtained diagrams of key aspects of the facilities and passed them along to Haruka and their own team of scientists.

But now the country's new leader wanted to speed up the process, to eliminate the UN's presence in the region as well as unite the two Koreas. Once Haruka convinced Kim II Jong-il that he could move his organization outside Japan freely, recruit top scientists, and acquire weapons-grade plutonium, Kim became convinced Haruka's plan could work. To Kim II Jong-il, it was like having a personal army behind enemy lines. Dear Leader was amazed at what resources Haruka had available to him.

North Korea's new leader, through resources of his own, had confirmed Haruka's purchase of an isolated ranch in Western Australia for about $400,000 as well as the payment of $110,000 for eight mining leases on the land. They had been gathering uranium ore since procuring this property almost a year earlier. Haruka had also recruited, from Russian's IV Kurchatov Institute of Atomic Energy, scientists who could build the nuclear devices he desired. Having two of these devices ready by the beginning of the next year was important to their plan.

What made Dear Leader especially eager to put their new strategy into play was realizing how much he could gain, with nothing to lose. Whether things went well or not, it would be too difficult to determine who made the initial strikes. And during that time, he would have the fourth largest military in the world poised for an invasion into South Korea. His people would then realize he was as powerful as his father had been, with as great a vision.

"In order to put our plan into play," Kim told his closest advisors, "we must work with utmost secrecy. I will not tolerate betrayal. Is that understood?"

"Yes, Dear Leader," each staff member replied. They clearly understood the implications of his message.

"When we've succeeded, the world will see how strong we are. Our neighbors will only rally behind us if we are strong. No one will intervene once we've made our country whole again. When you hear our plan, you'll understand how it will succeed." With a slight smile, he added, "We have nothing to lose."

Dear Leader began to tell them his plans about how the initial strike would be conducted from outside Korea. It would be done in such a way that the United Nations would be unable to determine who caused the initial attack. As a result, since they couldn't take action against an unknown threat, they would look weak. That's when the time would be ripe for our military to make its move south.

Everyone around the table smiled and nodded in approval as the details of the plan became clear.

Chapter 21

MATSUMOTO CITY, JAPAN

DECEMBER 1994

Early on Saturday morning, Captain Kelly Byrnes found herself sitting in the Matsumoto hospital's main-floor sitting area, waiting.

Kelly called earlier in the week to inquire about the Kono family, but the floor nurse could only confirm what the newspapers had revealed: Kono's wife remained in a coma. The nurse told her that Mr. Kono visited daily, but had not yet arrived. Since Kelly found talking by phone to be impersonal, and visiting his home was too intrusive, she decided to make an effort to meet him at the hospital.

The hospital was furnished in blond wood. Most hospitals were. They generally had no windows, so the architects tried to make them brighter by using light colors. Her theory was that it helped brighten the mood of those whose visits needed a lift. She had already decided she would spend all day waiting, if that's what it took to see Yoshiyuki Kono.

Kelly worried whether he would recall anything about her or even want to talk with her, or anyone for that matter. Almost three months had gone by and still he was the prime suspect in the investigation. Kelly felt she could stand by quietly no longer. She was determined to let him know there was someone on his side. Kelly knew that although he might be wary of talking with anyone, she had one big advantage when attempting this interview: she had helped save Kono's family and knew him to be innocent.

Byrnes, however, also had a special reason to be worried about interviewing Kono. She remembered her immediate boss's comment about not interfering with an ongoing investigation, at least in an official capacity. But, she didn't consider herself there in an official role. She was just a caring bystander, who wanted to see how the family she had helped was fairing.

She finally spotted him, entering at almost the exact time the resident nurse had stated, like clockwork.

As Kelly approach, she observed a police officer walking alongside Kono. Based on his behavior, she could see that he was there in an official capacity. He stayed at arm's length from Kono and a half pace ahead. The officer seemed leery of anyone in his path and glanced in Kono's direction. She wondered if he was assigned to protect Kono from the general public or vice versa. The media had set the mood for the local populace, showing Kono caused the gassing, taking their lead from the local police. Kelly confirmed this with the 200th MI Group.

Byrnes was careful to give the officer her full attention when approaching. She introduced herself, showing respect for the officer's position. Then she nodded in Kono's direction and explained that she had been the one to pull him out of his house during that faithful night. She could see that Kono was taking more interest in her now. The officer wavered, but only slightly until Kelly stated she was an army officer with the US embassy, visiting on her day off.

Relenting, the officer stepped aside. He suggested they talk briefly in his makeshift office. The local authorities had once used it for patient interviews during initial police inquiries, and it was now being used by him. Kono seemed relieved to have a sympathetic ear and told the officer he would like a moment with Kelly.

They stepped in, and the police officer stayed just outside the door.

"I know you're innocent," she told him.

"Thank you," he said, looking at her skeptically.

"I mean, I was there to help you because I saw it coming. Rather, I didn't know what was going on until after I heard you cry out and ran to assist, but I knew something was terribly wrong, and you weren't the cause of it." Following her awkward beginning, she explained what she had seen prior to assisting him.

Somewhat more encouraged, Kono asked, "Did you share this with the police."

"I tried to, but they didn't seem to want to listen to me."

Sadly, Kono added, "Yes. They don't seem to want to listen to anyone who wants to take my side, not that there are many willing to vouch for me at all. My neighbors have already tried and convicted me. I've received countless threatening phone calls. Someone even altered one streetmap, so that my home has now been identified as the 'House of Dr. Gas.'"

"The only group of people who do seem to believe me is a group calling themselves the Aum. Their Holy Master even sent me four books that he wrote and a letter inviting me to bring my wife for treatment at their private hospital. They even offered a musical tape to help her regain consciousness. That's where I got the idea of bringing my own cassette recorder, so I could play her Mendelssohn. I pray that this familiar melody might lure her out of the coma."

Seeing that Kono was working hard to maintain his composure and was definitely in the mood to talk, especially with someone who was sympathetic, Kelly said, "If you share what you experienced with me, maybe I can find a way to help."

Kono relented, and slowly began to unravel, once again, the story that he had shared so many times with those who had questioned him over the many weeks of interrogation. The police wouldn't believe that the chemicals found at his house were not for making herbicides, but for his hobby, photography. He tried to convince the investigators that it would have been ridiculous for him to have knowingly put his family at risk if, as they say, he knew enough about mixing chemicals to mix his own herbicide. Kono had endured his family's anguish in battling the physical ailments of the gas as well as the threatening public. He felt like a prisoner trapped in his own home.

He spoke with conviction, and his arguments were sound. When he finished, she could tell he wanted to cry. She reached out instinctively, gently touching his arm. She realized she had to lend a hand.

She could no longer continue doing her job, ignoring what was happening, thinking that the truth would eventually surface on its own. Months of work, sometimes years, went into preparing a case, but there was no telling how it would go once it got to court. She could only imagine how much harassment he would have to endure. All the while, although his daughters had recovered, his wife still lay in a coma.

Kelly knew she had to find a way to help. With all the resources she had, she could make unofficial inquiries.

Chapter 22

MINATO-KU, TOKYO, JAPAN

TWO DAYS LATER

*I**t's been six months since I arrived,* Captain Byrnes thought, *and Kono's situation still bothers me.*

Kono was still the primary suspect in the gassing investigation. Although frustrated at times, she had been able to gather a great deal of data about the incident.

Kelly had planned to be with Masa in Minato-ku today. She was anxious to get his perspective after he had promised to review the files she had compiled on the gassing.

However, she had to cancel this plan. She had been recalled to the embassy, to a meeting that included the assistant ambassador. Kelly would have to retrieve the files she left with Onishi at another time.

Feeling that she needed to talk with someone, she decided to call her friend, Carl. It had been a while since they last talked, and she wanted to update him on how things had been going since her arrival.

Through discussions with Major Northrup, in his role as the military police liaison to the local police, Kelly was able to share with Carl how she'd learned that the police were doing a good job. But she also learned that the various prefectures rarely shared information, and the national police agency was primarily administrative in nature with very little investigative experience. She suspected problems with the local investigative practices. They had still not changed their belief about the cause of the gassing. Captain Onishi reaffirmed much of this as well. After talking with him, Kelly believed Onishi was a vital resource as well.

Carl knew Kelly liked working with her counterpart, Masa, but was surprised at what she said she learned about his background.

"Prior to getting a commission with the Japan Ground Self-Defense Force, Masa spent time as a police officer with the Tokyo Metropolitan Police Department. He told me he had made the switch because he was tired of going after the small fish on the streets. Heavy hitters, like the Chakaku-ha, the Japanese Red Army, and the yakuza caused much of the country's problems," Kelly said.

"This information all come out over the time we worked together at the embassy." Kelly said. She knew Captain Onishi's involvement at the embassy had come as a result of his recognized ability, and, by choice he wanted to serve with those from whom he could gain insights on how best to protect his country. He joined his country's ground defense forces as an intelligence officer. As a result of their common interest, Masa and Kelly's relationship had grown.

Kelly also shared how Masa had her over for dinner to try his wife's authentic Japanese cooking. She had enjoyed entertaining their six-year-old son and daughter, who was two years younger. Sometimes she would join them at his unit's favorite pastime of volleyball, a sport that was recreational in nature but not taken lightly. She always got a good workout, something she enjoyed as a break from her regimented fitness program. The two enjoyed one another's company and developed a mutual admiration and respect for each other's talents.

"Masa even helped me find an apartment to rent close to the embassy." Kelly explained how this eliminated her long commute by rail from Camp Zama to Tokyo proper. "As a result, I'm closer to many of my activities," she said. Although she was allowed a great deal of latitude in this assignment, often she could be found either at the embassy with visiting foreign military or at special social occasions associated with embassy matters. But she preferred working at Minato-ku, headquarters of Captain Onishi's plans and operations department for the Japan Ground Self-Defense Force. She still made occasional trips to Camp Zama to monitor events tracked by the 200th MI Group.

After Kelly finished, Carl wanted to talk more about her experience with the Matsumoto gassing.

"I know dad told you I was there, and you probably already read about the incident in the 200th MI group's report," she responded.

"But I want to hear about what you witnessed," Carl said.

"I really don't want to talk about that," she said. "I've already put myself in a bad position with the 200th commander. I'm just not ready to go through all that again, at least not right now. And, I really don't have the time. I've got a meeting with the deputy ambassador in a little bit, so I'd better be going."

Chapter 23

US EMBASSY TOKYO, JAPAN

THE NEXT DAY

As soon as she entered his office, she knew something was wrong. Colonel Jackson, John Conklin, the deputy ambassador, and another man she had not met, were seated in Jackson's office. All looked uneasy as she entered, and either adjusted their ties or suit jackets, doing anything to avoid making eye contact.

Jackson was the first to speak. Clearing his throat, he asked Kelly if she'd like a cup of coffee and invited her to sit. His demeanor was brusque as he introduced her to the others. Kelly wondered if it was directed toward her or something else.

John Conklin was a political appointee, one of a small group of diplomats recruited for ambassadorship positions from Clinton's new team since taking office. Kelly had only met him once officially, when she first arrived. She had little occasion to cross paths with him and learned to appreciate how Colonel Jackson maintained a buffer between them. Conklin, like some diplomats, made it clear from the beginning that he didn't cater to the military. While many saw the military as a tool to be used once diplomacy broke down, a few, like Conklin, saw them as a hindrance to diplomacy.

The other man Kelly was introduced to was Vincent Baker, a CIA station chief out of Australia. Kelly knew there were CIA operatives throughout the Asia-Pacific region who would periodically check in with the various embassies, but she hadn't yet met Baker.

Colonel Jackson explained to Captain Byrnes that Conklin had asked for this meeting and stated, "Captain Byrnes, it seems that his office received a phone call from the Matsumoto Police Department… asking about you."

Kelly's eyes widened. Surprised, she said, "Oh?"

"Let's cut the pussy-footing around, Colonel," Conklin interrupted, "Captain, what the hell were you doing in Matsumoto interfering with a police investigation, and shaking up the locals, leading them to believe that we're involved in an investigation of an act of terrorism?"

"What?" was the only word Kelly could muster, completely surprised.

"Do you deny it?" Conklin asked sternly.

"No, I don't deny going to Matsumoto. But, you're saying that I interfered with an investigation. I never told them we're investigating terrorism. I don't know where you got that idea."

"Then why would the city of Matsumoto's chief of police call and tell me that one of his police officers said he talked with a Captain Kelly Byrnes, from the US embassy, who wanted to talk with their primary suspect in a major investigation they're conducting?"

"I simply went to visit with the man I helped during the incident they're investigating. I happened to be there when fumes overcame his family and helped get them out of their house. That's all."

"Yes, Colonel Jackson told me about your experience up there, but I'm concerned about why in the world you went back and identified yourself as an officer assigned to the US embassy. Once you did that, you officially involved us."

"Sir," she hesitated, looking toward Colonel Jackson for assurance, "I only wanted to reassure the officer that I wasn't someone who wanted to harm Mr. Kono. He has been harassed and even received death threats. Kono had stated, to the officer, that he remembered some lady had helped him that night, but wasn't sure it was me.

"Since the officer still seemed a little hesitant, even after I explained my role on that day, I added that I was on my day off and had traveled all the way from Tokyo, where I worked at the embassy. I didn't say anything about officially representing anyone or participating in any investigation.

I know I didn't say anything to him about a terrorist attack." She paused, trying to remember the conversation she had with Kono. "Unless, perhaps, he got this from Mr. Kono following our discussion."

"Well then, I want to make it perfectly clear now that we cannot afford to have any official involvement. I don't want you going out there again or stirring up the investigation any more than you already have."

"But, sir," she looked to Jackson for assistance. Seeing none she added, "I just wanted to see how he's doing. I know he's innocent."

Jackson, not giving any indication of understanding or support, simply said, "Captain Byrnes, we'll talk more about this later."

"Captain Byrnes, regardless of what is true or not, you must understand that this is not in the military's jurisdiction," Conklin said. "Any involvement, whether on a personal or professional level, would have negative implications. Since Mr. Baker was in the area, I asked him to be here today because if anyone is to get involved, it would be his organization."

Then Mr. Baker, who had been quietly listening, added, "I'm sure Captain Byrnes meant no harm in what she was trying to do," he said, laying on the charm. Kelly immediately felt like a schoolgirl being patronized, as if she were too naïve to know when she was in over her head.

Baker continued, "Any information you have, I'll be glad to take a look at. One thing that we first need to determine is whether there truly was an incident that indicates a terrorist event took place." With this comment, Assistant Ambassador Conklin dismissed himself after asking Kelly to share what information she had with Baker. Colonel Jackson followed him out.

Kelly hesitated at first, but then saw the benefits of reviewing even the most detailed information. Having just compiled her data, this would help her, once more, try and make sense of what had occurred.

As she proceeded, she sensed a feigned attentiveness. Baker hadn't requested that she expand on any aspect of the events. He seemed distracted. Then she noticed Baker's eyes.

It was obvious he was distracted by her physique. Kelly became increasingly uneasy and finally decided to ask if he was getting all of this and why he wasn't taking any notes.

He said, "I'll remember the important parts." There were times when she appreciated a man's gaze, but this was not one of them. She wasn't going to let this chauvinist write her off as one of those females who could be treated as an ornamental airhead. Kelly decided to quickly end her story with how the Aum had been the only ones who believed Kono's story.

Not surprisingly, Baker was indifferent to Kono's situation, but did add that he had heard of the Aum. "The locals in Western Australia reported that they are a religious cult who have been mining ore under a pseudo name, or so the aborigines believe," he had said.

This interested Kelly immediately, and she asked Baker to tell her more. Baker, showing surprise at her interest, asked why she would care about this group.

Kelly said she found his working in the outback with the aborigines fascinating, showing a personal interest in Baker. As much as Kelly detested this approach, it worked. Baker went deeper into the story that the aborigines had told him. How they had seen some cult members wearing what looked like space suits and carrying a container. After a pause in the conversation, Kelly thanked him for speaking up for her to the assistant ambassador and listening to her story.

"Listen," he said, "I'm going to be here through the weekend, and I was wondering if you'd like to have dinner with me Friday."

"The two of us?" she asked lightly. "You mean, like people who go out together?"

He tried a smile. "Something like that. Unless you think there's a taboo about intelligence gatherers possibly sharing secrets."

Kelly smiled in return. "Haven't you read the data on office romances? Tragic, and the woman always pays."

When he grimaced, she touched his arm, voice softening. "It's not just that, Vincent. And it's certainly not you. There's someone else."

"Sorry, I saw that you didn't have a ring and assumed that you were single."

"I am, but I'm not unattached. He's in Korea," she lied, thinking of her friend, Carl, and how he had stepped in to save her once before. She knew he'd step in again if need be.

The meeting was over, and they both excused themselves. She couldn't get to her office fast enough. Suddenly Kelly felt tired, drained. She needed a moment of privacy. She never felt so berated, belittled, and embarrassed in such a short time. She wanted to cry. She had just been reprimanded by the deputy ambassador, in front of her boss, and then made to feel like an inept airhead by someone who saw her as nothing more than a quick pickup.

She had given eight years of her life to the army. Other women had gotten married and had families, started their own business, written a novel, or sailed around the world. She had dedicated herself to being, what she thought, was a terrific intelligence officer. *How could I have gone from feeling so good about my career one day, to having made such a career-ending blunder the next?* she thought. The idea brought tears to her eyes.

Then Captain Onishi came in.

Chapter 24

US EMBASSY, TOKYO, JAPAN

SAME DAY

Onishi had gone to school in New Jersey and graduated with a degree in criminology. Somewhere along the line, he had also received a master's in psychology from Tokyo University. Like her, he was in his class B uniform with a sweater, different from the US uniform but designed for the same office comfort.

He had her file in his hand. "Your take on the threat is fascinating," he said, his eyes glowing with enthusiasm.

He went on, "I was going to leave this on your desk, but I'm glad I caught you."

She blew her nose. He had surely seen that she was upset, but he was tactfully pretending not to notice.

Onishi had obviously worked late to analyze her findings, and Kelly did not want to deflate his interest by telling him she had been ordered to stay away from Matsumoto and not get involved in their investigation.

"Take a seat," she said, composing herself.

"Congratulations on writing a very thorough and professional report!"

"Thanks."

"You must be pleased with all the work you put into it."

"I should be. But I just got chewed out by the deputy ambassador, in front of Colonel Jackson, for getting involved."

"Oh, him." Masa dismissed her comment with a flap of his hand. "He's a hot head, and everybody knows it. If you apologize nicely to Colonel Jackson, he'll have to forgive you. You're too valuable to him."

His offhanded remark was unexpected. It was almost as if he had known beforehand about her predicament. But if he knew about this, he knew she had been banned from the investigation. So why had he brought her the report?

Intrigued, she said, "You like my report?"

"The contrast between the 200th MI Group's summary and your report had me bewildered for a while, but once I was able to track the comparisons I understood."

He handed her his printout showing a brief of the 200th MI Group's summary, a summary of newspaper reports, and then a copy of her observations.

It did not tell her much, but she knew that Masa had checked every word for meaning.

"What do you make of it?" he asked.

She thought for a minute, but because she was too tired, and had resolved herself to the fact that she would be in no position to make a difference, she replied, "The police are prosecuting an innocent man because it makes them look good, as opposed to pursuing a group of thugs who released chemicals on a town of innocent victims, to either intimidate them or get back at someone."

"Well, that's in the right direction, but it's like you Americans like to say, 'short of the mark,'" Masa said with a smile. Then he continued, "Let's first look at the evidence and conclusions that the media has presented, based on their findings. They believe there was a lone suspect who inadvertently produced sarin while mixing a homemade herbicide in his back garden. His three children, wife, and even he fall victim as a result. They support this conclusion with the fact that the suspect's home is the building most upwind of any of the fatalities, where they confiscated nineteen types of chemicals. Some could be harmful when released into the air even when not mixed."

"For the most part, that summarizes their findings," Kelly responded. But now we know those chemicals were for his photography hobby, not for making herbicides."

"Right, but that doesn't change anything. The question now is: What is the advantage if they should draw these conclusions so rapidly? What benefit does it give to them?" Onishi asked.

"I see what you're driving at," Kelly responded. "First of all, the media, representing the public's emotional outcry, seems to have accepted the police conclusions rather rapidly because they don't want to acknowledge that there is a threat greater than just an accident."

"Now you've got the idea. Also remember that this makes the police look good. They found the cause quickly and have the culprit detained. This will stop any critical comments against the police department. The greater the problem, the greater the need to bring about an immediate resolution."

"I also understand," Kelly paused, fondly reflecting on one of the aspects of Japanese society she so admired, "your society has a very strict code of honor and trust. That makes it hard to understand how an individual could break that code, let alone a group who might unleash a massive chemical attack."

"That's right," Onishi said. "And don't forget your comment to the police about observing others in a truck. It could quickly be dismissed as being from an outsider, an American female, who really doesn't know what she saw."

"Okay, so we determined that the Matsumoto police would not want to pursue the possibility that there is still a group of criminals out there who wanted to do deliberate harm and don't really care about indiscriminately harming others. What next?"

Masa recognized how Kelly was coming alive once again and gave a small smile. "You called them criminals," Onishi reminded her. "You may be right, but they're intelligent, perhaps well educated, bold, well organized, and have a strong monetary backing."

Kelly shook her head in amazement. She was astonished by the way Masa drew conclusions from the evidence she did not see. "How do you know?"

"Just take a look at your own notes. You say you saw two vehicles that night, one a minivan that contained the lookouts, and another that looked like a delivery truck, which dispersed the gas. That sounds like they're organized to me. Not just off-the-street thugs, but highly educated ones. I don't know much about making this sophisticated gas they call sarin, but I'd be willing to guess that you'd really have to know what you're doing to produce it. And you've got to agree, it's a pretty bold move on their part to sit there in the parking lot long enough to disperse enough gas to cover so much territory. They had to have been there for at least twenty, maybe thirty minutes. Finally, I would also imagine that it's not cheap putting together an organization that could do this sort of thing, not to mention the vehicles they used. The people involved must have either been highly paid or highly motivated. Either way, that implies well-organized backing."

"What makes you think they made the gas rather than stole it?" Kelly asked.

"Because there were too many people involved in its delivery. You said that the boy you saved, and later interviewed, recalled hearing a number of voices in the back of the truck that had dispersed the gas," Masa added.

"All that makes sense," Kelly mused. "But what would motivate someone to do something like that?"

"That's what we need to look into next," Onishi said.

Kelly remembered her run-in. "I'm afraid I can't. Not after the little episode I just had with Conklin."

"Well, I can't do it without you," Onishi admitted. "We both need to get involved now."

"That's right, we…" Kelly heard the words coming from her office entry. Startled, she looked over and saw Colonel Jackson leaning against the doorway, a sly grin on his face.

Kelly looked puzzled. "Sir?"

"Like you said, there could still be a threat out there."

"How long have you been standing there?"

"Long enough to know that you and Captain Onishi will make a great team."

"But what about Conklin?"

"You let me worry about him. I sat in on his meeting with you to ensure he didn't get carried away. He does have a tendency to over-react. Saying anything would have just given him more ammunition. He's always like that with the military. 'Don't do anything' has always been his stance."

"So, the Matsumoto police weren't upset about me being there?"

"Well, they were a little concerned originally, but they really only wanted to confirm that you were who you said you were. They've been getting some rather unusual visitors up there. Some haven't been so legitimate. So you can't really blame them for being cautious."

"Why did you leave me alone with Baker?"

"Oh, him. That was Conklin's idea. Periodically these guys meet at the various embassies in the region, and he happened to be available. That's Conklin's way of emphasizing how this is not a military matter."

"Well Baker sure wasn't interested."

"I'm not surprised."

"Sir...he asked me out."

"Well, I can't blame him," Jackson said, with a smile.

Turning to Masa, Kelly said, "You knew about all this too, didn't you? Why didn't you say something?"

"If I had, you wouldn't have taken Conklin seriously. You had to show *some* remorse. If you knew the purpose of the meeting, you would have come in all fired up. That's not the way to approach him," Masa said.

"There is one thing Conklin said that we do need to take seriously, though," Colonel Jackson added. "You have to be careful about any official involvement. Be careful about how you gather information. Remember, Kelly, you are not to contact any Japanese authorities. Let others do that. Your job is to analyze what is collected. Captain Onishi, your contacts with the Tokyo Metropolitan Police Department could be helpful. If you can get some help from the national police department, great. But, none of this should interfere with your regular duties."

"No problem, my regular duties are to liaison with you. The only other major function I have is as an observer for an upcoming joint exercise. I have a few meetings to attend this weekend and next week at Camp Zama, but the exercise there isn't for a few more months."

"Fine. But it's best that you both stay away from the Matsumoto prefectural police. Let Major Northrup's military police handle that. They have more latitude in communicating with them. I'll call Major Jaegar at the 200th and tell him to give you their full cooperation and pass that on to Major Northrup. Northrup is in a position to better render assistance."

"Sir, when you talk with them, could you asked them to check on a group calling themselves the Aum. Their name keeps popping up, and I can't help but wonder that they may have something to do with all this."

"Did you say the Aum?" Masa queried.

"Yes. Why? Do you know about them? I understand they're a religious group. Is that right?"

"Oh, yes. They're a religious group all right. They haven't existed for very long, but they are evidently sizeable enough to have even tried their hand at politics."

"So they're well known?"

"Yes, but they haven't gotten involved in politics since they were unsuccessful at campaigning for seats in the Japanese parliament in the 1990 national elections."

"Where did they get their name 'Aum'?"

"I know that they were originally called Aum Inc. because it represents a Hindu mantra, or chant, and is said to incorporate the ultimate truth of the universe. Evidently that's where they got their name. Aum means truth."

"Well, that's what we hope to get to, the truth. I'll make sure Northrup understands the significance of this. Maybe he'll have something for you when you see him." Colonel Jackson looked at his watch. It was still early. "Periodically, I expect a brief on what progress you've made."

"Yes, sir."

Jackson excused himself, leaving both to consider how they'd proceed.

Just moments earlier Kelly felt drained, but now she was relieved. She knew she wouldn't be seeing Masa again until Wednesday, when they started preparing for a UN military exercise. Hopefully by then she'd have more information to share.

Chapter 25

TOKYO INTERNATIONAL AIRPORT -

TOKYO, JAPAN

DECEMBER 1994

Sergeant Arthur Stanley had no trouble picking Major Kurt Johnson out of the crowd of people walking away from the international arrivals gate. Most of the other arrivals were Japanese, and those who were American, didn't have his military bearing and prominent features.

"He hasn't been here before, but I've worked with him in Korea, in other exercises, so he knows the routine," Master Sergeant Davis had told Stanley. "Look for a guy who's about five feet ten inches tall, good-looking, and athletic."

Major Johnson, Stanley concluded, must be a sharp officer if Davis insisted that he be picked up by one of his own office personnel rather than catch a shuttle like most of the other reservists attending exercises. He spotted Johnson putting on his military black windbreaker.

Stanley hoisted his sign to be more visible to the man he believed to be Major Johnson. The reservist glanced at the sign, showed recognition, and veered toward him.

"Major Johnson?"

"Right you are…Sergeant…Stanley, is it?" Johnson said. He hesitated just long enough to first identify his rank and then read his nametag. He then smiled at Stanley.

"I'm standing in for Master Sergeant Davis, sir," Stanley said. "Let me give you a hand with your baggage."

"Thank you, Stanley." Kurt slipped his athletic bag from his shoulder and handed it over. "Where's Davis?"

"He's participating in what we call an 'In-Process Review' to brief the commander on what you exercise controllers will be doing once we get under way."

When they were in the camouflaged Bronco, Johnson said, "Well, I appreciate you meeting me, but I could have taken the shuttle or a cab."

"To Camp Zama?" Stanley blurted.

"Camp Zama? I'm talking about Tokyo."

"Sir, I'm supposed to take you to the BOQ at Camp Zama," Stanley said.

"I'm going to a hotel in Tokyo for a few days. That's why I told Davis I was going to arrive early."

"Sir? I...er...I thought you knew, sir. Sergeant Davis told me he talked with the colonel, and he arranged to have your orders amended because he wants you involved in the exercise evaluator meetings being held this weekend."

"Well I'm flattered, Sergeant, but that's the first I've heard about that. What makes it so important that I be included earlier than the original schedule?"

"From what I understand, they could use your branch expertise for the exercise. Rather than just injecting simulations that are not part of the original exercise, like they've done in the past, they want to see if we're adequately prepared to respond to an actual NBC threat. Since you'll now play a major role in the joint operations evaluation process, we need you as an evaluation team member rather than just as a controller for the exercise," the sergeant added.

"So, they've begun to see the merits of preparing for possible nuclear, chemical, and biological attacks and decided to enlist the expertise of the Chemical Corp in the evaluation process."

"Yes, sir. I heard they're going to focus more on a potential threat from North Korea, such as a Scud missile that can deliver nuclear, biological, and chemical munitions."

"Master Sergeant Davis didn't say anything to me about my orders being amended," the major mused aloud.

"Sir, he said he wasn't sure if the army reserve system could respond on such short notice. When he finally did try to call you personally, you had already left."

"That's true, the reserve's personnel command does mystify even the reservist at times, but they seem to get the job done when they really need to. Well then, to the BOQ it is. Lead the way, Sergeant."

Chapter 26

TOKYO, JAPAN

FIVE DAYS LATER

Kelly heard from Masa earlier that day. He told her he had been engaged in planning an upcoming joint exercise and met an American officer he wanted her to meet. Masa explained that the officer might be able to shed some light on the sarin gas used at Matsumoto, since he was a chemical officer. Consequently, Masa set up a dinner at his home and insisted Kelly come.

Masa was convinced they would all enjoy the evening, and knew Kelly would find this officer interesting. Kelly consented, primarily because she was anxious to share the information Major Northrup had passed on. Masa assured her they'd have an opportunity.

Johnson arrived at the Onishi's modest home, located in the southwestern suburbs of Tokyo, having accompanied Masa from the exercise planning session at Camp Zama. They considered it easier that way, since Kurt was unfamiliar with the area, or how to travel about Japan for that matter.

Kelly had made her appearance by car shortly after that. Her car was shipped from the states and had been delivered within a month of her arrival.

The introductions were made. Masa named off the gathered family members, followed by Kelly. Kurt greeted each one. Kelly was impressed by his congenial manner, and she couldn't help noticing how good looking he was.

Johnson was in civilian clothing, a well-cut gray flannel suit, crisp white shirt, and a red-and-blue finely patterned necktie.

The reception was warmer than Kurt expected, and the smells told him the dinner was already prepared. The house was filled with the aroma of seafood. Kurt trailed his newfound friends toward the rear of the house, with Kelly at his side. The smells of the dinner worked on him, stirring a rumbling in his stomach. Masa preceded him, blocking his view of the kitchen where he heard cheerful giggles coming first from the children then from Mrs. Onishi.

Mrs. Onishi stayed in the kitchen with her children while Kelly joined Masa to show Kurt around the house. The inside of the house was a study in simplicity. The floors were all inlaid with squares of fresh tatami matting, which gave off a sweet, straw-like smell. The frame of the house consisted of black-and-white wood beams, interspersed to create pleasing and understated geometric patterns. Sliding shoji screens, made of translucent rice paper, served to fill the rooms with a gentle glow from outside sunlight when the screens were closed, Kelly explained. Some of the sliding screen doors had been hand painted with seasonal landscapes or seascapes.

Kurt commented to Kelly on how intrigued he was by the Japanese ability to absorb foreign influences and at the same time keep their own traditions.

Mrs. Onishi announced that dinner was ready. They were called to a room to sit on cushions on the floor, which surrounded a low round table, covering a shallow square pit that contained an electric foot-warmer. Masa, Kelly, and Kurt sat around the table. Mrs. Onishi made multiple trips to the kitchen, where she tended to the children and gathered food to ensure everyone's plate stayed full. Mrs. Onishi assured everyone that having the children stay with her in the kitchen would make for a more congenial atmosphere, allowing them to visit with one another more easily. She also knew this was as much a business meeting as pleasure.

The threesome enjoyed a dinner of seafood and vegetable tempura. The batter coating the pawns, eggplant, sweet potato, string beans, and asparagus was so light it seemed to melt away almost instantly in their mouths. The cuisine was superb and the company enjoyable. Masa knew that Kelly would be anxiously looking for an opportunity to discuss developments in the gassing case, although she did seem distracted by his new guest.

Chapter 27

TOKYO, JAPAN

After the children left for bed, and Mrs. Onishi excused herself, the three officers settled in for a discussion.

Masa began, "While I did intend this to be a social gathering, we could benefit from having Major Johnson here for our discussion about the Matsumoto event. Over the last few days, I've had the opportunity to work with him and believe he can help us better understand what really happened up there. The other day we had a discussion about the various threats we want to bring into play in our joint exercise. That's when the subject of sarin gas came up."

Masa turned to Kurt and asked, "Major Johnson, would you tell Kelly what you told me?"

"Sure, but only if you call me Kurt, at least while we're not at work," Johnson began.

"Sorry, of course, Kurt," Masa said.

"I assume you mean about this Kono fellow we talked about," said Johnson.

Masa nodded.

"Well, if what you say is true—if the gas that spread across Matsumoto was found to be a sarin-like mixture—the chemicals that the police collected, whether they were for a herbicide or photography hobby, he couldn't have produced that gas."

"We know that," Kelly asserted, "but we need to prove it to the police."

"That's easy," Kurt said. "Herbicides couldn't result in the symptoms seen in Matsumoto." The chemicals used in picture development can be harmful, but their affects are nowhere near as devastating as that of sarin. Since they've already confirmed that the gas was a sarin substance, we need to let them know you can't make sarin from the chemicals they seized from Kono's house. The process to make sarin is quite complex. He'd never have been able to make it."

Masa joined in, "You realize, of course, this means whoever did this very likely brought in sarin that had been made elsewhere."

Directing her comments to Kurt, Kelly added, "We figured that. I even saw the truck that dispensed the chemical. But unfortunately, the police were quick to write off the possibility a late store delivery. Obviously they're having a hard time believing anyone would do this on purpose. That's why we're trying to show that Kono couldn't have done it. This information helps a great deal in proving that he's innocent."

Masa then asked Kelly, "What did you find out about the Aum from Major Northrup?"

Kelly saw how Masa was leading the discussion, allowing Kurt to assist and allowing Kelly an opportunity to share her findings.

Taking the cue, she added, "When Northrup inquired about the Aum, he found that the Matsumoto police had received complaints about them, but nothing that could be substantiated. Evidently, the local citizens are unhappy about a facility they're building nearby. The construction was supposed to be a food processing plant. When locals found that the two-story facility was actually going to be a new religious settlement, they complained. That's when the residents began receiving harassing telephone calls from Aum members. There is a land dispute case still pending between the Aum and the original owner who filed a civil suit to invalidate the sale. In fact, a panel of three judges is to make the ruling soon. And, get this, when they looked into getting more information from the judges, they found that all three had been affected by the gassing I witnessed. All three judges were staying in the same dormitory, which was directly affected by the gas. Thank goodness the winds shifted. I understand if that hadn't happened it could have been worse."

Kurt interjected, "Just be thankful that it was in the open. Although it's a very potent agent, it's nonpersistent, meaning it will evaporate within twenty-four hours, mainly due to its volatility. I understand all the variables that make the chemical the most dangerous were present, and there was only a light wind. The tendency of an agent to evaporate depends on its chemical composition, temperature, air pressure, and the nature of the underlying surface with which it comes in contact."

"If they were after the judges it must have been pretty important for them," Kelly added.

"I assume you believe they weren't necessarily expecting the ruling to go in their favor, Kelly," Masa said.

"If the Aum loses this case," Kelly clarified, "they would have to abandon one of their new Matsumoto settlements. There's their possible motive."

"But, that hardly seems enough of a reason for anyone to try and harm a whole community," Kurt interjected. "It only takes three milligrams to feel the effects of sarin, seventy-five milligrams to incapacitate you, and that's only if you come into contact with it for at least a minute. From what I understand, they affected up to two hundred people in the open air. They must have had a great deal of it to be able to put enough into the open atmosphere and affect that many people."

"That's why I said they had to have brought it from elsewhere," Masa reminded them.

Both Kelly and Kurt simultaneously seemed to sense that Masa had led them to the conclusion he had already arrived at.

"Maybe we need to take a closer look at what they're capable of and then examine their motives," Masa said.

"How's that?" Kelly asked.

Masa took a deep breath before beginning again, "Just a few months before you arrived, Kelly, a cousin of mine asked me for help in getting her out of the Aum. She secretly talked to me while we attended her father's funeral. What she told me caused me a great deal of concern. She feared reprisals if she tried to leave."

"Your cousin's a member of the Aum?" Kelly exclaimed.

Chapter 28

TOKYO, JAPAN

"Yes, she is with the Aum," Masa confirmed.

"Why would she join them?" Kelly asked.

"It wasn't really her choice," Masa clarified. "And I had to think long and hard before deciding to tell you," he confessed.

Kelly remained silent, realizing he was about to talk about a sensitive family situation.

"Kelly, when you first showed me your report that mentioned the Aum, you got my interest. I don't know what their motivation is regarding the events at Matsumoto City, but they're certainly capable of many cruelties. Unfortunately, my cousin is a part of that."

"Are you okay telling us about this?" Kelly asked.

"I think it's important that I do. Two years ago Mika was attending Tokyo University, performing at the top of her class, at least until she dropped out," Masa began. "I knew her father had become depressed following the death of her mother and assumed she had quit school to care for him. It wasn't until I talked with her at her father's funeral that I found there was more to it than that."

"You mean Mika and her father both got involved?"

"Yes. Mika told me her father originally went to find peace of mind by attending yoga classes shortly after losing his wife. The Aum sponsored those classes. Mika told me that she accompanied her father to appease him. She said she found their pressure tactics unwarranted. Her father had somehow gotten drawn in by the cult's mixture of science and spirituality. She told me how he talked about being deeply moved when the guru said he was the reincarnation of Jesus Christ. He had a mesmerizing voice also. She tried to dissuade him from getting further involved, but somehow they got him to donate a great deal of his money. She even thought they had forged his signature on some documents that showed he had transferred their home to them. When I asked how this could have happened, she said he didn't remember. When she inquired further, her father said the whole time period seemed pretty foggy. She couldn't prove anything but believed they had him drugged."

"Pressure tactics? Drug use? That does seem a bit much," Kurt added.

"Wait, it gets worse," Masa went on. "The Aum took them both to their Mount Fuji headquarters. They shaved her father's head and made him wear an electrode cap. It was supposedly to bring about a greater level of enlightenment, bringing his brain waves in alignment with those of the guru's. The device delivered regular shocks to the scalp. They had his money and documents that showed he was voluntarily doing all this, so Mika had to either go along with it or not be able to see him at all. She chose to stay. They didn't treat her the same as her father though, or the others who were supposedly going through their full initiation rites. They seemed to have a different purpose in mind for her."

"I can only imagine what it must have been like to live there," Kurt added.

"Mika was able to tell me a little about that, too," Masa responded. "She seemed almost trance-like when she described how they ate, slept, and dressed, needing permission to leave the compound. This, she explained, was all designed to keep them isolated from family and friends. She gave a vivid picture of what it was like there for the initiates. Most ate twice daily, usually unprocessed rice, seaweed, fermented bean curd, and tasteless vegetable stew. Those undergoing religious training, like her father, ate only once a day, either cabbages or dozens of tangerines. They were forced to eat it all, even if they threw up. Most only drank water that had supposedly been blessed by the guru himself, but Mika saw the drums the water was stored in. She said it had to be tainted, seeing the condition the drums were in. The drinking of tea, coffee, or alcohol was strictly forbidden. Even sleep was regulated. They got three to five hours per night, and even that was either on tiny plywood bunk beds or the floor where they worked. What better way to control people than to work them long hours, give little sleep, and poor nutrition."

"You say they had a different purpose for Mika?" Kelly asked.

"She was originally assigned to help in the design modifications and installation of air purifiers, supposedly to guard against poison gas attacks from an outside threat. Evidently they would often preach how the impure outsiders, who didn't understand their cause, would want to destroy them, and warned of an approaching apocalypse that would be initiated by foreigners. But she admitted she knew that the air purifiers were more likely to protect them from internal experiments. She said she had seen and heard enough to believe they're working with more than just chemical and biological agents. She was separated from those who were being initiated, like her father. She believed they were preparing her to get involved with something closer to the field she was studying at the university. She thinks that's also why they fed her better than other new initiates."

They all knew much more was yet to come and listened intently.

"She didn't work with the air purifiers for long. After her father was taken ill, they moved him to their Astral Hospital in Tokyo. It was then that she told them she wanted to be near him. A doctor told her that his care normally would be costly, but as a result of her father's dedication, they would provide free care. And if she did some special work, helping them manufacture some of their pharmaceuticals, they would allow her more freedom to visit him. She decided to go along with them since they couldn't afford any other options."

Masa continued to tell of the guru's personal involvement, "The guru, Asahara, summoned her himself. She was led to a small prefab building where Mika found him in meditation. An aide stood beside him. When she approached, Asahara opened his eyes and asked, 'Are you willing to work on a special project to help your father while he is healing in the hospital?'

"When she told him yes, Asahara's aide led her away, escorting her to a larger building next door. At the entrance she found a row of full-body protection suits, the kind used to shield people from biological and chemical hazards. She said they looked like space suits and described them as having thick plastic faceplates and heavy-duty plastic skin the color of faded orange. She was told to suit up. She believed they were testing her to see how much she knew and how willing and able she was to help them."

"That's funny, that's how Baker said the aborigines described what they saw," Kelly mumbled, not realizing Kurt had heard her.

"What?" Kurt exclaimed.

Kelly responded, "I was just thinking of a conversation I had with a man I ran into who had just been down in Australia. He mentioned that some aborigines had reported that a group of Aum members were seen in outfits very much like what Masa described. But this was in the outback of Western Australia. I can't help but wonder if that might be some sort of testing ground."

Not wanting to distract the group from Masa's story, Kelly quickly put the discussion back on track by saying, "Tell me more about Mika's father. What happened to him after they moved him to their hospital?"

Masa didn't miss a beat, "When she visited her father, he looked frail and weak and was covered with burns. When she asked about them, she was told that they were nothing to be concerned about. The nurse explained to Mika that he had been through what they called 'thermo therapy' designed to shed bad karma. She was told that sometimes the body has to suffer to enable the spirit to be cleansed. Evidently they had scalded much of his upper body. From what Mika described, the condition of the hospital was appalling. Mika told me about the inside of the clinic, how she was led to a narrow room packed with eight beds, a large portrait of Asahara smiling benignly hanging on a wall. Astral music echoed loudly through the place. Medicinal herbs were piled in the hallway. Sorrowful-looking patients filled the beds, their heads shaved. Amulets hung around their necks, supposedly to bring them luck. The interior looked shabby. She said cockroaches scurried along the floors, and when she commented about them, the doctor said they weren't allowed to kill any living creatures. Just looking at him, she said, she didn't have much confidence in the doctor's ability, his coat was filthy. The nurses were even worse. They wore casual clothes and displayed a surprising ignorance of basic hygiene. Even she knew you shouldn't empty bedpans into a sink. She was so alarmed, she knew she had to get her father out of there, but she also knew they wouldn't let him out if she asked—others had tried. She knew she couldn't do it alone either."

"What did she decide to do then?" Kelly asked.

"When she left, she said she was determined to get help. So, when she returned to their Mount Fuji compound, she worked hard to convince them of her loyalty while looking for others who were concerned about their operation. She knew, as isolated as they were from the outside world, she could only be successful working from the inside. The Aum had shown that they were powerful, successful in intimidating the local populace as well as the police. Their tactics had not only scared the local citizens, but kept the police in check as well, threatening lawsuits over their right to religious freedom."

Kelly added, "That clearly supports the information I received from Major Northrup. When I asked him about the police response to the harassing phone calls the locals received for challenging the Aum's Matsumoto settlement, he confirmed that these were well-orchestrated tactics designed to get what they wanted. They hoped to intimidate the locals enough to drop their land dispute case. Their tactics even included the use of expensive lawyers who threatened reprisals if the police further interfered with their religious freedom."

Masa began again, "So you can see how she might be concerned about being able to walk away. It took Mika another few weeks, but she finally did meet two others who agreed to help. One man was Kotaro Ochida, who she met when they worked together installing air purifiers in one of the labs. The other was Hideaki Yasuda, a friend of Kotaro's. Evidently, they both became disillusioned, from what she gathered, when Hideako's mother suffered treatments similar to what her father endured after being admitted to their clinic for Parkinson's disease. They were going to rescue her father, but when she returned for a visit to develop a plan for accomplishing this, she found that he had died the previous day. That's when she really became dishearten. She couldn't believe what she saw when she entered his room. They hadn't even moved him from where he had died. He was left in his bed, wrapped in a sheet. If it hadn't been for Kotaro contacting me on Mika's behalf, I believe the Aum hospital staff would have taken care of things in their own way. I wouldn't have known anything about Mika or her father. It was only during the funeral that Mika had an opportunity to share a great deal of this with me. Some I got from Kotaro. I've been trying to figure out how to get Mika out of there ever since."

Both expressed their sympathy before Masa was given the opportunity to continue.

"After her father died, they made sure she was not alone, so she had difficulty contacting me directly. Kotaro called me. When he did, he related the bizarre circumstances of my uncle's death. If I wanted his body for a family burial, or ever see Mika again, I'd better come to the Astral Hospital to claim his body. That's when I first had an opportunity to talk with her, but only during a family prayer. After that, we were only able to talk periodically by phone."

"It sounds like they're holding her hostage," Kurt added.

"They are, but not in the legal sense. That's the problem," Masa clarified. "That's why I've been so frustrated. She has been able to call me a few times, usually when she leaves the compound for duties elsewhere, but she told me she couldn't leave permanently. Upon arriving there, they made her sign papers that said she was subjecting herself to their religious practices and isolationism voluntarily. She's seen others who had tried to flee, only to be returned and put into solitude, placed on meager rations, forced to listen to loud music, and undergo 'thermo therapy,' for what they call 'being unfaithful.' Mika said they were rarely the same after that. They brainwashed them to believe that fleeing Aum was a most dishonorable act; it betrays the guru's love. They preach that a person will never find the truth, other than through them. Supposedly their name is based on just that, finding the truth."

Kelly explained to Kurt that the translation of Aum was truth.

"By the way," Masa continued, "their full name is Aum Shinrikyo or Aum Supreme Truth. Unfortunately, the only truth I've seen is that they want to increase their followers and the money they get when they join."

"There must be more to this than just money, if what you say is true about what they're capable of doing, especially conducting tests with chemicals and biological agents," Kurt added.

"You've got a point there," Kelly admitted. "I wonder what they have Mika working on now. Whatever it is, they sure don't want that information to get out if it's even more difficult to contact her now. Luckily, they still believe she is remaining faithful, as she is going along with what they want her to work on. Who knows what punishment they may carry out if she leaves. You said it was a few months ago when you got all this information from her. Do you know if she's still there?" Kelly asked.

"Unfortunately, yes," Masa responded. "I've been trying to work through legal channels to get her out, but that's been frustrating as well. I found a lawyer who has been working with a number of families in trying to get family members out. So far, it's been frustrating for the lawyer as well, but he is persistent.

"Those who have made contact with the Aum have only been able to confirm that she is, in fact, there, but on her own volition. They have the documentation to prove it. I even talked with the police chief, who is in charge of the prefecture for that area. He told me there wasn't much he could do. He felt helpless because their system doesn't allow him to intervene. He even admitted that he meets on a regularly basis with neighboring prefectures to share cases that they're working on, since they don't have any national investigative capability. The others feel the same frustration."

"You say you are still able to make contact with her?" Kurt asked Masa.

"I talk with Kotaro every once in a while, but only when he calls me. He told me he's had difficulty making contact with Mika lately. He said he has seen her but hasn't been able to talk with her because the group she works with often doesn't return to the compound until very late or sometimes only on weekends. Evidently, the new project they have her working on keeps her very busy. She seems more isolated than ever now. Kotaro did say he was able to overhear a conversation between Mika and a man named Mr. Mori. Mori made a reference to how Mika's new project was perfectly suited to her college training," Masa said grimly. "That makes it even more important for us to find out what they're up to and get Mika out."

"Why is that?" Kurt asked.

"Mika's area of study at the university was nuclear physics," Masa replied.

The looks of concern were evident—the room went quiet.

Kurt was the first to break the silence. "If this guy, Kotaro, can help us pinpoint where Mika is staying, maybe we can get her out of there."

Masa nodded slowly, thoughtfully. They both looked at Kelly for further comment.

Kelly dug into her purse, pulled out a pad and pen and began to write.

Masa and Kurt both looked at her in puzzlement.

"What do you have in mind, Kelly?" Masa asked.

"I'd like to think we can help Mika, but right now I just want to see what I can do to light a fire under the police," Kelly stated. "I'm going to write this NPA chief and see if we can convince him that they need to get involved."

Kelly began to make a list about what they knew.

Chapter 29

CAMP ZAMA, JAPAN

TWO DAYS LATER

After wrapping up their one-week planning session, a number of exercise players, observers, evaluators, and technicians were busy cleaning up their work areas. Although Johnson would have one more meeting the following day related to his role in the exercise, he had nothing pressing, so he could work with Masa and Kelly on their plan.

Kurt was prepared for the next stage of the exercise. Once he was needed, he'd be ready to provide a plan to keep the exercise players occupied. All he had to do now was wait and find out when his plans needed to be implemented in the overall design. Since Masa and Kelly were observers, they didn't have anything to do at this time. This allowed them to focus on how to best help Mika.

The three of them were in the planning room, adjacent to the United Nation's joint exercise control center, in a secluded section of Camp Zama. Charts and maps filled the walls, and binders, computers, and overlays lay on top of the tables that ran down the center of the room.

Although Kurt was scheduled to return stateside in a few more days, he wanted to help in any way he could. He wasn't ready to return home; he enjoyed being with his new friends. The next day would be the last planning day for the exercise, which was scheduled to begin at the end of the next month. It would also be a short workday since it was New Year's Eve.

At the planning room's farthest corner table, Kelly refined the letter she felt so critical to ensuring police cooperation. At one of the room's center tables, Masa shared with Kurt his thoughts about rescuing Mika from the Aum, if he failed using legal means. They leaned over a sketch of the compound that Mika's friend, Kotaro, had provided.

Kelly picked up her letter, stood, and walked over to join Masa and Kurt. "This is ready to mail now. Would either one of you want to take a look at it before I send it?"

Masa reached out for the letter and said, "Sure." He went back to the desk Kelly was using and sat down to read.

Kelly looked at Kurt. "Did Masa come up with a plan to help Mika?"

"You mean legally or otherwise?"

"Otherwise. I already know that Masa's been looking into who else might be trying to get a family member out of the Aum. He's just trying to figure out who to contact. Hopefully my letter will get the national police involved."

"If we do have to get involved…"

"We?" Kelly said.

"Well, yes. I assume you'll want my help too," Kurt responded. "Especially if plan B is needed."

"But don't you have to get back home soon?" she asked.

"I do, but I won't be gone long. I still have to be here when the exercise starts the end of next month."

"What's your family think about your being gone so much?"

"No family, no attachments, and this is more exciting than my civilian job."

He's not married, Kelly thought. "What kind of civilian job do you have that allows you to be gone so much?"

"My business partner and I own a chemical company and are both in the reserves. Either one of us can manage the business. He's gone more in the summer and fall while I'm gone mostly during the winter months."

"Okay. So what did you and Masa come up with for plan B?"

"We think the direct approach through the front entrance is the best way," Kurt said.

"You think you can just waltz right in?" Kelly asked.

"No, that's where you come in. We figured you'd provide the distraction we need."

"Are you sure you'll be able to find her?"

Kurt, looking at the sketch, pointed and said, "Based on Kotaro's description, we think this is the dormitory where Mika is staying."

"Is Masa sure this sketch is accurate?"

"As far as he knows," Kurt said. "But, I'd feel more comfortable with an actual photo," Kurt said carefully. "That's where I thought you might help."

"Oh?"

"When we were at Masa's the other day, you mentioned the 200th MI Group as being a resource. Do they have access to satellite imagery?"

"Yes," Kelly said, hesitantly.

"Great. How about asking for a satellite picture?"

As much as she saw the logic in this, she dreaded the idea of having to deal with the arrogant Major Jaegar, something she'd prefer to avoid. "I'll have to give that some thought," she said.

Masa returned from reviewing Kelly's letter.

"Catchy title, 'Some Thoughts on the Matsumoto Sarin Attack.' I only have one suggestion. Rather than sending it without identifying the writer, how about we use initials. That at least gives them the pretense that we may identify ourselves later, implying it might not be safe to do so now."

"That sounds like a good idea," Kelly said.

"I think that about wraps things up for the day," Masa said. "Care to go to the O Club, you two?"

"Great idea."

Chapter 30

CAMP ZAMA, JAPAN

SAME DAY

Rank has its privileges. In this case that meant that the commanding officer of the 200th MI Group was driven in a government issued sedan to the officers club, where he normally left his car, just across from his BOQ billet. The officers' club was where he spent much of his off duty time.

Major Chuck Jaegar was a somewhat overweight officer who looked like an amiable enough leader of men, until you saw his eyes. He was wearing a battle dress uniform that, although frowned upon, was starched and tailored to help camouflage his rotund figure. After graduating from college and receiving a commission, Jaegar was granted a delayed entry into the army so he could attend law school. However, he was not able to practice law as a judge advocate general because he hadn't passed the bar exam on any of his three attempts. As a result of his postgraduate education, he was allowed to enter the army as a captain in the intelligence corp.

Major Jaegar spotted her sitting in the corner of the O club's Rathskeller bar; even from the back he recognized her neatly cut page-boy that bounced as she talked and moved her head about. Captain Onishi sat at her side. Jaegar recognized the Japanese officer as the one with her the same night she tried to upstage him. The other, a major, he didn't recognize. While she was a great looker, he didn't think she was very intelligent.

As Jaegar approached their table, he could hear Kelly explain to the major, "...the Japanese have been struggling psychologically, having accomplished a great deal economically. They still use traditional cultural practices, believing the team more valuable than the individual—working to maintain social harmony. But, the current environment includes Western influences that celebrate individual ingenuity in a free-market system. The result is that Western cultural influences create a struggle to retain a sense of continuity in the midst of change."

"I see," Kurt nodded, then looked up to see a newcomer approach.

"Oh, so you do recognize the appropriateness of being a team player," Major Jaegar interjected.

Flushed, Kelly tried to ignore the remark, as Masa stood to introduce Kurt.

"I've been told to provide you all the support you need on your quest to gather facts about the Matsumoto gassing," Jaegar stated. "For starters, I promised the defense attaché I'd be more than happy to show you around. Since I saw you sitting over here, I thought I'd extend the invitation."

"That's very kind of you," Masa said politely.

"Yes, well, anything I can do to keep in good standing with the embassy and your ground defense forces."

At least he's honest about needing to be on the good side of embassy personnel. He's supposed to provide us support.

"How did you know to find me here?" Kelly pursued.

"When Colonel Jackson called me about providing support, he said that you might be down this way. I knew you'd eventually wind up here. Everyone does sooner or later."

"Well, if you'll excuse me, I'll head out—" Major Jaegar began.

Johnson interrupted, "What a coincidence, Captain Byrnes and Captain Onishi were just discussing how they were looking forward to seeing how you operate to support this region." Looking at Kelly and Masa, Kurt quickly continued, "Tomorrow we'll be reviewing how we're going to handle the message traffic for the exercise. So there's no real need for either Onishi or Byrnes to be there. That would be the perfect time for them to get an orientation, wouldn't it?" Looking at Major Jaegar, he added, "Of course, only if that's all right with you, Major."

"Of course," Jaegar said awkwardly, trying to size up this new major.

"Great, I'll see you tomorrow then?" Kelly tried to sound appreciative.

"Fine, see you then," Major Jaegar said. He turned and made his way to the far side of the club.

Kelly looked over at Kurt as Jeager excused himself. Kurt couldn't help the big grin on his face. Masa knew he had set this up in order to access the 200th MI's satellite imagery capability. Kelly would have to swallow her pride she decided.

"Okay, I'll do it," Kelly sighed. "But, if we're committed to helping get the police involved, we still have a great deal of information we need to gather. Masa, the next time Kotaro calls, tell him we need to know anything he can tell us about what goes on inside the compound."

She then looked over at Kurt. Pretending to be upset, she said, "Thanks a lot."

"My pleasure, ma'am," Kurt responded with a big grin.

"Kelly and I will drive by and take a good look at the place while you're gone, Kurt," Masa added.

"That sounds great. Remember, I'll be back next month, just a few days before the exercise begins. Let me know if you're successful in getting the police involved and Mika released through legal channels," Kurt reminded them.

"Otherwise, we plan on getting Mika out ourselves, agreed?" Masa added.

The others nodded their agreement.

Chapter 31

KOBE, JAPAN

JANUARY 1995

etween the bomb's steel casing and the crate's lead lining, little if any radiation readings could be detected. A casual observer, upon first viewing the crate, would see the words of warning about x-ray equipment. However, Mori was more concerned about meeting the shipping standards overseen by the hazardous cargo officer aboard a vessel. Hopefully, the radiation symbol, combined with the words of caution, would explain any radiation emitted by the crate.

A small, ground-detonated atomic bomb. How brilliant.

Yes, it would explode and destroy plenty in the immediate area, which was the primary purpose, but it was not the main reason Mori supported Haruka's plan. Haruka had convinced those in Pyongyang that radiation was necessary. The radiation would make it impossible for UN forces to offload anywhere near Pusan for a counteroffensive. Radiation from the second bomb, in Japan, would also cause people to evacuate much of Tokyo and the surrounding area. This would result in the Japanese people turning to the Aum for guidance.

Exploding the first bomb near Japan's heartland was genius. Mori understood the implication. Polluting the air with radioactivity would destroy the immediate area, make a great deal of the surrounding area uninhabitable, and start a chain of events that would soon put them in charge. All this would happen with the backing of the Japanese people, who would lose faith in their own government as well as the

US military forces in the region. Their illustrious guru had already predicted this Armageddon.

While the UN, Japan, and Korean forces were busy making accusations and trying to determine who might do such a thing and why, the people would rise up against those who had sworn to protect them. Then, before the government could counter the criticism of their ineffectiveness, they'd find their attention being diverted to stop North Korea's invasion of the South. Little did they know how vulnerable the US was. The UN's efforts to bring in reinforcements would also be futile.

The bombs looked big and heavy, but the bomb specialist had assured Mori a common flatbed truck could easily transport them. This backup plan would have to work for now, since the training of pilots for their newly acquired Russian made helicopter had not yet been completed. The two devices' combined weight was as much as a full load of passengers the helicopter was designed to carry and would have allowed them to make their delivery much quicker and easier. Now Mori had to consider the time it would take to deliver the bombs using ground transportation.

The timing on all this would be critical. Mori's part was tricky enough, ensuring that the bomb in Japan detonated well before the one sent to Korea. One would be placed just across the island, near Yokohama, and set off on his command. But that was all still dependent upon the positioning of the second bomb in Pusan's harbor. It was one thing to develop a bomb and ensure it detonated when it was suppose to. It was another to guarantee they arrived in their precise locations as planned.

At the back of a large warehouse in Kobe, behind locked and guarded doors, were the bombs. They lacked the final fuse mechanism, but were almost ready for the final step. One sat fully encased in its box, ready to be shipped to another carefully guarded location. Its fuse and timing mechanism would be inserted later, once it was determined when the countdown would begin. The other lay tightly strapped to its wooden pallet, not yet encased in its wooden box. The outer casing lay off to one side. It still needed to be lined with lead before the bombs went in the container with the radiation symbol and a stamp showing the words "Handle with Care, X-ray Equipment."

Mika cautiously watched Mori as he checked on their progress. She knew he understood the basic concept behind the bombs operation, but didn't bother himself with the details. He was interested enough to want to understand how each of his weapons' systems worked, but not in intimate detail.

The bomb specialist pointed at the nearest bomb, where Mika was working. "It doesn't look like much considering how it will be bringing on Judgment Day," she heard the specialist tell Mori. "It's bigger than what we originally had hoped we would need, but that's because we couldn't refine the uranium as much as we wanted," he further explained.

She knew what he meant. Depending on the refining process used when purifying the U-235 for use, the minimum amount to start a chain reaction would vary depending upon the purity of the material. For pure U-235, it was 110 pounds. But uranium is never quite pure, so in reality, more was needed to reach supercritical mass. The actual mass needed to facilitate a chain reaction. That's why they needed a larger container.

Mika knew the facts only too well. They had developed the thousands of porous barriers in their centrifuge to achieve a relatively high concentration of U-235. Two percent pure uranium is found in reactor fuel. If pushed further, it could yield up to 95 percent pure uranium for use in an atomic bomb. That process had cost them a great deal of time, energy, and money to develop. The process used centrifugal force to separate the two isotopes, U-235 and U-238.

"Have you been able to determine its destructive power yet?" Mori asked.

"The explosive force is determined by two things. Depending on the refinement along with the design of the warhead and the altitude at which it detonates, the explosive force of an A-bomb can range anywhere from one kiloton to twenty megatons. The higher the altitude when it's detonated, the greater the blast effect, but there is less radiation fallout."

"So you say it will yield less destructive power if at ground level?" Mika detected a tinge of concern in Mori's voice.

"Oh, don't worry. It'll more than take care of the port facility you want to destroy. While there will be more fallout than with an air burst, the amount will vary depending on how close the ship gets to shore and if the package is offloaded prior to its detonation." Either way, the area won't be inhabited again during our lifetime, unless they can remove all the contaminated soil.

They're going to destroy a port? But which one, when and why? Was this true for both bombs? Mika wondered.

"Then we'll just have to ensure it goes off when we want it to," Mori indicated to the bomb master.

"That's what she's working on now," the specialist indicated with a nod toward Mika.

"How do you know it won't go off prematurely?"

Mika was careful not to make eye contact and continued to work, not knowing if she or her supervisor was being asked.

"Would you like to answer his question?" the supervisor asked, looking toward Mika.

"I would be most happy to," Mika said faithfully, again being careful not to look directly at one of the most powerful of the guru's lieutenants.

"The plastic explosive will be packed in this location," Mika pointed to the empty internal compartment. This charge, when ignited, will violently inject the two payloads together, welding them to achieve critical mass within one millionth of a second. As you can see, these are not in place as yet. The lead shield around the bomb's payload is primarily to prevent its radioactivity from short-circuiting the internal circuitry and causing an accidental or premature detonation. To further ensure there was no untimely accident, the fuses will not to be installed with the plastic-shaped charge until just before shipment," Mika added. "I don't know when that will be."

The bomb specialist, angered by her impertinence, quickly interjected, "We will tell you when it is time."

"I do not wish to be bold," Mika quickly bowed her head. "I only wish to ensure I fulfill the desires of his holiness in a time that pleases him."

"That's all right," Mori said calmly. "She has earned the right to know at least that much. We have about a month to complete final preparations and put the bombs in position, so it seems we're well ahead of schedule, thanks to enlisting capable workers such as your helper here," he said as he looked at her supervisor and nodded his head toward Mika.

Mika knew the Aum considered focusing on the most elite colleges for recruiting as a brilliant move. There they were able to find the brightest minds. They often spoke of how those students, under great stress to achieve, seemed to be most disillusioned with how society had become corrupted. The drive to attain materialistic wealth was one reason so many were willing to give away their wealth. Once recruited, a select few would be carefully screened to ensure their loyalty before selectively matching them with the project they best fit.

Mori then looked right at her and said, "You being a true believer will be justly rewarded. There's a great deal more I can't tell you right now, but when our Day of Reckoning arrives, I'll have a place for you, out of harm's way."

The bomb master was next to speak. "Then, if what you say is true, we no longer need the work detail that has been coming here each week from Mt. Fuji headquarters. I'll just have them clean up a few things and send them back the end of next week. Mika should be able to complete the assembly of the fuse mechanism and prepare the cases for shipment by the end of this week. The only thing left to do will be to activate the timer." He reached down and flipped a switch. "Now that it's activated, all you have to do is pull a pin that will be inserted here," he pointed to a small hole drilled into the faceplate, "Once the pin is pulled, the twenty-four-hour clock will begin."

Mori clarified, "That will be just before the ship sails, since it won't take too long for it to reach its destination. Once there it won't be offloaded for some time. Whether it's aboard ship or off loaded, it will still be in the port area, accomplishing our goal."

"Those working on the bomb have worked faithfully," the bomb master added, "but I don't need them after today. I know that I can complete any final touches by myself, between now and when we ship. If I do need any additional help, I can use my security team. I give you my personal guarantee."

"As you wish," Mori responded.

Mika had seen this type of jealous behavior before. The bomb master was like any other middle-management worker. They would do anything to gain recognition from those working most closely with his holiness, or to gain a position of higher stature. Sending the bomb maker's team of workers back to the compound was no surprise. There were many others, like the bomb maker, who were not only paranoid about outsiders, but who might want more recognition as well.

Mika had been closely scrutinized and controlled while going through her apprenticeship. Until now she was careful not to bring attention upon herself. She knew they had not only been testing her skills but loyalty as well. Little did they realize her loyalty was to her father, not to them or their cause. Once she had seen how they had treated her father and caused his death, she was convinced those in charge were not honorable people. She had seen even those who might be respectable be convinced to serve in a most shameful way. That was when she decided to find out more about their plan and put a stop to it, if she could.

Mika had earned confidence from her superiors and now was in a position to make a difference. She realized that what she was participating in was wrong, but also knew that if she escaped or did not participate, they would find another to do the job. Escaping had not been an option anyway. She had seen what they did to those who escaped. If she didn't help, she would have been put on meager rations and subjected to punishment that would have made her into another one of the malnourished zombies she saw back in the compound. Now at least she could sabotage their plans. Besides, what else did she have left to live for?

Meeting the specifications of the diagram was not all that difficult for Mika. The tricky part was sabotaging the fuse. *If she could incapacitate the fuse mechanism in such a way that it still looked operational, they would deliver a bomb that would not explode.*

Still, Mika was concerned about how Mori watched to see who was too curious. Her time there was limited. She would have to make her move soon.

Chapter 32

KOBE, JAPAN

FIVE DAYS LATER

The shaking lasted less than half a minute. It would be several days before an official account of the deaths and devastation was issued, but the people of Kobe knew it was bad.

In an office-size room at the corner of the warehouse, Mori awakened from his cot with a start. Once he realized it was an earthquake, he rolled out of bed and lay prone underneath it, next to the warehouse's outer wall. Although the room was dark, he knew it must be early morning.

After the shaking was over, he got up and made his way to the inner warehouse door, checked his watch, and determined that it was a little before 6:00 a.m. Fearing damage to his project, he quickly dressed and ran into the warehouse.

From an adjoining room, Tomomitsu Nogami, Aum's security chief, had also emerged. They both moved quickly to the bombs' location to assess the damage. They found one crate damaged beyond repair. A forklift had fallen across it and crushed its wooden container. The neighboring crate was untouched. Concerned about retrieving his precious cargo, Mori quickly ordered Nogami to get some help, to free the damaged crate.

Shortly after Mori walked around the debris and pulled off a couple broken planks, Nogami and three of his guards returned to help.

"I left two others at the front entrance to guard against unauthorized entry," Nogami said.

"Good idea," Mori replied.

It took all of them together to push the forklift back to an upright position.

"I need a team to start rebuilding this crate," Mori said.

"I'll leave these three here to help you until we get the right people and equipment to complete the job," Nogami stated.

Mori listed what he needed to make the repairs then turned to walk outside. As he reached the exit, he turned to Nogami and said, "Let our bomb master know I want him back here as well."

Nogami waved to acknowledge that he'd heard.

Mori walked outside. Looking toward the harbor, he realized he had bigger problems. Transporting the bomb to Pusan would not be easy. But it would be a few more days before he could find his way down to the wharf to determine what the challenges were. He noted that he had another omen to pass along to Haruka and the guru.

Mori's most immediate concern was his package. He knew emergency groups would be coming, but not right away. Search and rescue teams would be busy with the many structures that were heavily damaged, including those housing local residents. The Aum's warehouse showed little damage compared to many nearby. His first action would be ensuring the bombs were hidden in their crates before visitors got nosey.

It wasn't until late on the third day following the quake that two city building inspectors stopped by. They insisted they had to make a cursory inspection of the facility so they could tag it. They carefully explained that tagging meant putting a red sign outside the main entrance, indicating that it had already been checked. That meant that the building was safe to be occupied. The tag would preclude others from needing to bother him further.

The next day another visitor warned Mori that access to any facility would be denied unless they were actually running a business or providing support for emergency relief. Realizing the warehouse didn't look much like a business, Mori came up with an idea.

To ensure he could access the warehouse, Mori put his Aum forces to work the next two days and turned the forward section of the warehouse into a makeshift aid station. As a result, emergency response coordinators allowed Mori to accomplish two things at once: covertly secure his precious cargo while providing a public service. Performing good deeds would also be helpful in recruiting new members.

In just a week, Mori had gotten Tomomitsu Nogami and Yoshihiro Inoye, the chief of intelligence, to help with this work. While Nogami's team provided security for the bombs, Inoye supervised the medical facility and recruiting efforts. Dr. Tomomasa Nakamura was also brought in to tend to the patients. They hoped that by taking over what was normally the government's job, the people of Kobe would see the Aum Shinrikyo as having shown *ninjo* (warm heartedness) for the *giri* (faithful).

Once this plan was put in motion, Mori shifted his focus to transporting his package to Korea.

North Korea's troops were beginning to move into position.

Chapter 33

KOBE, JAPAN

ONE WEEK LATER

During the first week following the earthquake, Mori sent out followers to evaluate the local damage. From their reports, he knew there were a couple of routes open for him to drive where he needed to go. Rubble had been cleared from some of the main roads. Mori knew that he needed to go to Kobe's port authority office to determine the status of the terminals, or what was left of them.

Although Kobe's port authority office, near the inner harbor, was only three miles away, it took nearly forty minutes to make his way there. Once there, he inquired about the harbor's shipping status. No ships would be scheduled to leave any time soon. The harbor had been damaged more than he realized. The most assessable and useable of the wharfs were the older ones that could only take ships with the shallowest of draft. Most of the docks that had been destroyed were for much larger container ships. The more he learned, the more he became concerned about finding a ship that could meet his timetable. He had been ahead of schedule; now he would be lucky to meet the deadline.

He shared his concern with a port authority worker. Letting the man know that he was leading a major medical team to assist during this time of crisis, Mori said it was important to find a ship he could load equipment on. He had found a sympathetic ear. He didn't get into specifics, and the man seemed too busy to inquire further, but he did want to help. He showed Mori a shipping book that was revised daily and showed all shipping movements throughout the region.

After spending some time going through the printouts, he saw a tramp steamer listed that could fulfill his needs. It fit the criteria of being able to moor at a shallow pier and was destined for Pusan. Going back to the man who originally assisted him, he discovered how to request that ship for a shipment. Once that was accomplished, he moved on to his next task.

Mori wanted to relocate the bomb closer to the pier it would leave from. Moving it out of the warehouse put Mori's mind to rest, knowing that aftershocks were still causing havoc in the area. This would allow him to respond more quickly to any loading opportunities. It was also important to report progress to the boss, especially since Haruka knew he'd be conveying the plan's status to the North Koreans.

Mori selected a site and received authority to move his crate to the new location.

Now that Mori had coordinated for the final positioning of the bomb, he decided it was a good time to make a more thorough inspection of the outside of the bomb. It would be prudent to inspect the inside as well.

Mori went to talk with the bomb master. Proud of his accomplishments, the bomb master was more than happy to oblige.

The bomb master got two of Nogami's security people to assist and had them open the end of the crate. Then they pried up the lid to the bomb's encasement. Seeing that the only damage from the earthquake had been to the crate, not the bomb, they looked more carefully at the inner core, being careful to avoid going inside the lead lining of the casing.

Seeing that Mori was pleased with the condition of the bomb, the bomb master started closing the lid to the encasement when Mori said, "Wait. I want to see the timing mechanism."

The bomb master set the lid off to the side, reached in, and pulled the mechanism out.

Explaining how the mechanism worked, once again, he pulled out the devise and deactivated the switch. Pulling it out further, a loose wire caught his attention.

Chapter 34

SEOUL, KOREA

SAME DAY

"Look here," the photo intelligence specialist said, pointing with a pencil at a series of aerial photographs laid out on the table. "Here's Haeju and Kaesong. The distance between the two is about seventy kilometers, yet they seem to have only positioned a battalion-sized unit in a sector just south of here," pointing between the two cities, "and just north of this waterway."

He pointed to another photo, "I don't get it. Over here they've placed a brigade-sized element to establish a defense perimeter. That seems to be their typical way of doing things. Why would they assign only a battalion to cover such a large area over there? It looks like someone made a major blunder during these training maneuvers. And why are they conducting these now? They announced a major training exercise, but the bulk of the troop's maneuvering shouldn't begin until the end of the month."

"That's interesting," the warrant officer replied, turning the photo for a better view, "especially knowing the quality units they have there." Looking up, he saw the CO glancing his way and caught his attention. "Major Walker, you want to take a look at this?"

"Sure, Chief. What have you got?"

"There seems to be an inconsistency in their deployment tactics. If you look in these different sectors, you'll see that battalion and brigade sized units have dispersed fairly consistently throughout these areas."

The CO looked closely at the various photos.

"Now, look here, sir," the chief warrant separated the photos he was looking at, and pushed them toward the CO.

"I see," the CO said. "Their dispersion looks deliberate to me. See here? The pattern looks consistent. If it were in error, one or two companies would be clumped closer together. But just to confirm, let's get more shots and see if this pattern is consistent as they redeploy elsewhere." Turning to the first photograph, he said, "Let's also take a look at the type of terrain they seem to be interested in and get a closer look at their equipment. I can't help but wonder why that one battalion is being given so much maneuvering space, and why there and now?"

"Yes, sir," the chief responded.

Major Walker had already talked with each of his two warrant officers and senior NCOs to get their feedback on their sections of expertise. Now he needed some quiet time in his office to think.

Major Walker had heard the announcement, like everyone else in the American sector, that "Kim II Jong was scheduling a training exercise to determine their level of readiness now that he was the new commander in chief," but he didn't like what he saw. Walker couldn't help but wonder if their deployment indicated something wasn't right. Radio intercepts from within Korea were consistent with what was expected for an exercise, but there was also an inordinate amount of message traffic outside the country. He needed to see the infiltration reports once again, see if another set of eyes drew the same conclusions.

He picked up the phone and called the G2 office.

Chapter 35

SEOUL, KOREA

Brigadier General Byrnes's aide de camp had plopped a thin stack of papers down on the desk in front of him an hour earlier. They were the latest intelligence reports from the international peacekeeping units and headquarters stationed in Korea. Byrnes received these reports at his office in Seoul regularly. Somebody, either the head of the forwarding agency or his assistant intelligence officer, had highlighted the significant sections with a yellow marker.

His eyebrows went up. Buried deep among the routine troop movements, weapons deployments, and other miscellaneous satellite photos were some disquieting reports. Although it was well known that the North Koreans were gearing up for tactical exercises, previously announced by the North Korean government as training exercises, all indications were that they were more expansive than in the past.

Further, one report, from Major Carl Walker, was of particular concern. He had considered the positioning of some elite units, observed by satellite photos, as particularly noteworthy. The tactical spacing seemed generous, almost implying that they were preparing for battle in a nuclear environment. *Was this by accident or by design?* The first satellite photos could not eliminate the possibility that their positioning might be the result of poor planning. However, other photos seemed to show the same consistent dispersal whenever these units moved, concentrating along the hills and valleys surrounding the waterway.

Some were expected deployment practices that precede major engagements, but other reports showed more movement toward the

South, with increased coded message traffic between the North and their operatives in the South. Even more concerning was an increased exchange with operatives in Japan. Although Byrnes didn't have enough evidence to support his feeling, he believed this might all be explained by stalled talks at the negotiations table. However, he only had these unsubstantiated reports and his instincts. He knew he couldn't go forward with just a hunch.

General Byrnes looked up at Colonel James Sullivan, his assistant intelligence officer. "There is too much message traffic going on between North Korea and Japan."

"Yes, sir," Sullivan spread his hands. "But who? And, if it's not the military, what kind of organization could provide that level of threat?"

"The CIA have any ideas?"

Sullivan shook his head. "No, sir. Not that they're much interested. Langley doesn't see the NBC threat as even a possibility. The organizations they've been shadowing either have been dormant or don't have the know-how to pose any significant threat."

"Since all evidence shows North Korea has stopped nuclear research and has a very limited delivery capability, they must be up to something through outside resources," Byrnes said.

"Yes, sir," Sullivan responded. But, so far, we've only received that one report, regarding what the doctor in Pyongyang overheard, indicating a possible connection with a religious group in Japan. Who'd ever believe some religious group would have the ability, let alone a desire, to work with North Korea and help them develop a nuclear arsenal. If somebody else told me that, I'd certainly have a hard time believing it. If it is true, and the North Koreans are communicating through a religious organization, that's beyond our jurisdiction."

"Shit," Byrnes grimaced. "Kim Il Jong could be working with almost anyone from China, Russia, Japan, or anywhere else for all we know. While everyone's attention was on his father while he was president, no one knew what his son was up to. But, again, if the information we've received from this North Korean doctor is legitimate, there's a religious group in Japan we've got to find out more about."

"True," Sullivan nodded.

"We need to find out who they've been making contact with. While a religious organization doesn't seem like a credible threat, we can't reject anything until we know more." He thought back over conversations regarding expanding his intelligence network to incorporate those in positions in the various embassies. "Look, Jim, direct our people to start gathering evidence, even if it seems unrelated—anything odd or out of place."

"Even rumors?"

"Right. One thing's for sure. The embassies could be a greater resource than the CIA." Byrnes thought for a moment. "Look, I'm flying down to Japan next week for a conference with Colonel Jackson. Have this put together in an organized fashion and I'll take it with me. Then we'll see if the boss can shake loose a few more resources so we can follow this up on our own."

Sullivan nodded. "Sounds good."

"In the meantime, I'll recommend to the boss that we alert defense forces along the border. Even though they've announced training maneuvers, the massing of troops beyond the norm, especially along the border, is always unnerving. We don't want to be caught unprepared." Byrne's jaw tightened. "Some son of a bitch may be out there building alliances inside Japan's borders, and I want to find out who the hell it is."

Chapter 36

TOKYO, JAPAN

THE NEXT DAY

Haruka was angry. It was not just Mori's report regarding a traitor in their midst. Clear action was needed to be taken to rid themselves of another major headache. A man who was a major threat against all that Haruka had carefully orchestrated.

"I'll take care of the woman who sabotaged the bomb. But you'll need to get a few of your people together for a mission of your own." Haruka made it clear he wanted the lawyer to disappear.

Sakamoto had taken too many of the Aum missing-family cases. At least twenty-three families had asked the attorney for help. Their children had joined Aum and then simply vanished from their lives.

Gathering several lead medical and security staff, Mori explained the situation to them and what needed to be done. But not before he had his chemist put together a few items for the doctor's medical bag. The group then made their way to the lawyer's home.

There is no other way. "You must take the whole family, if necessary. There is too much at stake to allow him to continue his practice another day," Haruka had said. Membership was doubling, money was pouring in, and there were plans to expand further overseas. Haruka blamed Sakamoto for fostering a hysterical atmosphere against the Aum. The lawyer was heading up a campaign against them and had formed a society that supported the families of abducted Aum members.

Taking the distance into account, Mori timed their arrival at the lawyer's apartment for the middle of the night.

When it came time to abduct their target, they found the feat wasn't as easy as expected. First, Sakamoto's fourteen-month-old baby awakened. When he started to cry, one of the guards quickly suffocated him. Then the wife, hearing her baby's muffled cries, began to stir.

The team quickly surrounded the bed. Mori placed one hand across the wife's face and the other on her chest to pin her down, while the doctor prepared the syringe. While Mori's attention was diverted toward the doctor, Sakamoto's wife pulled Mori's hand to her mouth and bit as hard as she could, drawing blood. Mori yelled out in agony and pulled his hand away.

In the struggle that followed, the doctor dropped the syringe. Sakamoto's wife reached out again, this time grabbing a small chain that hung about the doctor's neck. It broke and dropped to the floor. Distracted by his search for the dropped syringe, the doctor did not notice the chain with his Aum badge was missing. That's when another team member hit her on the head and strangled her.

The doctor finally located the syringe in time to inject Sakamoto. Although the lawyer fought viciously, even after being injected with the toxic fluid, he would be dead in just minutes.

It had taken thirty minutes to complete their task. All three bodies were wrapped in blankets and thrown in the back of the group's cars.

Once back at their Mount Fuji compound, the bodies were disposed of. Pajamas and bedding were burned. The drums, used to hide the bodies, and shovels were tossed into the Sea of Japan.

There would be *almost* no evidence of what had transpired.

Chapter 37

TOKYO, JAPAN

THE NEXT DAY

Since learning of Mika's predicament, Masa had saved every newspaper clipping related to the Aum. Through them, he had learned that Sakamoto was the lawyer handling missing persons cases related to the Aum. Sakamoto had even formed the Society of Aum Supreme Truth Victims and began negotiating on the parents' behalf. After meeting with him, Masa was certain he had found the right man to help. It was no wonder he was heartbroken when he read the news article that Sakamoto's whole family was missing.

The lawyer had made a positive impression on Masa during his first visit to the young attorney. Upon entering Mr. Sakamoto's office, Masa quickly became aware of his easygoing manner. It was no wonder so many families were drawn to this man with the messy hair, thick glasses, and a ready smile. Masa had even been invited to join the support group. Masa did attend one meeting, only to hear the frustrations of others who had already tried communicating with the Aum directly.

Following the gathering, Masa talked with a gentleman who shared how he had even tried to force his way into an Aum compound where he believed his wife and daughter were staying. Once inside, he found himself immediately surrounded by a number of Aum members who blocked him from going any further. A man who introduced himself as Mr. Haruka stepped forward and told him he would have to leave or he would call the police. The man still insisted on seeing his family, but to no avail. The police were called, but he left before they arrived, knowing his actions would not be productive.

Kelly had sent her letter to Takaji Komatsu. To their pleasant surprise, it was subsequently printed in the newspaper. However, they understood the local police were still reluctant to get involved. *Religious freedom* was still the Aum's cry. While there was no indication that the National Police Agency had gotten involved, publication of the letter did seem to cause more citizens to publicly speak out against the Aum.

That's when Masa decided now was the time to make contact with an old friend. He'd go visit Komatsu himself.

Late morning, following reading about the Sakamoto family, Masa sat in the empty office of the chief of the National Police Agency, located in the heart of Tokyo. Takaji Komatsu, whom he called earlier, was in a morning meeting and was expected to join him shortly. Normally he would be required to wait in the visitors' area, but being an old friend and former partner of the chief, Komatsu directed his secretary to let him wait in his office.

Masa looked about the Spartan looking room. The only objects on the desktop were a computer monitor, a telephone, and a photo of an attractive woman and two cute children, who stood next to Komatsu. A few police academy pictures were scattered about one wall that ran along the side of the desk. Masa's eyes lingered on one photo in particular that showed him standing next to Takaji.

Masa heard the door open and turned to see Komatsu enter. He was a bit older and more worn looking than Masa last remembered, but his intelligence was still evident. The chief was a slightly built man with dark-brown eyes that matched his now thinning hair. Takaji smiled when he saw his former partner.

"Masa, it's great to see you," Takaji said, reaching for his hand as Masa stood to greet him. Masa sat back down as Komatsu motioned for him to do so, and then he circled behind his desk to sit. "Thinking of leaving the army to come back and join us? We'd love to have you. The intelligence gathering you've become adept at dealing with would be very useful here, particularly while trying to coordinate between our various agencies."

Masa looked surprised.

"Oh, you think I haven't been following your career?" Takaji smiled.

Masa quickly recovered. "My boss might have something to say about that. But I'll have to admit, every once in a while I wonder what I'd be doing if I'd stayed."

"Number one in your class at the academy, and top rated in every assignment you had. I expect you could have been my executive officer," Takagi said with a smile.

Hearing his mentor give him such high praise, Masa blushed.

Takaji laughed, "Well, you didn't come here to talk about the good old days. You said on the phone that you had some questions about the Aum Shinrikyo and a possible witness who was willing to testify against them. What's your interest in them, if you don't mind my asking?"

"I'm not sure if my interest is so much in them as it is in why I believe you should be pursuing them."

"We're still monitoring but can't find a way of going after them as yet. That's why you got my interest when you said you had a possible witness who was willing to testify against them."

"You've been monitoring but not pursuing," Masa mused, thinking maybe he wasn't ready to talk about his cousin.

Komatsu sensed his friend's hesitation. "What do you know about the Aum Shinrikyo?" the chief asked.

"It's relatively new, as a religious organization, is headed by a blind guru, and has political interests, although that fizzled out after losing during the 1990 elections. I believe a man by the name Mori is one of his top lieutenants."

"That pretty much sums it up," Komatsu said. "That man you mentioned, Hideo Mori is his full name. He primarily works for a man by the man named Kiyohide Haruka. While the guru, Ashihara, is their religious leader, Haruka seems to be the main power behind the scenes. Mori is one of a few of Haruka's associates he seems to work with most closely. There's been talk for some time that they still have aspirations to govern this country. The word on the streets is that they're well organized and have even created a series of ministries, much like our government. They've recruited from the government as well as police officials and universities. They've even built up their own army, called the 'Army of White Love.' We believe they've killed a number of their own members, but we can't prove anything."

"At least I'm glad to hear you have been looking into them," Masa said.

"I'm always interested in hearing new information," Komatsu said. With that, Masa and Komatsu shared, with each other, what they each knew.

Toward the end of their conversation, Komatsu said, "We still have a number of others missing, too."

"Actually, that's what brought me here," Masa said. "I had been in contact with a lawyer named Sakamoto to help get a friend out."

Komatsu raised his eyebrows. "Oh, so you're here to check on the missing Sakamoto family?"

"I'm here because Sakamoto was my last hope to help get someone else out of the Aum. Someone you may want to use as an eye witness, who can testify against them."

"A friend?"

"Actually, my cousin," Masa confessed softly.

"You want to tell me about her?" Masa's friend asked.

Masa told him how she got involved, and finally what she'd been working on.

"Masa, if you can verify this information, I can investigate; if not, I can't take any action," Komatsu said.

"So, you can't help me?" Masa said.

"Sorry, my friend, but my hands are tied. Let me tell you something. Not too long ago, I received a letter from someone who seemed to know a great deal about the Aum. It was valuable information that told us what they've done and how dangerous they are, but unfortunately that letter was sent anonymously. So, unless I have someone willing to verify the information, I can't do anything. I get the feeling some people want to help, but they're too afraid to identify themselves, for fear of retribution."

"Have you been able to determine the origin of the letter?" Masa asked innocently.

"No. We don't even have the original letter anymore."

"What do you mean?"

Takaji looked at him with a sly smile. "We had it in a file. But, it seems that someone pulled it from our records and decided it would be more useful to the media. All I know is it ended up in the newspapers. Thank goodness they didn't use my name."

"You don't seem too upset at that," Masa said.

"You won't hear me say this in public, but someone sending that letter to the newspapers is one of the best things that could have happened."

While Masa knew his friend could not legally take action, he also knew Komatsu would do what he could, if he could. He chose not to tell the chief of the personal investigation he and Kelly had been pursuing, nor how he was beginning to feel the inevitable need to do something more himself.

Now he could honestly tell Colonel Jackson, during his next meeting, that he had pursued all avenues against the Aum.

PART 3

Chapter 38

US EMBASSY, TOKYO, JAPAN

TWO DAYS LATER

"The ambassador will see you now," the executive assistant to the US ambassador in Japan said, and held open the door to an inner office.

Captains Kelly Byrnes and Masa Onishi rose from the lobby's light-brown leather couch and walked toward the office entry. They were expecting to conduct their briefing with Colonel Jackson, so they were a bit surprised to be led into the ambassador's office instead.

As the two captains entered, they saw Ambassador Murdock sitting at the head of a rectangular conference table. To the ambassador's left, Deputy Ambassador Conklin sat facing them. The two army officers who were seated with their backs to them, turned to greet the captains as they entered. Furthest from the ambassador was Colonel Jackson. Between Jackson and the ambassador was Brigadier General Byrnes.

"We were the ones who caused you to have to wait so long out there," General Byrnes said.

Captain Byrnes looked surprised, then smiled and nodded. They had been in the outer office for a little over an hour. Looking at the ambassador, Kelly said, "Excuse me, sir, but I was under the impression that Colonel Jackson wanted us here to brief him on the Aum situation."

"Well, yes. That's right. There may very well be a danger out there, as you said, that can be construed as a threat to Japan's national security." The ambassador looked at General Byrnes and then back to Kelly before continuing. "The general is here because, after discussing a situation they're monitoring in North Korea, it was felt there may be a connection and more far-reaching implications to what you've been dealing with." Following a short pause, he continued. "I'm sure he'll make his purpose clear at a suitable time."

Kelly, realizing that it would not be appropriate to press any further, turned and gestured toward Masa and introduced him to the ambassador and her father. "He's assigned as a liaison officer, from Japan's Self-Defense Forces."

"How do you do?" Ambassador Murdock said. "We met once before, didn't we?"

"Yes, sir, but only briefly, when I was first assigned a little over a year ago. You have a good memory, sir."

"Good work doesn't go unnoticed around here."

"Thank you, sir."

General Byrnes acknowledged the comment with a smile and then looked at Jackson. He made a *let's get to it* gesture with his index finger.

Colonel Jackson began, "As the ambassador stated, General Byrnes and I met initially to discuss the situation in Korea. The reason you two had to wait for so long was because we were discussing the situation before you arrived, and we wanted to get the ambassador read in on what we know. We believe he also needs to hear what *you* have to say." He then took a fat, business-size envelope from his interior jacket pocket and handed it to Captain Byrnes.

"Take a look at that, Captain Byrnes," Jackson said.

Kelly opened the envelope and took out the sheaf of paper.

"What is this?" she asked.

"Before we talk about your little escapade at Matsumoto City, and what you found out from Captain Onishi's cousin," Jackson said, "it might be a good idea for the two of you to have some idea why we're so interested in hearing what you have to say."

It took Kelly just a couple of minutes to read the top page, "Executive Summary."

"This appears to be an intelligence assessment of North Korea's military movements," she said finally, "but I don't understand."

"Read the next page," Jackson responded.

Kelly read some more. She saw that the document had been printed on Brigadier General Byrnes's stationary and was not an official intelligence brief.

Kelly said to her dad, "Is this your personal assessment of what's going on in North Korea, sir?"

"Yes, but we haven't been able to confirm enough to send this up the chain of command. I came down here to talk with Colonel Jackson about the possible threat from the north, I also wanted to let him know that since we don't know how credible the threat up north is, or what outside help they're getting, we need to keep an eye on any religious groups that may be suspect. Now, Joe tells me he believes it is credible, that he may have a religious faction in mind, and you're right in the middle of it."

Kelly let out a deep breath and said, "I'm glad you're here. If the implications are as listed in this letter are true, the situation may be nastier than even we suspected and would confirm our worst fears. That's assuming we can confirm that the Aum group we've been dealing with is, in fact, the same religious organization that has been working with the North Koreans."

Kelly handed the assessment to Masa, who read the documents.

By the time they had compared notes, they all knew they were talking about the same religious group. They further understood the frustrations felt by local and national police agencies, and were particular concerned about Mika's possible involvement with a nuclear weapon.

The Aum connection was confirmed with both North Korea and in the Sakamoto family's disappearance. Masa also confirmed General Byrnes's information that the Soldiers of White Love Army was the same one Mika had told him about during her father's funeral. Finally, Masa shared how the chief of the National Police Agency had evidence connecting the Aum to the lawyer's missing family. Those who abducted the Sakamotos had left a badge belonging to the Aum.

Now, they just needed to figure out what to do about this.

The ambassador called in his administrative assistance to arrange for a direct flight back to Seoul for General Byrnes. He then stood, signaling that the meeting was over. The others followed his lead and stood as well. They were being excused.

They all had roles to play now.

Chapter 39

BASE OF MT. FUJI, JAPAN

THE NEXT DAY

To find privacy, Haruka and Mori stood in the printing center of the Aum's Mt. Fuji compound. The machines' loud racket covered their words. Mori's conversation with Haruka had him feeling flustered.

"Informing North Korea of our setbacks won't do any good," Haruka assured Mori. "The wheels have already been set into motion. Once they start moving a whole army, they can't just put plans on hold. They've already partially mobilized some selected units. In two weeks, all their forces will be in position. Once that occurs, the main part of the training exercise will commence. They can maintain that level of readiness for only a few weeks before they have to start shutting down operations. You have to ensure your job is completed during that time."

It was apparent to Mori that he, and he alone, would bear the burden of responsibility for making the North Korean's plan work.

"If you remember, when we first agreed on this operation, you said you could handle it. You would be the one to send the signal, setting off the first bomb in Japan," Haruka continued, "letting the North Koreans know when they should mass their forces for the final push south. You have the *honors*, the *responsibility*. We're all counting on *you*."

Mori realized Haruka had cleared himself of any responsibility. Mori was beginning to regret his earlier boastfulness when he first took on the task. At that time, he saw only an opportunity to move up in Aum's hierarchy.

"As far as your problem with the traitor goes, however, *that* I *can* help you with," Haruka offered. Then with a smile, he added, "But I'll let Ashara have his pleasure with her first. Once in a while, we should try and keep him happy as well. After that, with Ikuo Higuchi's help, Nogami will make her disappear. Higuchi can supply whatever drugs you need."

With that, Haruka left the printing facility to find Higuchi and Nogami and send them to Mori.

Just below where Mori and Haruka had been standing, Mika had been restrained most of the week in a secret basement.

Mori was through with his questioning of her. Now he was ready to rid himself of her traitorous burden.

Chapter 40

BASE OF MT. FUJI, JAPAN

SAME DAY

I t wasn't quite dusk as they drove along the base of Mt Fuji. As was almost always the case this time of year, the temperatures dropped quickly as the sun went down. Pedestrian traffic was nonexistent and motor traffic was light. Slowly, the late model sedan cruised past the rectangular encampment for one final look. The car's three occupants were careful to scan the towering walls and gatehouse. They wanted to ensure there were still only two guards manning the front gate, as noted during the preceding two weeks.

Kelly and Masa had conducted a series of scouting missions as they awaited Kurt's return from the states. Although the two had promised Kurt they'd wait for his return, it was really a matter of exhausting all other options before taking this action. The legal approach and police intervention were no longer possibilities, so now it was up to them.

From the satellite photos, supplied by Major Jaegar, they got a clear picture of what they could expect inside the compound. Masa and Kelly had agreed that Kurt's plan was the best option. A simple, straightforward approach. They would walk in the front door.

Kelly stopped about a quarter mile away, far enough to ensure they could not be seen exiting the car. Masa and Kurt had already gone over how they would conduct their infiltration. They had not worked together before, but found military operational protocols very similar in approach. Like doctors discussing a delicate brain operation, no detail was left to chance. Their success depended on it. Radio and hand signals were agreed upon well in advance. Kelly waited to make sure they were in position before she got back behind the wheel of her sedan.

Directing the vehicle to the front of the complex, Kelly completed a U-turn and stopped just a few yards shy of the front gate. The two guards stayed in position until it was obvious that the beautiful Caucasian woman needed assistance.

Byrnes stepped from the car, carrying her roadmap in such a way that it would be clear to anyone watching she was lost. She was wearing light-tan slacks and an oversized green sweater. The sweater was loose fitting, allowing a radio to be attached to her belt holster at the small of her back.

The two security guards moved to assist. Kelly was quick to speak, talking in English, looking relieved to have found someone to help. She realized that her façade as an American tourist who lacked an understanding of the Japanese language was working to her advantage.

A moment later Masa Onishi and Kurt Johnson slipped in past the front gate.

The two officers, in civilian clothes, were no-nonsense as they moved surreptitiously through the compound. Masa led the way to ensure the coast was clear before waving Kurt forward as they proceeded. Masa always made the first move knowing that he stood a better chance of blending in, in the event of discovery. He had carefully draped a robe over his pants and shirt, prior to entering, to better blend in with the white-robed residents in the event of being discovered. Speaking the language helped also.

Kurt, on the other hand, knew he couldn't blend in as a foreigner and didn't speak the language. Since he wore blue jeans, a denim shirt, and a light ski jacket, if he got caught, he expected that he'd just get kicked out of the compound as a nosy American exploring the area.

They moved clockwise around the compound, hugging the outer wall, following a series of vertical beams that supported cross-timbers, along a covered walkway.

Masa crossed an open area that lay between the buildings lining the front and back walls of the complex. He stood next to one that was labeled Satian 7. Up ahead he could see their objective, the dormitory. Masa made his way along the side of Satian 7, and when he reached the corner, he motioned for Kurt to hold his position.

Masa indicated that he spotted two people. The two stayed in place until Masa motioned Kurt that it was clear. Once Kurt joined Masa, he was informed that one man had gone inside while the second stood outside the entryway to Satian 7.

"Something, or someone, in there must be important if they have a guard inside this compound," Masa said. "Neither of the men had on the robe typically worn by most of the Aum members."

"That's curious," Kurt said.

"When Kotaro called last night, and I told him we were coming for Mika tonight, we talked for a while. During that discussion, he told me more about what we could expect. He said Satian 7 was the most mysterious of all the buildings. It's considered to be the holiest. Only a chosen few were admitted. He said it held a golden image of Shiva on an altar, on top of which were placed the bones of Buddha, which Shoko Asahara claimed to have brought back from Sri Lanka."

Other than the two men Masa had seen, there was no one else walking around the compound. Kotaro had mentioned that would be the case for this time in the evening.

"We need to find a way of getting to the dormitory without that guard seeing us," Masa said. They both looked at their objective, a three-story building where many of the Aum members, hopefully still including Mika, resided. "The last we heard, while you were gone, was that Mika was staying on the third floor, supposedly along with others who worked with her on special projects."

Masa and Kurt backtracked until they found a better way of approaching the dormitory without being seen by the guard. They located a back entry to the dormitory that was not locked.

As Masa started to enter, Kurt said, "I'll continue along the far side of the dorm to explore the immediate area and wait out of sight. You'll only hear from me if someone comes."

Kurt radioed Kelly to keep her informed before moving on to explore the next set of buildings and seek another means of escape. He continued along the compound's back wall until he came upon something he remembered from the satellite photos, the illustrious Guru's home. Kurt saw that it was not lavish on the outside, but wondered what amenities remained unseen.

Kurt crept between two buildings to peek out into the center of the open area, but quickly ducked back when he saw three figures approach from the far corner he had just circumnavigated. They continued to walk directly toward him. He blindly backed up, feeling his way by placing his hand on the outer wall of the guru's home. Just below the eve of the covered walkway, he stumbled on a drainage cover. He froze, hoping they would not see him in the dimness of the covered passage. Luckily, the two men were too focused on the lone female figure walking between them.

Chapter 41

BASE OF MT. FUJI, JAPAN

SAME DAY

M asa walked past the offices on the first floor of the dormitory then climbed to the third level, where he found a series of tiny rooms honeycombed throughout the floor. When he entered what he understood to be Mika's room, he found it empty. He then checked to see if anyone was in the neighboring rooms. Everywhere he looked, everyone was quietly lying in bed. Some had electrodes attached to their heads and looked weak and filthy. Only one took the effort to look up at him as he checked for recognizable features, but no one said a word. He began to wonder if he had received the correct information when he saw a robed figure walking in the hallway, heading his way.

Masa stepped back into Mika's empty room and hugged the inner wall, waiting for the person to pass. He heard the footsteps stop just outside the entryway. Masa realized whoever it was, was not going to pass by. The stranger stepped into the room. Masa quickly reached out and covered the stranger's mouth while easily restraining the slim figure. "Don't scream or you'll regret it," Masa stated. "Do you understand?"

The man nodded.

"Good, now tell me where Mika Hiroshi is. I understand this is her room."

Masa uncovered the man's mouth. "You must be Masa. I'm Kotaro. I came here to warn you that they've taken her away."

"Where? For what purpose?" Masa asked.

"I didn't find out until today that she hadn't been in her room for some time. I only just heard that they had hidden her away for purposes of meditation. That would mean they want more control over her and suspect a loss of trust. Just a little while ago, I overheard Haruka telling a man named Nogami that the guru wanted to see her personally. I think they took her to one of the other buildings in the compound."

"Show me," Masa insisted.

He followed Kotaro down the stairs to where Kurt was waiting. Finding him not far from the back entrance, he explained what Kotaro had told him.

Kurt said, "I may have seen her. When I went looking around, I saw two men and a female walking from the printing facility to the guru's quarters. She may still be there."

Kotaro and Masa followed Kurt as he made his way back toward the guru's home. When they arrived there, they circled its outer wall until they found a side window slightly ajar. There, they stopped. They heard two men talking inside.

Their tone seemed stern and argumentative, Kurt thought.

When they heard a woman talking, Masa confirmed they had found Mika. The anguish in Mika's voice made Kurt realize she was in a serious predicament.

They stood silently, feeling precious seconds tick by. Each was deep in thought, trying to think of what to do. Kurt didn't need a translation. He could clearly see the frustration in Masa's face.

Finally, one of the men left. Kotaro was the first to speak. Looking at Masa Kotaro said in Japanese, "I feel sick. There is nothing I can do that would not put me in jeopardy as well." Masa translated the obvious conclusion to Kurt.

"There's only one guard there now," Masa said, then began to make a move toward the door.

Kurt held his arm up to stop him before Masa could take his third step. "Wait, Masa."

"How can you tell me to wait? She's family."

"I know," Kurt said, "but if you barge in now, the situation would only get worse. There would be more than just the bodyguard we'd have to deal with by the time we got to the front gate."

Kurt could see Masa calculating what lay between their location and the compound's front entrance.

"Then I suppose you have a better idea?" Masa queried.

"Better than storming in," Kurt responded. "Listen, I think I know how we can pull this off."

"I'm listening," Masa said.

"I could cause a distraction, but I don't speak the language. You'd be perfect for causing a distraction since Mika's your cousin," Kurt continued explaining his plan.

When he finished, Masa turned to Kotaro and made the plan clear in Japanese. When he finished, he turned back to Kurt and nodded, "Okay, I'll do it."

"Great. I'll contact you as soon as I can. Be ready to help us into the car once we're out the front gate. If I find another way out, I'll call you on the radio."

Masa made it clear to Kotaro what their options were, and that his role was to assist only if he wouldn't be discovered. Masa pulled his robe over his head and handed it to Kurt before moving toward the front gate. His next task would be best performed in his regular clothes.

Kurt found a bench near the front of the building and placed it below the window. Standing on it, he and Kotaro could plainly see the back of the guru's bodyguard and the front of Mika as they looked into the spacious room.

"Kneel here," the guru's bodyguard ordered. Mika slowly dropped to her knees on the straw tatami mat in the center of a room, which was barren of any furnishings other than a single large futon against one wall.

"What do you want of me? I told you that I have been faithful. I have done everything that has been asked of me. Why else would I work such long hours to ensure we complete the task so judiciously?"

"Yes, you have done well, until you sabotaged the project," the guard said.

"I told you. I must have forgotten to attach that one last wire."

"Then why was it cut?" the guard asked impatiently.

"I clipped it because I was going to strip off the insulation and reinsert it, to ensure I had a better connection," she lied. "I must have been sidetracked and not gotten back to completing the task," she added.

"Either way, you now have an opportunity to show your allegiance to the guru. Feel fortunate, for only a few have the opportunity to rise to a higher level of enlightenment."

Before Masa left for the front entrance to the compound, he had explained to Kurt that Mika had no other option but to go along with whatever they wanted to do with her. To not go along would admit guilt, or so Kurt was told.

Mika did not look her captor in the eyes but held her head up now, showing pride and conviction. Kurt was surprised to see how pretty she was as the guard untied her long black hair, letting it fall down the back of her robe. The light of a dim, single wall lamp and scattered candles seemed to make her face glow.

"You are fortunate that the guru is looking kindly on you," the guard said, adding a slight smile.

"What do you mean?" Mika's voice quivered.

The guru entered from a back room and sat just feet in front of Mika, on the foot of a futon.

The guru then asked, "Are you a true believer?"

Mika answer, "I am."

"Then are you willing to do what is necessary for God?"

"For God, yes," Mika said indifferently.

"Then you may disrobe," his eminence said plainly.

"What?" Mika said with surprise.

Kotaro pulled Kurt just below the window and said in his broken English, "Now is good time for Masa to bring some attention on himself."

Kurt could only look at Kotaro in puzzlement. Although he knew Mika was in a predicament, he did not understand what had been said.

They both looked back through the window.

"You heard him," the guard said. The guard walked over, stood directly in front of her, and placed a hand on each side of the neck of her robe. He then pulled the neckline apart until the tear allowed the dressing gown to fall over her shoulders to the ground, before he again stood off to her side. Mika's hands hung meekly at her side. There was nothing she could do.

Kurt could see that the guru was not looking at her directly, and that the high priest was, by and large, blind. He realized that that action was more for the benefit of the guard than it was for the guru.

Kurt looked around the room for an alternate escape plan. Before he could find a more immediate solution, he heard the cavalry coming to the rescue. Kurt knew the noise he heard was from Masa.

While he couldn't make out what Masa was saying, he could hear him yelling at the top of his lungs. He was sure the commotion could be heard all across the grounds.

The guru directed his bodyguard to find out what the commotion was about. The guard hesitated, directing Mika to stay where she was, and then followed the guru's command.

Before they could be discovered, Kurt and Kotaro jumped down from the window, returned the bench to its original location, and watched from around the corner of the building. Aum members were arriving from all the surrounding facilities. Everyone's attention was directed toward the man making the disturbance.

They could see Masa standing in the middle of the compound yelling. The guards, looking confused as to how this man had slipped past them, ran up to the ranting intruder and immediately restrained him. Kurt could see one man Kotaro identified as Mori taking charge of the situation. He was looking at one of the two guards and pointing toward the front of the compound. Kurt surmised that Mori was directing the guards to escort Masa out the front gate, just as they had hoped.

Now was when Kurt knew he had to make his move.

Chapter 42

BASE OF MT. FUJI, JAPAN

"Kotaro," Kurt said. "There's a drainpipe between those two buildings. Do you know where it goes?"

"Yes. To river," Kotaro pointed.

"Is it big enough for us to crawl through?" Kurt asked, using his arms to indicate what he meant.

"Easy for me, harder for you."

Kurt felt it was worth a try. "Wait here," he said.

"Where you go?" Kotaro asked.

"To save the fair maiden," Kurt said.

Now it was Kotaro's turn to look puzzled.

Kurt silently watched the spiritual leader's bodyguard return, then he moved to the window once again. As he had hoped, he heard a discussion then saw the outside door open and the guard reemerge. Kurt thought the guard would have told the guru that it was Mika's relative who was making all the noise and assumed they were going to move her. Kurt was relieved when he saw the guard pulling Mika behind him.

Mika attempted to hold her torn robe together, to cover her body. The guard ignored her humiliating predicament and continued to drag her along. Kurt followed, looking for an opportunity to subdue him. He didn't want to try anything out in the open. The pair didn't go far, just next door to the printing facility. Kurt followed close behind.

Kurt waited for a moment before proceeding to the front door. When he snuck a quick look inside, he didn't see Mika or the guard. He stepped in and began circling the room. Not until he heard Mika's voice did he make his way to a stack of boxes that had been moved to one side. Next to them, a hatch lay open, and below was a dimly lit room.

Kurt peered through the hatch and saw a man leaning over Mika with something in his hand. Mika, her eyes wide, clutched her robe with one hand and reached out with the other toward what the man was holding.

Fluid shot out from the end of a needle.

Kurt responded immediately. He squatted on the edge of the hatch opening, turned, and slid down the rails of the ladder.

The guard turned to look at him and froze. It took him a moment to realize the newcomer was an unwanted intruder, but Kurt was upon him before he had a chance to respond. With one solid punch to the side of his head, Kurt landed him flat on his back. The syringe skidded across the basement floor. Kurt prepared to hit the guard again, but saw he was out cold.

Kurt then turned to Mika, who stared at him, fear in her eyes.

Kurt met her gaze, gave a smile, and tossed her Masa's robe. "Here. Put this on. I can't have my fair maiden catching a cold."

Mika complied, pulling the robe over her head, while Kurt turned his back and scoped out his surroundings.

Without a word, Mika stood and joined Kurt. He led the way up the ladder checking that no one had heard the commotion from above. Once he had pulled Mika up through the opening, he closed the hatch, latched it, and slid the stack of boxes over the top. He then offered Mika his hand. She took it, holding it weakly, as he led the way, between the guru's house and the printing facility.

Kurt found Kotaro right where he had left him, next to the drain cover.

Kurt removed the grate, lowered himself into the basin, and waved for Mika to follow. She looked frail but willingly complied. Once Mika had dropped below the surface, Kotaro carefully replaced the cover, and then watched the area until they were out of sight.

Kurt was first to crawl through the narrow passage. It was a tight fit for his broad shoulders and limited his arm movements. He thought about how much easier Mika's petite body must have been able to maneuver, just a few feet behind. Kurt estimated that the darkened passage would run nearly a hundred feet to the ravine behind the compound, reaching the creek bed above the river that he'd seen in the satellite photo. It was cold but dry. He could only imagine how much water might have flowed through there even in moderate rainstorms. That would have made the situation difficult, he thought.

Kurt's arms began to ache, and he decided to rest for a minute before pushing on. He had to chuckle to himself when he remembered a conversation he had with a friend before leaving Seattle. How he enjoyed the reserves, and these trips, because of the adventure. He had been in tight places before, but not quite like this. Kurt thought about what had drawn him in to this excursion. The idea of being in a foreign land had always been intriguing, but being with Kelly was a strong draw.

He felt Mika's hand on his foot and decided to move on.

Kurt sensed he was near the end of the tunnel because he could hear the roar of the river. He reached the end and slowly pulled himself out of the last segment of pipe. It was dark now, but he could make out a few rocks and trees along the hillside.

The coast was clear. At least there were no indications that they had been followed. Kurt suspected that the guard he knocked out would be coming around soon, if he hadn't already. While his pounding on the hatch might go unnoticed, he suspected the guru would be asking about the guard shortly.

With that in mind, and hearing Mika had reached the last part of her journey, he made another quick scan of his surroundings before reaching in to assist. Mika looked exhausted. She appeared to have used up all her strength to make it this far. The ordeal she had gone through must have been grueling, Kurt thought.

Kurt gently assisted her out of the end of the pipe. He lifted her upper body, allowing her legs to gently stretch down to the ground. Once she was ready to proceed, Kurt drew her close to his side to provide support as they moved parallel to the river below. Although haggard, Mika seemed more than willing to put as much distance between themselves and the compound as possible.

Kurt maintained the same direction until he was free of the clearing that bordered a dry creek bed that descended to the river below. Once they had moved well within the tree line, they began to negotiate up the bank. Kurt knew they were headed toward the spot where Kelly originally dropped Masa and him off, before they infiltrated the Aum compound. However, he didn't know how far they had traveled, and it was getting darker by the minute.

Kurt first heard a commotion from the compound behind them and then saw lights in the direction of the Aum facility. He decided this would be a good time to try and raise Kelly and Masa on the radio.

He made the call and Kelly's response was instantaneous. Kurt assumed that since last hearing from him she was assuming the worst. Following a brief description of where he thought they were, Kelly told him to head straight for the road. She said she'd flash the car headlights on and off.

Kurt grabbed Mika's hand, but her legs began to give out so he lifted her into his arms and picked up the pace as he traversed the last of the slope. He was finally on open ground. Based on the power lines along the road, he knew he didn't have far to go. Soon he saw headlights blink up ahead, less than a hundred yards away.

He also saw more activity in the direction of the Aum complex. Lights now appeared along the road, illuminating the trees. He moved rapidly for the vehicle.

The back door was open. Kurt quickly set Mika in the car. He guided her across the rear seat, jumped in beside her, and pulled the door shut. Kelly had the car engine running, and with Masa in the front passenger seat, they quickly proceeded to put distance between themselves and their pursuers.

Chapter 43

US EMBASSY - TOKYO, JAPAN

THE NEXT DAY

"Sir, we've got new information about the threat, and it is nuclear," Colonel Jackson said into the speakerphone to General Byrnes.

"Is your information credible?"

"It's as good as you can get. Captain Onishi's cousin was part of the Aum and worked with the bombs."

"You said *bombs*, plural?" General Byrnes asked.

"Yes, sir. Two. While we don't know their target, we believe there is a chance they could still be where she last worked on them. But, we'll need to move quickly, sir," Jackson said.

"What's their last known location?" Byrnes asked.

"Kobe, Japan."

"The heart of the earthquake," Byrnes mused aloud. "With the devastation the city has incurred, that could mean they might have difficulty moving them, especially with the roads being as bad as they are."

"Yes, sir," Jackson said.

The ambassador and his deputy, as well as Captains Onishi and Byrnes, sat around the ambassador's conference table. This time they sat quietly, letting Colonel Jackson bring General Byrnes up to date. They already had a discussion about the necessity to take some kind of immediate action. Even Deputy Ambassador Conklin was no longer playing the devil's advocate.

Late into the previous night, Mika's three rescuers had questioned her at Onishi's home. They had stopped only after it became evident that everyone would benefit from a good night's sleep. But before anyone could settle in for the night, phone calls had to be made.

Onishi called his friend, Takaji Komatsu, who assured him the police would provide the protection needed for Mika's safety. A twenty-four-hour watch would be maintained at Masa's home as long as she was there. Captain Byrnes had called Colonel Jackson at his home and gave him a report. That's when Jackson set up the meeting at the embassy to update the ambassador and his deputy, as well as to get Kelly's father involved.

To the police, Mika was a critical asset that would allow legal action to be taken against the Aum. Having a witness come forward to testify was critical to their success.

"What I find particularly troubling," the ambassador said, "is when I try to understand what would draw the North Koreans and an obscure religious sect in Japan to work together."

Colonel Jackson responded, "We can probably assume that their motivation is to work together to achieve a common goal."

"I can't help but think it's related to the problems we're encountering at the negotiations table," the ambassador added.

"We can no longer consider it a coincidence that they're conducting a large-scale training exercise concurrent to the stalled negotiations," General Byrnes said. "And now we see that they have ties to an organization developing weapons of mass destruction. I'm even more alarmed. Our intelligence indicates the North Korean troops are training to work in a WMD environment. I can't help but consider that Kim II Jong is not just conducting a training exercise but using that as an excuse to mass his forces for a move south."

The ambassador said, "But why would Jong be willing to risk his position as North Korea's new leader by committing his military? He must know that they'll only get pushed right back to where they started, once we send in UN troops. It doesn't make sense for him to try what they attempted back in the 1950s."

General Byrnes responded, "Unless his intent is to have the Aum involved with that as well." Byrnes paused. He wanted to consider the implications of what he had just said.

Colonel Jackson said, "You think they may be intending to destroy something strategically significant for both North Korea and the Aum?"

The room went quiet as everyone thought about what that might be.

"A port facility," Kelly interjected. "This morning, before I left Captain Onishi's, Mika said she overheard talk that one of the targets is a port."

"That would make sense," Jackson continued, "if they're targeting a port that is intended to supply reinforcements. My guess is that Pusan would be the logical target. That's our biggest port facility, capable of offloading a lot, if not most, of our military cargo. Hell, it's no secret that we've used it almost exclusively for deployment operations over the years."

"I agree," General Byrnes said. "If they did that, it would make it pretty tough to respond fast enough to stop them from taking over South Korea. That would make it almost impossible for us to even establish a foothold anywhere on the peninsula. That's got to be their port target."

"But how does that help the Aum," the ambassador asked, "and what's the second bomb for?"

"Maybe one is just a backup, in case something goes wrong with the first one," the deputy said.

"Maybe," the ambassador replied.

"That's the million-dollar question," the general responded. "What else do we know about the devices they plan to use?" It was obvious he wanted to hear what the others had to say.

"From what Mika said, both bombs are probably ready to be deployed by now, and may have already been moved out of the warehouse," Masa said. "Mika said they were just putting on the finishing touches. Who knows what's happened to them as a result of the earth-quake. They could have been destroyed for all we know."

"We could only hope," Captain Byrnes added. "But, we've got to send a team in right away in to confirm their status."

"We've also got to be cautious. If we send people out in the public, we don't want to alarm anyone," the deputy ambassador cautioned.

"I agree," the ambassador said. "To send any kind of a military force in to recover the bombs now might only cause greater problems. We've got to be very careful how we go about this. We have to think about a possible worst-case scenario. If the bombs are not there and we bust in, they'll know we're onto them. That could make things more difficult. We've got to find out more before we strike, and when we do, we've got to do it right. We've got to get higher-level backing, too. Once we get in there, and our own people confirm what Mika has shared with us, then we'll be able to mobilize all the forces we need."

General Byrnes then asked, "Captain Onishi, I know you shared with me the National Police Agency chief's apprehension about taking action based on unconfirmed reports. But do you believe he'd be willing to get involved with us now, knowing that we may have confirmation on the presence of weapons of mass destruction?"

"With Mika's testimony, I'm sure he's willing to support police involvement to pursue kidnapping charges. But if they do have a nuclear bomb, he'd feel more comfortable teaming up with us. He lacks the resources we have. He would still have to get permission at a higher level," Onishi responded.

"A joint operation," General Byrnes interjected.

Kelly saw the advantages of this. "Sir, how about a joint recovery effort for earthquake victims? We would fit right in with all the other rescue workers, and have the response force immediately available if they're needed. What better way to gain access to their facility and conduct a little reconnaissance of our own?"

"That just might work. Any recommendations on who we could send in?" General Byrnes said.

"Major Northrup would be a good person to take the lead on this, with a few volunteers from his group at Camp Zama," Colonel Jackson added, "I would also feel better if Captain Byrnes went along. She's about as capable and well read as anyone else I can think of."

Captain Byrnes and Colonel Jackson both looked at her father. They saw the hesitancy before he nodded and gave his daughter a smile.

"Good. Make sure Major Northrup's thoroughly briefed. We don't want him to take any unauthorized actions." The general knew he had to send in someone who knew the situation and could be trusted to make good, on-the-spot judgments.

"Captain Byrnes, if you're going to be part of this team, remember you're only there to gather information and report back. Is that clear?" With that said, Colonel Jackson knew he was addressing what was on the general's mind.

"Yes, sir," Kelly responded.

"Well, somebody better start doing something," Murdock said. He sounded frustrated. "How the hell did we get ourselves so involved in the first place? This Aum group should be a national issue, not ours. As much as I hate to say this, I agree we've got to get involved."

"Sir, if I might suggest..." Captain Onishi was anxious to find a way to make their involvement go forward. "I know Chief Komatsu of the National Police Agency has been monitoring the Aum situation. I talked with him not too long ago. He works with many of the different prefecture police departments, especially the Tokyo Metropolitan Police Department. Perhaps he, in coordination with his assets, could put a force together. The TMPD is also the biggest and most well-trained force we've got."

"That's worth talking with the Japanese government officials about," the ambassador said. "General, I appreciate what your people here have already done. They've exposed something that we wouldn't have otherwise found out about. Let me know what I can do to support you. If you're right, we've got more than just a local religious organization going astray here. I can't imagine what is motivating these people to do what they're doing."

"That's the key question, Mr. Ambassador," General Byrnes responded. "That's what we need to find out. Captain Onishi, you said they were involved in politics earlier. Tell me more about that."

"They tried to get control of twenty-five seats in the Japanese parliament. Even the guru ran for one of the seats, but every one of them lost. Ever since then, they've been preaching that Japan is doomed. They say the United States is Japan's enemy. Anytime something goes wrong, they claim their illustrious guru predicted it, and that it's just another sign of the apocalypse."

"Interesting," Colonel Jackson said. "That just may be their motivation. To prove the guru is right, they have to create a set of circumstances that convinces the Japanese people of just that. The strategy of teaming with North Korea is ingenious. Setting a bomb off in Korea, so close to Japan, would fulfill one of the predictions."

Then Kelly asked, "What if the other bomb is more than just a backup? What if it were set to explode outside Korea, say in Japan itself? Wouldn't that make it more difficult to place the blame on the North Koreans? In fact, we'd have a hard time retaliating if we weren't sure it was really them, right? We really couldn't take any action unless, or until, they actually invaded the South with their forces."

The ambassador was the first to speak. "My God! That's got to be it. That's what they're trying to hide, their involvement in the whole scheme."

General Byrnes said, "Whatever their plan, we're going to get to the bottom of this. Colonel Jackson, any military assets you need beyond what you have available, just let me know. I'll make sure you get what you need. Mr. Ambassador, use your diplomatic channels to expedite matters. I suggest that you listen carefully to what Captain Onishi has to say about what police assets should be brought in. Perhaps we can still make this a Japanese operation. I know you're concerned about intervening where we don't belong. Obviously time is of the essence."

"I agree," Murdock admitted. "Hopefully, by the time the Japanese authorities catch on to the magnitude of the situation and find a way to respond to it, we'll have some answers of our own. Make no mistake about what I'm saying. We're getting ready to take action in dangerous territory. What we want to accomplish is in our national defense interest, but we cannot go forward until we get a 'go' from our own higher-ups as well as the Japanese government."

With that, the meeting ended. Phone calls needed to be made.

Chapter 44

THE WHITE HOUSE — WASHINGTON, DC

SAME DAY

General Byrnes returned his phone to its cradle and leaned back in his chair. The call to the pentagon had been long. Laying out the facts and timeline was involved but necessary. The final decision was now in the hands of those in DC.

The four star's aide de camp took the information General Byrnes had just given his boss, the chief of staff of the army, General Gordon, double-checking what he could against the last CIA briefing and compiled it into a briefing paper and a slide presentation. Gordon had told his aide to bring it over to the White House Situation Room as soon as possible. The aide pulled the paper copies of the briefing one page at a time from the printer, not looking to see if they were even in order. He knew he could complete that in the car on the way to the White House.

When the aide entered the conference room twenty minutes later, President Bill Clinton was on the phone. Gordon motioned for his aide to come forward and give him the executive summary of the briefing. The aide handed it to Gordon, who immediately separated the pages, slid one copy over to the president, and another set to the secretary of state, whose face turned darker.

The president scanned the paper and said into the phone, "Interesting." He leaned back in his chair and gave the aide de camp a thumbs up. He seemed somewhat tired. But as usual, his voice was so calm he could have been chatting at a social gathering.

"We've got enough information to believe it's more than just a theory about what that religious organization in your country has been trying to do in conjunction with the North Koreans. The evidence is rather incriminating and seems to have created quite a dilemma for us."

The aide started up the laptop presentation then slid it toward the president, at Gordon's direction. A wry smile came over the president's face. He looked like a poker player about to reveal a royal flush.

"I'm looking at the satellite image of the exercise right now," the president said. "The intelligence I'm receiving tells me that they're about as close as they can be right now to posing an imminent threat, if they chose to move south. That means, if they don't stand down within the next few days, we will remain at a high alert until this situation changes." He was scanning the notes next to the slide. "That is when the Aum could take whatever action they are planning, presumably to signal the North Koreans to make a move south."

The president listened carefully to the Japanese prime minister's response.

Looking at General Gordon as he responded, the president said, "This cooperative effort is imperative if we are to stop this catastrophic event."

The president again patiently listened.

"Well, Mr. Prime Minister, our people are prepped and ready to take action. All we need now is your authorization to be part of the joint team," the president said. He sat up straight. He was laying his cards on the table. "Do you really think we can afford *not* to take any action if our assessment is correct? This problem affects not just your country but the whole region. We've got to take concrete steps toward coordinating our forces within the next twelve hours. In the meantime, I've authorized our people to go forward with putting a response force together. It would be most advantageous to us both if you were to take the lead on these efforts and keep us involved since we don't have time to get your folks read in on the problem."

The president listened, nodding as the Japanese prime minister spoke. Gordon slid out one of the sheets from his report, placing it so the president could see.

"Well, that's very good," the president said finally. "I'm told you could use some help in recovery efforts in Kobe. That's also where we believe they've transported the bombs. Like I said, we have reason to believe they may have two."

The president smiled as he listened to the Japanese leader's plan for cooperation. After a minute or so, he interjected "With all due respect, we need to put this plan into action as soon as possible. I understand what you're saying about not alarming your people and having your police force take the lead on the investigation. You should go ahead with the legal process on kidnapping and possible murder charges, but we have no time to spare. You've got to allow us the flexibility to look beyond that." Although the president hid his concern, this was the first indication he felt apprehension over the prime minister's hesitation about an immediate action.

After discussing the situation for a while longer, the president finally said, "Great, if you hand the phone over to Ambassador Murdock, I'll pass the phone to my secretary of state."

The secretary of state talked for a moment longer and said, "Thanks for helping, Ambassador Murdock," and then hung up.

The president had been perusing the papers handed to him during the secretary's conversation.

"They'll cooperate," the secretary announced, when he saw the president look up. "Ambassador Murdock assured me he'd monitor the situation closely, and General Byrnes and his people have no problem with the Japanese police force taking the lead. The ambassador said the prime minister understands the working relationship necessary to diminish the threat. But, he says they still seem stunned that anyone in their country is capable of such actions."

"I can understand that," the president said. "I'd like to think it's not possible either, and I understand his concern about not wanting to alarm the Japanese citizens, but there are some security issues here we cannot ignore. The small response force we're putting together using their local assets should be adequate for now."

"We've just received carte blanche to seek out the terrorists in Japan," Clinton stopped and looked directly at General Gordon.

"General Gordon let's make sure General Byrnes has whatever support we can give them. We can't afford to screw this up. While I hope they're wrong about what the Aum may be trying to accomplish, I also know we need to handle the situation correctly. We need to alert our forces in Korea also."

"Yes, Mr. President," General Gordon replied. "I'll give them priority on any satellite photos they may need as well as transportation and other equipment."

"Beyond providing whatever intelligence we have, it's now up to Japan's National Police Agency," Gordon sighed.

Chapter 45

CAMP ZAMA, JAPAN

FEBRUARY 1995

"Prepare to get your teams loaded on the choppers," Chief Komatsu yelled over the roar of the helicopter's rotor blades.

He'd just reviewed and briefed his new command, the ad hoc joint task force. At his side, his administrative assistant was making notes on what the chief considered significant. Gathered around them were four officers assigned to assist him in their mission: Major Northrup, Major Johnson, Captain Onishi, and Captain Byrnes. Standing near two Sikorsky UH-60 Black Hawk helicopters—made available through US army channels—were eight police officers selected from the Tokyo Metropolitan Police Department, eight US military police officers, and two US army bomb disposal specialists. Onishi also had a newly enlisted assistant assigned to him, who would work jointly with Komatsu's administrative assistant. Whether they were police or military, every member of the task force wore battle dress uniforms.

"Once again, welcome aboard," he said to his officers. "I know a great deal of thought was put into choosing each of you to be part of this special unit. I just hope we're acting soon enough."

They all nodded, understanding the chief's sentiment.

Days earlier, Major Kurt Johnson was surprised to receive a call from the office of the commander of UN forces in Korea, asking if he could have his orders amended on the pretext that he was extending his stay to provide chemical expertise for a special project. III Corp had an exercise coming up in two months, and they would appreciate his assistance in developing a realistic scenario for that exercise. In reality, the caller had made it clear that they wanted an expert in his field who was available immediately. Someone, preferably, who didn't need to take a great deal of time getting read in on the situation.

The teams were now waiting to load up in the two Bell model "Black Hawk" helicopters that had been attached to Major Northrup, for use to support the chief's task force. Major Northrup was the lead commander for the American soldiers. Northrup was also well versed on protocols when working with the Japanese military, as were his men.

"Thanks to information provided to us by a former Aum member," the chief glanced at Onishi, "we now know the location of the Aum warehouse in Kobe. We can't waste any more time."

"Okay, load 'em up," the chief yelled.

The UH-60 Black Hawk had replaced the UH-1 helicopter in the late 1970s. These models, with their upgraded twin-engines, allowed transport of up to thirteen troops depending on their equipment needs.

They would arrive in Kobe within the hour.

Chapter 46

KOBE, JAPAN

The heavy-duty forklift laid the crate gently into place.

Mori's workers had moved the crate from Aum's Kobe warehouse to the pier's reception area. Although it was now out of Mori's control, he had been careful to watch its every movement inside the pier's warehouse. While in the terminal storage facility, he was permitted to watch the operation, but only if he stayed out of the way of the port workers and wore a hard hat. The workers were strict about how things were done.

As much as he wanted only his people to handle the package, he knew it was out of his hands now. But he would have an Aum security team keep an eye on things. Now that the package had been positioned, two-man teams, provided by the Aum's security chief, would ensure the crate was secure until it left the harbor. Mori wanted to make sure no one tampered with it.

Shortly after the crate had been positioned in the terminal warehouse, the truck that Mori had sent back to the Aum warehouse showed up at the terminal, again. The driver frantically waved to get Mori's attention, which surprised Mori. The driver was supposed to park the truck back in the Aum's warehouse, next to the other bomb, where it would be loaded onto the flatbed truck later. Eventually it would go to their northern facility to be prepared for its final position.

The quick arm movements of the driver indicated that he was distressed and wanted to make an immediate entry to the port facility. But the terminal's guard seemed adamant about not allowing his return.

Finally, as Mori continued to watch, the guard made a gesture toward a spot outside the perimeter fence, and the driver quickly backed the truck up and drove over to an open space along the fence.

Only then did Mori see the other case resting on the back of the vehicle. It had not been secured to the vehicle. The driver got out of the truck cab and ran through the gate to where Mori was standing. Out of breath, the driver gasped while explaining how he'd quickly loaded the crate without strapping it down due to the arrival of some visitors.

"We've had visitors before," Mori said.

"They were the police and American military," the driver exclaimed. "I thought it best to load the truck and leave there as quickly as I could. I didn't know anywhere else to go."

Mori assured him that he had done the right thing, directed the driver to stay with the truck, and went to the port's office phone. He made a call back to their warehouse to get more details. When a man answered, Mori said, "I understand we have some more visitors. Tell me about them."

He carefully listened to the report while his small security detail waited outside.

Although Mori had some anxiety about unwanted visitors, he knew visits from earthquake response teams were not uncommon. He'd dealt with a number of these in the last couple of weeks. He was sure he didn't have anything to worry about. Even if the visitors had entered the back of the warehouse while the bomb was still there, all they would have seen was a single crate marked as x-ray equipment. The rest of the warehouse had been emptied.

The man on the phone told Mori, "They said they were a security team who were told to conduct a sweep of the area to ensure everything was secure. They said there had been some looting lately and needed to search every building. They said they were also conducting a safety check."

They couldn't know, Mori thought. "We already had people come by for a safety check," he said.

"Seemed like they were just double-checking," the man on the phone said.

"Did you let them into the back of the warehouse?"

"We had to. They insisted. I'm just glad the others got the crate loaded and out of here while we were still talking," the man said.

Mori thanked him and hung up the phone.

He decided caution was called for. Mori walked out to the driver and directed him to requisition tie-downs to secure the case on the truck. He then selected four guards to accompany the second package and dispatch it to the spot they'd originally selected. Then he pulled in the rest of his team to inform them about the next move.

The following morning they would transfer the crate, destined for Korea, from the pier's warehouse to another resting place. The tug would take it from there. It wouldn't be long before it would be on its final journey.

A tramp steamer, out of San Francisco, was due to arrive in just a few days, before proceeding to Pusan and then on to Alaska. It was a 254-foot freighter. Although more limited in capacity compared to the much larger container ships, it was able to take on a few pieces of cargo and was available for their shipment.

Chapter 47

KOBE, JAPAN

SAME DAY

The ad hoc joint task force was making its way back to Kobe's EOC a little before noon. Having discovered that the Aum warehouse was empty, Chief Komatsu was returning as quickly as he could. Komatsu and the rest of the team were sure they couldn't have missed the Aum's bomb movement by much. All indications were it had been there but had been moved somewhere else.

There was also enough information to determine the bombs had been moved not long before the team arrived. The team had found only a forklift, a small stack of lumber, and an empty container. The rest of the warehouse was almost empty. Even the front section that was used as an aid station was being dismantled. Aum members were packing up the last of their equipment.

Major Johnson remembered that Mika had stated the bomb crate had "Handle with Care X-ray Equipment" stamped on it. He found the same stamp on the lumber piled next to an empty container. With that, they were also able to determine the size of the bomb's container. When Johnson used his Geiger counter, he discovered low levels of radiation, enough to indicate the bomb had been in the area.

One of the MPs, who examined the forklift, discovered that the engine was still warm, so they knew it had recently been used. When checking the surrounding area, the TMDP officers found witnesses who had seen a flatbed truck leaving the rear of the warehouse within the last hour. It was last seen heading toward the harbor.

Returning to the EOC had been almost as difficult as when they left there to get to the warehouse, even though the route they used had them avoiding the red zones. Red indicated areas that were too dangerous or sensitive for anyone to enter, other than authorized rescue teams or engineers inspecting structures. Trying to quickly move from one location to another was frustrating. But thanks to Onishi's assistant they had access to all the ground transportation they needed.

As they passed along narrow streets that had been cleared of rubble just a week earlier, they could see that the devastation was widespread. On either side of the roadway lay piles of concrete and cinderblock where buildings once stood. The few people they saw rummaging through the debris were all but unrecognizable in their overcoats, with masks or scarves that covered their mouths and noses, protecting them from the grime that coated everything in sight. There was still ash in the air from the fires that continued to smolder.

Chief Komatsu was anxious to have the team return to the EOC as quickly as possible. Having struck out at the warehouse, he knew his next option relied on getting the phone records he'd requested prior to leaving Camp Zama. These records would hopefully tell him which piers were called from the Aum's warehouse. Knowing that a bomb had probably been moved toward the harbor, he needed to narrow down which pier they had communicated with. The sooner that was established, the sooner they could put an end to this madness.

Upon arriving at the EOC, Komatsu and Onishi headed straight for the fax machine, while Northrup recalled the helicopters to pick them up. The pilot's orders were to go to the nearest airfield to refuel and be ready to return on short notice. The rest of the team gathered their gear and prepared to board the choppers. Kelly asked Kurt to help her set up the satellite phone that had been issued to her. She needed to keep Colonel Jackson apprised of their progress.

Chapter 48

KOBE, JAPAN

Komatsu looked at the fax and frowned.

"It looks as though the Aum called most of the piers, some more often than others. They even made a few phone calls outside the city. Some time or other, we may need to check those locations out as well," Komatsu said to Onishi. "Unfortunately, it looks like it's not going to be as easy as I'd hoped to narrow down our search."

"Maybe I can find a way to help," Onishi said. "If I call the Kobe port authority, they should be able to tell me which piers are no longer functional."

"That would be helpful," the chief said. "Let's get down to this terminal first," Komatsu said, as he pointed at the EOC's map that showed a terminal not far from their location. "The emergency director here told me there's plenty of activity there, and the Aum made calls there. You can make your call from there."

"All right, I'll go tell Major Northrup to pass the word that we'll be heading out as soon as everyone's on board."

Just getting the helicopters loaded was a task. In a space that could normally accommodate two helicopters, a medevac helicopter, similar to the UH-1 "Huey" that the Black Hawk had replaced, was already taking space on the tarmac. This landing spot consisted of a flat area that was partly paved and potholes filled with gravel. Surrounding the landing area was a series of wooden barricades. An ambulance was parked alongside an extended antenna that was lashed to the ground with a windsock flying from it. Roughly fifty yards beyond, a gathering of media antenna vans were clustered along the fringe of what was once a large parking lot.

Komatsu watched the first helicopter, which had lifted off the tarmac and was holding its position above. Once his Black Hawk was loaded, they joined the helicopter overhead. It was just minutes before they arrived at the pier and landed between two cranes that were damaged and not in service. Komatsu's administrative assistant and Onishi's enlisted assistant stayed behind at the EOC to coordinate other means of transportation.

After landing, Onishi and Komatsu went to the main office while the rest of the task force broke into two-man teams to better search the cargo. Komatsu talked to the site superintendent, to apprise him of their purpose, while Onishi found a phone to use.

Onishi gathered the information they needed regarding shipping conditions, once he'd been able to reach the port authority. He quickly reported to Komatsu what he'd found. Of the twenty-seven possible berths, only three cargo-handling facilities remained operable. Five of the other oil tanker facilities were operable, but temporarily excluded for consideration since they were not taking on cargo. The container facility they were at was functional but had limited crane capabilities. The earthquake had damaged some of the cranes and their rails. Another pier was only accepting ships that could load and offload using their own onboard lift capabilities. Another neighboring pier was usable but couldn't be accessed due to the inability of ships to clear a damaged bridge and pass through a narrow canal.

Many of the larger container ships had bypassed the port of Kobe, to offload somewhere else. It was too costly to wait offshore until a berth opened. A ship waiting at anchor lost thousands of dollars a day when not moving cargo.

There were a number of old Liberty ships anchored offshore, waiting their turn to access the harbor. These ships could more easily maneuver through the damaged waterways and could operate out of the shallower piers. While the container ships were more cost efficient, handling more cargo in a single transport, the Liberty ships were still convenient, transporting goods to the lesser-developed countries that did not have deep ports.

With this information, they began to eliminate possibilities through which the bomb could be transported.

Chapter 49

KOBE, JAPAN

Kurt helped Kelly with her satphone. At least he could be useful until the task force began opening containers. Then he'd be busy with his Geiger counter. Kelly invited him to stay after she connected with the embassy.

"It'd be nice if you stayed," Kelly said, "in the event I have a communication problem or a question you can help me with." Kurt and Kelly had become a team of their own.

Weather conditions and satellite positioning were optimal. Kelly was pleasantly surprised to hear instantaneously the familiar ring of a telephone.

Jackson took the call. As soon as he realized it was Captain Byrnes, he called Ambassador Murdock's assistant on the intercom and activated his speakerphone.

Once Murdock got the word, he joined Jackson.

"Afternoon, sir," Captain Byrnes began. "I'm currently in Kobe, at one of the terminals. We arrived a little while ago. The team is just getting ready to search containers destined for Pusan."

"What led you there?" Jackson asked.

"Although we struck out at the Aum warehouse, we found witnesses who saw a flatbed truck with a crate on the back, leaving the warehouse and heading for the harbor. We're acting on the probability that they're targeting a port facility and that they'll be shipping from here. We've narrowed down the search the best we can for now."

"This is the ambassador," Murdock said. "It's just the two of us in Jackson's office now."

"Yes, sir. Hello," Byrnes said.

"How did you narrow your search?" the ambassador asked.

"Chief Komatsu has phone records that show which piers had been called from the Aum warehouse. Captain Onishi called Kobe's port authority and was able to find out which facilities were still operational. Between those two parameters we were able to narrow down the possibilities."

"Sounds like a good start," Jackson said.

"We've been able to identify sixteen ships that are scheduled to dock in Kobe over the next thirty days," Kelly responded. "Due to a number of other considerations, we've narrowed down the search to two container ships and three regularly scheduled freighters, at least for now. The other vessels, although capable of limited cargo space, are tankers designed to carry grain or oil. The only cargo they carry is limited to what is brought on board by the crew. That normally wouldn't include a crate the size we're looking for."

"Whatever avenues you find possible, you must encourage the chief to pursue," Jackson emphasized. "Time is of the essence. I can't stress that enough."

"The chief understands that," Byrnes said. "As each new ship arrives, we'll concentrate on them, but in the meantime we'll start sweeping every berth area that is operational. Chief Komatsu is being careful not to spread our team too thin. He has told the local authorities just enough to ensure we get their cooperation and pass on any relevant information we need. Starting this evening, local officers will be watching each area. If any of them see any unusual activity, they know how to reach the chief. If we don't find anything during the normal workday, we plan to meet with the harbor superintendent first thing in the morning to determine our next step."

"Good work," Jackson said. "Is there any additional support we can provide from here?"

"Besides the piers that were called by the Aum, we've also identified a number of other places they called around the country. I don't know if it'll do any good, but if you can get some people to watch those sites, maybe we can learn more about what they're up to. If you call the chief's office they should have a copy of that phone list."

"Consider it done," Jackson said.

"Thank you, sir. I'll call again when we find out anything new."

Chapter 50

KOBE, JAPAN

THE NEXT MORNING

Every available local police officer in the prefecture had been mobilized to assist the already strained resources of the Kobe emergency response force. Police officers from surrounding cities, as well as those who had returned to duty after caring for their own families, were now filling the ranks.

Through Chief Komatsu's insistence, a team of over twenty men and women were dispatched to cover all dock areas that were operational, whether they had been searched by the task force or not. They would conduct security checks throughout the night, while the task force rested. The police were to report any unauthorized, suspicious, or unusual activities to the emergency operations center. Chief Komatsu's assistant, working together with Onishi's assistant, would be at the EOC to forward any critical information and collect these reports in the morning to bring to Komatsu.

The night patrols that conducted the security checks were told the importance of their duties. If they found any suspicious activity, they were not to take action, but report it immediately and wait for the task force's arrival.

Komatsu told these officers what to look out for but not enough to cause widespread panic. They were told: "*Intelligence reports indicated that a group of anarchists would be attempting to take advantage of Kobe's chaotic situation. They were to be considered dangerous and were known to have explosive materials. Police were not to intervene but report their observations immediately. A quick response team would be mobilized to the site, with bomb disposal experts.*" Beyond that, information was need-to-know only.

The ad hoc joint task force had worked late into the night until Komatsu found the resources to relieve them so they could rest. Cots and blankets were made available from the EOC. They also acquired two vans to meet the team's transportation needs. Komatsu's task force would continue their search following his morning meeting with the harbor superintendent.

The group had been operating on the premise that this morning's schedule showed seven ships at berth or scheduled to dock that day. Also, one container ship was scheduled to leave, and another would immediately take its place at the pier. Both had cargo destined for Pusan as well as other ports-of-call. There were also three freighters scheduled to arrive, with only one that was destined for a stop in Pusan. They would focus first on those vessels destined for Pusan.

Relatively rested, the task force was prepared to continue their search. They split into two groups, both with local police officers and US military police, for the purpose of searching two adjoining container yards. After scrutinizing the bills of lading that listed what was in the container, they opened each to physically inspect its contents, paying particular attention to the description and size. In some cases, they also checked the packing list to see if an x-ray machine had been listed.

The search teams were well underway when Komatsu's assistant arrived with the police reports that had been consolidated at the EOC. Major Northrup monitored the teams as they reported by radio from the two container yards. Byrnes, Johnson, Onishi, and Komatsu stayed at the facility's main office. While Byrnes and Johnson reviewed the reports from the previous night's patrols, Komatsu and Onishi met with the superintendent to review the day's shipping schedule.

By the time the four officers finished going over the schedule and reviewing the reports, the search teams had begun to report in by radio. They weren't finding anything.

Once Byrnes and Johnson had gone through their reports, they joined the chief, Onishi, and the superintendent. The task force completed their search of the piers that either had a ship moored on site, were expecting ships to arrive shortly, or were scheduled for Pusan. Northrup radioed in his report to Komatsu, showing no success, shortly after Kurt and Kelly joined Komatsu. Once Northrup signed off, Onishi shared what they'd found out from the superintendent. That summary didn't seem promising either. The frustration on everyone's faces was evident.

Byrnes, remembering one of the police reports she'd just read, turned to the superintendent and said, "I read something from a night patrolman. A report that described a barge being loaded off one of the piers. I don't remember hearing that mentioned." Looking at the superintendent, Byrnes asked, "Is it listed on your shipping report?"

The superintendent explained, "No, it's not. This document only shows those vessels that would receive direct billings from the Port of Kobe. It does not reflect any vessels subcontracted to support the major shipping companies. The barges are mostly used locally, just around the harbor."

"In other words," Byrnes said, "the barge supplying support to one ship could be subcontracted to support another vessel?"

"What are you getting at?" Komatsu asked.

Onishi, picking up on what Byrnes implied, looked at the superintendent. "Could that barge be taking freight to a ship that's still anchored in the bay?"

"Sure," the superintendent responded.

"Which ship could it be supporting?" Kelly asked.

"Let's see," the superintendent scanned the list of ships scheduled to enter port. He then stood quietly, trying to recall which ones were anchored offshore. "My guess is that this barge would be supporting the *Northern Star.* At least that would seem the most logical. I know that it's anchored just beyond the channel where the barge is located. That channel isn't open to large vessels because the damaged bridge isn't capable of opening." He again scanned down the list of ships on his list. "That ship does not appear on this list. It's not scheduled to tie up along any of our berths."

"That could be significant," Kelly interjected, scanning the faces of the others. Looking again at the superintendent, she asked, "Can you check to see where that ship is destined?"

"Sure. I'll have to make a call back to my office, though. That's where we keep records of ship-to-shore communications as well. All ships coming in have to request passage through harbor shipping lanes. Just a minute and I'll check."

The superintendent went to a neighboring office.

Komatsu pulled out his handheld radio and contacted Major Northrup. The chief directed him to gather everyone up and return to the office.

Moments later the superintendent returned, only to confirm what they feared. The *Northern Star* was scheduled to transport freight from Kobe to Pusan, before moving on to Alaska. While they still hadn't confirmed the bomb's location, they knew that this was their best bet. They needed to move fast.

The superintendent said that the barge had been scheduled to transfer a limited number of goods aboard the *Northern Star*. It was scheduled to complete loading and leave that same day.

It took almost fifteen minutes to assemble the teams before redeploying to the site. They could only hope that they'd arrive in time.

Chapter 51

KOBE HARBOR, JAPAN

"**G**ood news, the ship hasn't left yet," Komatsu informed those gathered by their vehicles.

Komatsu's team was transported in three military jeeps, while the US squad was deployed by helicopter. Komatsu and Major Northrup had reconfigured their teams. While conducting their searches, they'd divided into two joint operations teams. Now they needed to make a change.

They had determined that the ground-transported group would primarily consist of Komatsu's police officers, while Northrup's MPs and bomb disposal experts would take to the air. US forces would be on-call, while air support would be a backup, to be called in as needed. In the meantime, the US team would reconnoiter the route between the ship and the barge. If the police did find the bomb, the helicopter could be called in to deliver the bomb disposal experts.

As Komatsu's team arrived alongside the pier, they could see that the barge had departed. About a kilometer down the canal, they spotted a tugboat pulling a barge.

Komatsu ordered his team to stay in place while he ran inside the terminal office. His most senior officer accompanied him inside. Spotting the first port employee, Komatsu flashed his credentials and demanded to know how he could contact whoever was operating the tug. Pointing toward the canal, it was clear which vessel he was referring to.

"I've got a ship-to-shore radio right here," the man at the counter said.

"Great, tell him to stop for boarding and prepare to receive further instructions from me." Komatsu then turned to his senior officer and ordered, "Get the radio frequency for that boat. I want to be able to communicate with him with our radio if need be."

"Yes, sir."

The man at the counter was already writing the frequency on note-paper, which the officer grabbed and put in his pocket. He and the chief walked outside, where they both watched the tug begin to veer toward the side of the channel.

As the two made their way toward the pier, they saw the tug change direction once again. This time he angled back toward the center of the waterway. Komatsu snatched a pair of binoculars from the officer at his side and peered out at the tug. Focusing in on the wheelhouse, he could see more than one figure at the helm. One stood by the wheel, while another was pointing something at his head. Komatsu handed the binoculars to his senior officer and asked him what he saw.

"It looks like someone's forcing him to maintain his course."

Komatsu ran back to the terminal office. He grabbed the radio microphone and ordered, "Tugboat, this is Chief Komatsu of the National Police Agency. Tell me your intentions. Why have you diverted back to your previous course?" The radio went silent, not even static was heard.

"I know he's receiving you. We just checked communications moments ago," the man at the counter commented.

Komatsu asked the port employee, "How many men on that tug?"

Normally they've got a three-man crew, but I know there are at least two extras, maybe three, who aren't part of the crew.

"Who are they?" Komatsu asked.

"I only know that they were authorized by the tug's head office. I originally thought they were friends of the crew, but overheard the crew mumbling something about their boss allowing others on board to check out their operations," the man responded.

"Well it sure looks like they're in charge now," Komatsu said. He motioned for his senior officer to accompany him outside where they discussed a plan of action. His officers loaded into two of the three jeeps and quickly drove off through the terminal gate. Komatsu then called Northrup and told him his plan. He would need some equipment from Northrup while he put his diversion into play.

Komatsu stood at the terminal observing the tug slowly make its way toward the end of the channel.

"How on earth do they think they can get away from us?" he said out loud to no one in particular.

Chapter 52

KOBE HARBOR, JAPAN

Komatsu could see the helicopter lift up from the damaged bridge at the end of the canal. It appeared as if it had been traveling inland over the water and had moved skyward only to avoid the bridge. In actuality, Komatsu knew it had stopped above it just long enough to drop some equipment before swiftly sweeping back along the channel to join him at the terminal.

"Now we'll start the diversion," Komatsu said to the local law enforcement officers who had begun to gather around him. Komatsu ordered these officers to engage those on the tug from the water's edge, using a bullhorn he had acquired from the terminal office.

While the local officers made their way on foot down along the canal, Komatsu stayed next to the terminal building, awaiting the helicopter's arrival.

Komatsu knew his officers were already in place. The helicopter and local forces were his diversion. The helicopter landed, and Masa, Kelly, and Kurt offloaded and stood at Komatsu's side.

Turning to Onishi, Komatsu asked, "Masa, you man the radio in the terminal while Byrnes and Johnson watch the tug and barge. I'm going to control things from the air."

"Sure," Onishi responded and began to stride toward the terminal building. Byrnes and Johnson both nodded and turned to follow Onishi.

As Onishi left, Komatsu added, "And see if you can get me a damn boat. I don't want to be caught unprepared if they cut the barge loose and run."

"Understood," Onishi responded.

The tug was now approaching the bridge as Komatsu boarded the helicopter. Once on board, it quickly lifted and sped off to approach the tug from the rear. The pilot, taking his cue from Komatsu, hovered just over the back of the barge. From this position Komatsu engaged the tug's occupants using the helicopter's onboard speaker system.

"Attention all personnel of the tugboat *Majestic,* this is the police," he began. "You are ordered to steer your vessel to dockside and prepare to be boarded. If you do not comply, we will take charge of your vessel by force. Proceed to the portside pier where you see the local police waiting."

As the tug moved below the bridge, Onishi manned the terminal's radio, while Johnson and Byrnes watched the drama unfold from the second floor, just above the terminal office.

Kelly and Kurt both scanned the tug and barge with binoculars. The helicopter maintained its position over the barge as it moved forward. Kelly saw that the helmsman was looking ahead and maintaining his course, heading toward the *Northern Star,* anchored only a kilometer beyond the bridge. Another man, standing by the helmsman, scanned the horizon and periodically looked back at the barge, and tracked the helicopter's whereabouts. Little did he know that his greatest threat was directly overhead.

On the barge, Kelly noticed two men standing toward the bow. She could not tell if the two were part of the crew and wondered if there were more on board.

Kurt's elbow nudged Kelly as he stood beside her. "Look below the helicopter," Kurt began. "Just behind the boxed crate in the center of the barge I saw some movement."

Kelly yelled down to Masa to alert the chief that there might be someone else on the barge.

Onishi made the call, just as he saw action on the bridge.

Chapter 53

KOBE HARBOR, JAPAN

Three figures descended by rope from the damaged bridge and lowered themselves onto the tug. Two of the police officers landed on the deck, just forward and to the port side of the wheelhouse, while a third landed on the wheelhouse roof. All three quickly disengaged from their ropes.

The two officers on deck climbed the steps to the wheelhouse to enter the portside door, while the third went to the starboard side of the roof. As the officers entered the wheelhouse, the Aum gunman dashed out the starboard door. They left him to the officer on the roof and quickly checked the condition of the tug's captain.

"I'm all right, but please check on him," the captain said. He was holding the wheel with his left hand while pointing to another crewman lying on the floor in the rear of the cabin. One officer stayed to check on the unconscious crewman while his partner left to catch up with the Aum gunman.

The captain told the police officer that the visitors had come aboard with authorization from their head office. Supposedly, they wanted to see how operations were conducted under adverse conditions.

After the armed intruder left the wheelhouse, he jumped the railing. As he crashed to the deck, his gun flew from his hand. The officer on the roof sprang from the overhang just as the man went over the rail.

Seeing there was no time for him to retrieve his weapon, the unarmed man turned and ran toward the stern of the tug. Arriving

241

there, he began to lunge for the cable leading to the barge, but the officer grabbed the back of his shirt and swung him into the winch, which released the cable. The officer then pushed the man down and pinned him against the side of the steel railing. By this time, one of the other officers arrived at his side to assist. The gunman was turned facedown and cuffed.

Three men watched from the barge as the tow cable began to sag. Only one of the men was a crewmember. One Aum member stayed hidden at the rear of the barge. He had completed his work inside the crate and was using his handheld radio to summon a ride. All he could do now was watch and wait, hoping he had not yet been discovered. When he saw the cable pulling the barge drop below the waterline, he saw his chance to escape.

The speedboat he had been waiting for was now rounding the bend up ahead and heading toward the barge. All he had to do now was cause enough havoc to distract any pursuers.

He saw the crewmember walking to the side of the barge. Seeing his opportunity, the Aum member shoved him, causing the crewmember to fall overboard. He then summoned his partner. Using a crowbar from nearby, the two pried on the cable that was looped about the starboard post. It took both of them to unfasten the cable before they ran to the edge of the barge to await the speedboat.

After receiving Onishi's radio message, Komatsu had the helicopter check for the man hidden among the crates. By this time, the two Aum members on the barge had been able to release the starboard line. This brought excessive tension on the portside line, which caused the barge to lose its alignment with the tug.

Simultaneously, a speedboat pulled alongside the barge as it drifted under the bridge. The helicopter rose over the bridge and descended on the other side.

Seeing the condition of the barge and tug lines, and knowing that there was no crewman left on it, Kelly contacted Onishi. He quickly radioed the information to the tug, and the captain immediately slowed.

Three more police officers repelled down to the barge, which was now below the bridge, but not in time to stop the two men from leaving the barge. The powerboat was already clearing the bend.

Komatsu radioed the officers to look for the crate.

"It's probably near the rear of the barge," Komatsu said.

The helicopter was already following the powerboat.

The helicopter hadn't gotten far when Komatsu received the first of two radio transmissions from the barge and the tug officers. The first call confirmed that the captured terrorist was anxious to show where the bomb on the barge was. He confessed that there was another bomb that had already left Kobe by flatbed truck, destined for Yokohama. However, he also said that he didn't know if it was going there directly or not.

While the first call wasn't enough to turn the helicopter around, the second one was. The officers on the barge had found the crate and determined that a timer had been activated.

"No wonder the man we captured wanted to cooperate," Komatsu said, after assessing the situation. He then instructed the pilot, "Take us back to the barge." Taking off his radio headset, he yelled to the two bomb specialists. "Okay gentlemen, here's where you earn your pay. Get ready to offload."

The helicopter lowered to just inches off the edge of the barge, allowing the two American bomb experts to jump aboard.

Komatsu radioed Masa at the terminal, "Masa, what's the status on that boat?"

"It should be rounding the bend shortly," he replied.

"Great. Direct the crew to join us at the barge. We'll need some help getting the line from the tug secured. Then get my jeep and join us at the dock, just past where the tug is now. That's where the local police are heading, too. That's the closest site we can get to without turning this thing around."

"I'll be there as soon as I can," Masa replied.

"One more thing, Masa. We're going to be busy for a while, so before you leave, ask Captain Byrnes if she can contact my assistant at the EOC. Tell him to notify other police prefectures between here and

Yokohama. I want them to be on the lookout for any flatbed truck with a large crate on it, heading toward Yokohama. I know that's not much to go on, but that's all the information we have for now. Unfortunately, we don't know if they were going straight there or diverting to one of their own facilities first."

"Will do," Onishi replied.

Moments later, Onishi jumped in Komatsu's M-151 jeep and passed through a security checkpoint established by the local law enforcement officials.

Near the water, Onishi saw the bomb disposal experts huddled around a crate on the barge with a pilot boat tethered at its side. Police were questioning one man in handcuffs, while the other sat hunched over, wrapped in a blanket. He had a pool of water under him.

Onishi approached Komatsu. "It looks like you had some success here," Masa said.

"Not as much as I'd hoped, I'm afraid," Takaji said. "I was so focused on securing the barge and the bomb that by the time the pilot headed out to search for the powerboat, we had no idea which way to go." Komatsu looked upset.

"The pilot boat wasn't the only one I sent your way," Masa said.

Komatsu looked puzzled.

With a big grin, Masa pointed off into the distance, past the barge, and out into the harbor.

Komatsu turned and saw the helicopter flying low over three vessels heading their way. Two small coast guard patrol crafts flanked either side of a powerboat.

He looked back at his old partner, shook his head, and with a smile said, "You're still the best partner I ever had."

"Forget it. I'm not coming back. I like where I am," Masa stated firmly, with a grin.

Komatsu laughed. "I thought as much, but how about you stay here and help me wrap up this situation. Perhaps you can ask your American friends if they can make a sweep along the major roadways between here and Yokohama. Maybe they'll be able find the truck by air."

"Oh, the burden of watching over an old partner," Masa sighed.

"The Americans have a few resources of their own. You may have noticed that they didn't have any difficulty deactivating the device."

"Yes, I saw that. The troubling part is we now know the Aum are more dangerous than we thought. They were willing to set off the bomb locally." Searching his surroundings, to see if anyone else was listening, Komatsu added, "The timer was set for fifteen minutes." He paused. "It took the bomb specialists ten minutes to get to it. Even if they'd headed straight out of the harbor in that powerboat, I'm not so sure they would have cleared the blast area."

Moments later the helicopter landed, Major Northrup came over to Onishi and Komatsu, while the local authorities secured the terrorists.

At that moment Byrnes was already on her satphone, making contact with the embassy.

Chapter 54

KOBE, JAPAN

MIDAFTERNOON, THE NEXT DAY

Captain Byrnes spread out a series of fax sheets across a table at the EOC.

Kelly led Northrup through the pictures, as Johnson and two senior NCOs looked on. The rest of the US task force was gathered nearby.

The 200th MI Group had sent satellite photos by fax to Kobe's EOC. On these photos, Major Jaegar had indicated the properties owned by the Aum.

"Great, these are a lot clearer than I expected," Northrup said.

"As you can see," Captain Byrnes began, "the sites that have an arrow pointing to them or are circled belong to the Aum."

"Hmm, most of the Aum properties are located around Tokyo and west of Yokohama," Northrup stated. These are the main thoroughfares, between Kobe and Yokohama. If we follow this route until we arrive here," Northrup pointed on the map, "we can view even the side roads that run parallel to the main highways. With our binoculars, it shouldn't be too difficult to spot a flatbed truck with a crate on the back."

Byrnes, Johnson, and the two senior NCOs nodded.

"At this point," Northrup said, specifying where the roads split, "we'll have to decide if we want to continue along this eastern route to Yokohama or head further north," Northrup said. "Any thoughts?"

One of the NCOs asked, "Where are the police focusing their search?"

"I would imagine they're paying closer attention to the more direct routes to Yokohama," Northrup said.

"The Aum only have a couple of sites up toward Mt. Fuji," Kelly said. "I can't help but think that there was a reason Mika was billeted up there."

"Where was she staying?" Northrup asked.

Johnson, recognizing the compound on the fax, pointed, "Here's where she stayed."

He looked closer. "But I don't see where they might put their truck. There's another property just up the road, but it doesn't look like there's much there either," Johnson said.

"Anyone have any better ideas?" Northrup looked at Johnson then the NCOs. "Very well," Northrup said. "Mt. Fuji it is. Let's get everyone ready to load up the helicopter."

Northrup look at Byrnes. "Captain Byrnes."

"Yes, sir."

"You have a little bit of time before the helicopter arrives, so you might want to contact Colonel Jackson and let him know where we're headed," Major Northrup said, looking at his watch.

While the rest of the team moved their equipment to the helipad, Johnson took Byrnes's gear and joined the others while Byrnes called Jackson.

On the satphone, Captain Byrnes confirmed receipt of the images at the EOC sent by Major Jaegar. She then told Jackson which route they were taking and why. She also told him, "As I mentioned when I called you from the waterfront, Chief Komatsu is going to be tied up there for a while. But the chief has already gotten the word out to all prefectures between here and Yokohama to monitor the roadways. That's another reason we're taking the more northerly route." Byrnes also explained that Komatsu asked for their help finding the other truck, rather than wait for Komatsu's team to leave Kobe. Byrnes reaffirmed that their role was to do nothing more than observe and contain, as needed, until Komatsu's force caught up to them. They would also keep Komatsu informed as to their whereabouts, either directly or through the chief's administrative assistant at the EOC.

Kelly finished and left to join the others on the tarmac just in time to see their helicopter landing.

Chapter 55

IN THE SKIES OVER JAPAN

EARLY EVENING, SAME DAY

The helicopter lifted from the EOC tarmac and headed over the hills to the east. The chopper contained an all-American team.

Soon the rubble of the city of Kobe was lost from view, and they were flying over hilltops, this time following a primary road as it angled its way to the northeast. When they reached a fork, where the arterial split, the helicopter veered north.

It was easy to see what the pilot used as a beacon to guide them. Mt Fuji's cone-shaped peak could easily be seen in the distance as the late afternoon's sun highlighted its magnificence. *This may be known as the land of the rising sun, but the setting sun is just as beautiful,* Kurt thought. *There's no better spectacle.*

Even though the task force had split up, leaving behind their Japanese counterparts, they knew time was too great a factor to return to the embassy and wait for the next call. They could only hope that their reasoning would take them to the right place. Komatsu made it clear that he would be joining them as soon as he could. Takaji also said that he'd had placed a team of police officers on standby in Tokyo when they suspected the bomb was near. This special unit could arrive in a short time by helicopters provided by US army forces. Komatsu and Onish had become quite a team.

The helicopter neared the Aum facility Masa and Kurt had entered. Approaching from the southwest, the Black Hawk rose toward Mt.

Fuji's peak and swung to the east. This placed the sun at their back as they descended. They hoped to view the compound without anyone distinguishing them from any of the other sightseeing aircraft that typically flew in the skies over Mt. Fuji.

As they got closer, Kelly recognized the road they had driven a few times prior to Kurt and Masa's infiltration. She got the attention of the pilot and, using the intercom, described the area. What she didn't realize, however, was that Kurt's attention was drawn elsewhere.

Less than a mile southwest of the structure that Kelly was now pointing at, Kurt noticed more buildings that he realized hadn't been visible in the satellite photos. Some were tucked into the hillside and all were covered by vegetation. He also spotted an obscure road that wound its way well off the main highway to those facilities. It didn't look more than a mile from their original destination.

Byrnes was still guiding the pilot to their destination, so Johnson poked Kelly to get her attention.

Kelly turned and gazed out the starboard side of the helicopter to where Kurt was pointing. The complex the two viewed seemed much more substantial than the compound the pilot was focusing on. Since the wind was gusting and their flight helmets made it difficult to hear, Kurt had to yell to Kelly, "It looks to be more like a military training facility than anything else. What do you think?"

"It also seems close enough to the Aum compound that…they must own all those buildings as well as the land that was marked on the satellite photo. That might be worth looking at." They both glanced around at the others, whose attention was fully focused on what the pilot was saying on the intercom about the Aum compound.

Northrup pointed in the direction of a small clearing a few hundred feet closer to the main road, about fifty yards in from the access route that led south toward the military compound. He said, "If we need to set down, that seems the most likely spot, so far. But let's circle around and see what else we can see."

Most of the flight team maintained their attention on the Aum facility. Kurt and Kelly, however, became more intrigued by the complex to the southwest. Kurt pulled out his binoculars and began looking more closely.

Kurt saw a flat, open field with a structure off to one side that appeared to be more like two, two-story barracks connected by a single-level common-use area. *Possibly a dining hall,* he thought. Just outside that hall were a string of exercise stations with chin-up bars and a succession of horizontal ladders with metal rungs. Just down the way from the billets, a series of sandbags were stacked in walls that bordered on either side of some dirt mounds. Kurt told Kelly that they looked like firing positions directed toward the hillside. Kelly nodded.

They both continued to scan and saw what seemed to be a makeshift heliport in another clearing closer to the main entry road, a few hundred feet from both the main entry road and the northeast corner of the clearing, opposite a corrugated building. Then their eyes simultaneously fell on the flatbed truck parked alongside a large, corrugated metal building. It looked like what they had been looking for, but it sat empty.

Kelly immediately informed Northrup of their findings over the intercom. Northrup, in turn, directed the pilot to change course. The helicopter swung back to land at their initial landing site, which also was the best location for their new destination.

As the helicopter continued toward the landing site, Kurt zoomed in with his binoculars to view the facility more closely. That's when he saw a helicopter that didn't look anything like a Japanese- or US-made aircraft. Kurt handed his binoculars to Kelly and pointed in the direction of the building.

Kelly focused on the open door to the facility and carefully scanned the inside. She saw the helicopter with its blades folded back and informed Kurt it was a Russian-made M-17. As the Black Hawk began its descent, she saw movement inside the hangar. Looking more closely, she noticed people moving about. There was a large lift near the rear of the helicopter.

"Uh oh," Kelly muttered.

"What do you see?" Kurt asked.

"I think I saw the crate," Kelly said.

Again, Kelly activated her intercom and conveyed her observations to Major Northrup.

After landing, Northrup's two teams, directed by his NCOs, dismounted and established a secured perimeter while the pilot had his crew secure the aircraft. Northrup's teams lined up facing south toward the wood line, in the direction of the airstrip's hangar. Northrup instructed them to disperse along the wood line and keep at least five yards between each man.

While the troops headed for the wood line, Northrup called in Kelly and Kurt to clarify what he expected of them, "I'm going to take our two NCOs and take a closer look at the hangar. You two stay here. Johnson, I need you to help Byrnes with the communication equipment. Byrnes, radio Komatsu and give him an update. Then set up the satphone and monitor our radio communications. I want you to be prepared to relay information as needed to the embassy and Komatsu."

"Got it," Kelly and Kurt both responded.

Major Northrup caught up to his team, saw they were correctly positioned and called for his two NCOs to follow him. They moved through the trees, toward the M-17 helicopter.

Kelly pulled out the satphone, while Kurt secured the radio. They selected a location between the helicopter and the main road to set up their equipment. Kurt walked over to the Black Hawk to see if he could see Northrup from there while Kelly made a call to the embassy.

From the Black Hawk, Kurt could no longer see Northrup or any of his people. They had been gone for just over fifteen minutes.

Having worked their way to within fifty yards of the hangar, Northrup and the NCOs checked for the bomb. Just seeing the crate was not enough to take action. They knew they were not to make contact unless there was a direct threat or the Aum tried to move the bomb.

The two NCOs returned to their squads without Northrup. Once they briefed their teams on what they'd found and Northrup's location, they were to maintain their positions along the tree line. One NCO directed one of his men to find Major Johnson and have him join Major Northrup.

"Be careful," Kelly told Kurt, as he left to find Northrup.

Kurt asked the enlisted man why the major wanted him.

"I don't know, sir. I was just told to get you up there ASAP."

"Okay. Let's go." Kurt stayed close behind as the MP led the way through the brush.

As they got closer to the south edge of the tree line, they both lowered to a crawl. The NCO pointed to Major Northrup's position and turned to join the others. Major Johnson crawled up alongside Northrup.

Northrup pointed to the side of the building's entrance. "Look over there. Do you see that barrel?"

"Yes," Kurt responded.

Northrup handed him his binoculars and said, "What do you make of it?"

Kurt scanned the entrance and then zoomed in on the barrel. It was sitting between the entrance and a truck. While he couldn't read the Japanese sign posted just above the container, he was able to recognize the symbols on the side of the container. "I don't know what's in that container, but the symbol indicates it's toxic."

Kurt adjusted his binoculars and tried to get a better focus. "It's hard to distinguish the lettering since the printing is black on dark green, and the container's rotated so I can only see part of it." Then he looked more closely at the truck parked next to the barrel and realized what might be in the container.

"While I can't make out the canister's contents, that truck does match the description Kelly gave of the one used to disperse the toxic fumes at Matsumoto."

"You mean that might be a nerve agent?"

"Possibly," Kurt admitted. "I recommend we act on the side of caution. I'll go back to my kit and get you some atropine injectors, just to be on the safe side."

Kurt quietly made his way back to the helicopter.

Chapter 56

BASE OF MT. FUJI

Haruka, Mori, the security chief, Nogami, and a young, up-and-coming lieutenant, Higuchi, had just exited the Aum compound and gotten into a sedan. Higuchi drove, with the security chief riding up front, and Mori and Haruka seated in the back. The car pulled out and headed toward their other complex, where Higuchi, not long before, had the second bomb offloaded in the hangar. Just a mile up the road, the M-17 helicopter was being prepared for the bomb's final leg of its trip by newly qualified pilot and crew.

As the car made its way up the road, Mori was clearly on edge, concerned that all he'd worked so hard for would not come to pass. When he got word that the first bomb had been disarmed and the security team captured, he was less worried about his boss's response than he was about the North Koreans.

Haruka had struck out at Mori, saying, "We can't afford to have this one bungled, too. Hopefully, setting off the last bomb will enable Pyongyang to turn their army south. We can still make this work if we move fast enough."

A flustered Mori responded, "Everything was planned out perfectly. We had no idea the authorities would intercede." Gesturing toward Nogami he added, "Perhaps if security were tighter, they wouldn't have intercepted our bomb."

Realizing that bickering among his lieutenants would not help the situation, Haruka placed his hand on Nogami's shoulder to calm him and indicate that there was no need for him to respond. He could only think of how the North Korean president might view their failure. "It doesn't really matter how the police were able to find it. What matters now is carrying out the second part of our plan."

Haruka was still convinced that planting the second bomb could be effective. "If we successfully complete this part of our goal and destroy a major portion of the American fleet, that will hinder any UN response to North Korea's invasion. It will also lead our believers to see that we are capable of predicting catastrophic events. Other converts will join us. Our illustrious guru has made predictions like this in the past. Not so grand, but effective. Once our country men and women see how ineffective the current administration is, they'll clamor to join us and want to be part of building a new order for this country."

As hollow as Haruka's statement may have sounded, even Mori became more hopeful. Perhaps Haruka was right, Mori thought. If they succeeded in setting off the second bomb, North Korea's invasion could succeed. And if they didn't succeed, Pyongyang would have greater concerns than Mori's failure.

Their car was approaching the turnoff when Nogami saw the silhouette of an American helicopter in a small open field just off the entry road. He told the driver to pull over. The foursome exited the vehicle and walked to a group of trees where they could stay hidden and see the helicopter more clearly.

The group made their way forward and then stopped abruptly when they heard a woman's voice. They could see that she was using a radio.

Haruka turned to Nogami. "No matter how many people they brought, our Army of White Love can easily overcome them. Go alert them now."

The blow to the back of her head stunned Kelly. Before she could react, hands grabbed her and a rag was shoved roughly into her face. The last thing she remembered was the satphone falling to the ground.

Chapter 57

MT. FUJI COMPLEX

Rummaging through his flight bag in the rear of the helicopter, Kurt found the chemical kit that contained his atropine injectors. Before heading back to Northrup, he walked behind the Black Hawk to check on Kelly. He figured he'd share what he and Northrup had found, but she was nowhere to be seen.

Not far from where he last saw her, he discovered the satphone lying on its side. Kurt realized something wasn't right. He picked up the handset and put it to his ear.

"Hello," he said.

"What happened to Byrnes?"

"Major Jaegar?" Johnson asked.

"Yes, I was talking with Byrnes. She was relaying some information when she stopped midsentence. What's going on?"

Knowing the animosity between the two, Major Johnson said, "She's not available right now. We had an alignment problem with the satellites, but we got that corrected. I know she was giving you an update, so let me finish. Here's how we stand for the moment. The crate is not an immediate threat at this time. We believe we can contain the situation if need be until the Japanese police arrive, but I'm afraid we may have other concerns to deal with besides the crate. We may have spotted the chemical dispersal vehicle used in Matsumoto."

"Anything we can do for you?" Jaegar asked.

"Not at this time. We'll let you know if we need anything."

"Can I talk with Captain Byrnes now?"

"Can't right now. She's on the radio with Chief Komatsu. Sorry, I've got to go." Without giving Jaegar time to respond, Kurt quickly disconnected, he had noticed dust rising near the main road. As he got closer, he spotted a car heading in the direction of the Aum's main compound.

Remembering the importance of getting Northrup the injectors, Kurt located the pilot.

"I have to check something across the road. Could you have one of your men take these injectors up to Major Northrup and monitor the satphone until I get back?"

"Can do. Glad to be doing something until it's time to power up again," the pilot said. He then summoned a crewmember.

Kurt knew the best place to start his search was the compound up the road.

His adrenaline was pumping as he neared the facility. Still a ways off, Kurt saw a woman pulled from a car by two men.

Kurt thought about the guards at the entrance. He knew he didn't have time to make a concealed entrance. There was no time to waste.

Like a football linebacker, he ran straight through the guard at the gate, knocking him back against compound wall. The guard's head hit hard, and he went down. A second guard stepped forward and received Kurt's fist squarely between the eyes. Kurt didn't need to see how the second guard was; he knew he wouldn't be getting up any time soon.

Johnson had stopped just inside when he heard a scream. A man's scream.

As Kurt rounded the corner of a building, he saw Kelly and two men outside a partially opened freight container. One of the men was holding his arm.

Kelly was trying to claw at the other man's face. She wasn't making things easy for them.

Approaching quickly from behind, Kurt drove one man headlong into the container, where he crumpled to the ground.

Kurt helped Byrnes subdue the second man.

"Kelly, are you all right?"

"Oh yeah, having a great time," Kelly responded. "And you?"

A third man appeared from around the corner of the container. Kurt hit him with a fury that surprised even him. Only when the man was down did Kurt recognize him as Mori. The same man had escorted Masa out of the compound during Kurt's escape with Mika.

Byrnes and Johnson had just begun a quick retreat when they heard gunfire.

Chapter 58

MT. FUJI COMPLEX

A s Byrnes and Johnson ran, they realized the gunfire was coming from the vicinity of their helicopter.

When they arrived, they saw the crew initiating takeoff procedures.

"The firing has been coming from that area over there," the crew chief pointed. "Major Northrup radioed for us to prepare for take-off. Obviously there's no longer a concern about drawing attention to ourselves."

Kurt retrieved the radio and handed Kelly the satphone. He contacted Northrup on the radio and asked for an update.

"My NCOs have told me they've encountered a substantial force, but not necessarily an experienced one," Northrup said. "Although we may be outgunned, they're keeping their distance. We're staying in a defensive posture for now."

Northrup suggested to Johnson that he go airborne to get a better view of the situation and report back. Northrup wanted to stay on the ground where he could best command his men.

Byrnes reestablished herself at the communication center while Johnson left in the copter.

What Kurt saw as they rose above the trees astounded him. More men wearing fatigues were flowing out of the barracks. Some had already entered the trees to Major Northrup's left, joining the others already in place. It was obvious their intention was to try and roll up his flank. He also saw a separate squad of men gathering, across an open field, to the right side of the barracks.

Kurt raised Northrup on his radio and shared his observations. Hearing of the reinforcements moving to his left, Northrup ordered one of the NCOs to take his team and shift their line to face that threat.

"No casualties yet," Northrup told Johnson. "They seem to be trying to figure out what to do for now."

Johnson said, "I just hope they don't decide to do something stupid once they increase their numbers. They may feel less cautious once more join them."

"Our highest priority is to safeguard the bomb. So if we have to pull back to the hangar, we will."

"Understood," Kurt said. "Something else. I saw a smaller group gathering in the trees, across the field in front of you. At first I thought they were trying to get a better look at what you're doing. But I see they're now working their way toward the hangar. Watch your right," Johnson warned.

"Will do," Northup responded.

Moments later Kurt's pilot received a radio call from Chief Komatsu. His aircraft had just rounded Mt. Fuji and its silhouette was coming into view. Kurt conveyed instructions to the pilot to land so he could meet up with the chief. He also called Northrup to report Komatsu's arrival.

Johnson briefed Komatsu and Onishi as soon as they touched down.

Once the Japanese team joined Northrup, Northrup filled them in on the Aum's movements.

Komatsu's team circled wide to the right, around the rear of the hangar. From there, he was able to observe the workers inside. As a result of all the gunfire, most were crouched behind the M-17 helicopter. Only two had weapons, and they were keeping an eye out the front of the hangar.

The Komatsu's group entered the hangar from the rear and encountered no resistance. The two armed men quickly dropped their weapons after seeing the weapons pointed their way.

The bomb was secured and the workmen were tied up, but the situation was far from stabilized.

To meet the threat that was making their way along the far side of the field, Komatsu posted three of his officers in the trees near the back corner of the hangar. Two of his men were left to guard the prisoners and one accompanied Onishi. Onishi was to ensure contact was maintained with Northrup's flank.

The chief exited the rear of the hangar to join his three officers outside. Onishi directed his men to a secure location between the corner of the building and Northrup. This allowed them to both monitor Northrup's right flank and maintain contact with the chief's team.

As Onishi stepped from behind the vehicle to make his way back to the hangar door, a barrage of bullets began to hit all around him. The gunfire came from across the field.

Masa promptly ducked back behind the truck. The volume of fire was intense at first. Then Masa heard shouting and the firing ended as abruptly as it began.

Onishi realized why they stopped as he gazed at the chemical tank next to the truck.

They must have realized the danger they were placing themselves in, Masa thought. *The wind is blowing toward them.* Seeing the combatants moving further to the right, Onishi told a guard inside to warn Komatsu.

An exchange of gunfire erupted again, this time between the Aum and Komatsu's officers behind the building. Once the combatants encountered resistance, they stopped firing.

The chief's last order to the task force was clearly heard over the radio, "Hold your ground."

To the west, the sun continued to drop below the hills. There wasn't enough light to make out a silhouette, but everyone's attention was drawn to the east. A distinctive sound reverberated from that direction.

The low roar of multiple helicopters grew louder as they closed from the east. Sporadic gunfire continued to emanate from the Aum troops on both flanks, but the task force held their fire.

As the gunfire tapered off, the helicopters could be heard more clearly.

"Our special unit from Tokyo has arrived," Komatsu announced to his men over the radio. He then switched his radio frequency and notified the special unit commander where his troops were located.

A short time later, the helicopters conducted a quick touch-and-go long enough to allow the special unit to offload behind the Aum's forces.

Komatsu announced on the radio again, "Hold your positions. Let our reinforcements sweep across your front."

Once the Aum realized they were surrounded, they were rounded up with little resistance. Finding themselves in the dark between two forces, confusion reigned, and they threw down their weapons and raised their hands.

Chapter 59

PYONGYANG, KOREA

TWO DAYS LATER

"How much longer?" Kim Il Jong asked his foreign secretary as he poured himself another drink.

With no feel for the ship's actual arrival time, Kim's foreign secretary could only shrug indifferently. "You've received all the reports that I've seen. I don't know any more than you. When our contacts in the South notify us, we'll know." He knew he was taking a risk talking to the president this way, but he also knew he had to be candid and maintain a confidential air if he wanted to keep his trust.

Kim downed his drink in one swig. "I am sick of waiting around like a pregnant cow. We can't keep up this ploy much longer before we lose the element of surprise. We either go within the next three days or risk looking suspicious."

Kim stood once again and began pacing around the room before settling in a chair. "We should have received some sort of message by now," he said. Kim scanned the papers on the table before him, checking the battle deployment positions more closely.

"I was hoping we would as well, Dear Leader," the foreign secretary said. "All the rail cars are in place and have been for some time. So many supplies have been moved forward that finding room for more is a concern. All troop-moving vehicles are in place, ready to mobilize our soldiers at your command."

Kim stared at the military situation map. A few photographs lay scattered about, showing the southern outposts along the border. The head of the North Korean army moved up beside him.

Kim muttered, "We should have known better than to trust this Haruka."

"Maybe it's not Haruka who's at fault here," the foreign secretary said. "He said he tasked Mori with this part of the operation."

"We're at the point now, Dear Leader, where we must either push forward or stand down," Kim's military commander said. "Staying at this level of readiness is risky. We've already received reports that troop buildup is occurring across the border as well."

A senior intelligence analyst entered the room, walked to the foreign secretary, and handed him a message. The secretary read it carefully and said, "Mr. President, this is a report from one of our agents in the South. While the Aum were transporting the bomb to the vessel, the police intercepted it and captured a few Aum operatives. Evidently they had a bomb specialist who was able to disarm it...an American."

"So, it had been activated?" Kim asked.

"Yes. According to the report, a team of Japanese police and Americans were there to help."

Seeing concern on the president's face, the general said, "The South Koreans have crack troops, but even with the thirty thousand UN troops there to support them, they won't have a chance against our overwhelming forces. We currently have three-to-one superior strength within striking distance of the border. We can muster four-to-one superior strength within twenty-four hours and five-to-one within seventy-two hours."

The president just nodded, gazing across the information on the table. He then turned his head slightly toward the general and in monotone said, "In a few days we'll break them at the border. Then what? As long as the UN can gather reinforcements through Pusan's ports we'll have another stalemate at best."

The foreign secretary said, "There's been no indication they captured the second bomb."

"Even if they haven't," Kim Said, "we have to assume the operatives they captured told them all they need to know. Even if they succeed in detonating the other bomb that doesn't change our situation."

Kim pushed the photographs aside. "We have been claiming, through diplomatic channels, that this is just an exercise, yet across the border the South is building up their defenses. I can't help but think they've known all along. Even if Mori is successful in detonating the second bomb, the United Nations forces won't be indecisive in their actions."

President Kim sat back in his chair to think. "The last thing we want is to face off with United Nations troops, once they've been reinforced. Withdraw to our bases," Kim said quietly. "All we can do now is withdraw."

"But, Mr. President, we have the strength to push them out. We're ready," the foreign minister urged.

"Yes, you're right," President Kim agreed. "But unless we destroy their port of entry, we will not succeed." He paused to let these thoughts sink in. "Stand down," he emphasized again.

"Yes, sir," the general looked at the foreign secretary and then back to the president. Hearing no further discussion, he stepped over to the door and looked back at the president, who solemnly waved for him to leave. The general snapped to attention, saluted, and took his leave.

Looking glum, all the foreign secretary could do was sit with the president and wait for further orders.

"Mori needs to know that failure has a price," the president said quietly.

The foreign secretary looked at the president.

"One thing my father taught me," Kim said, "was the virtue of showing patience before making a judgment about one's allies or enemies. Another was to show no mercy."

The foreign secretary quietly stood and exited the room. He knew what had to be done.

Chapter 60

TOKYO, JAPAN

Major Ted Northrup, Major Kurt Johnson, Captain Masa Onishi, and Captain Kelly Byrnes, along with the other task force members, had endured what seemed like endless debriefings over the last few days. They covered everything from joint training, police and military protocols and practices, and communication as well as equipment needs. When they thought they were done, the military officers were told to report for one more meeting at the US embassy in Tokyo, to meet with Colonel Jackson, Brigadier General Byrnes, and Ambassador Murdock.

When they reached the ambassador's office, Captain Byrnes was first to enter. Her father greeted her with a big smile and a warm hug. Once she was released from his embrace, she noticed Major Carl Walker standing just behind the general. Kelly embraced her dear friend as well. "Carl, what are you doing here?"

"I invited him," General Byrnes responded. "Since he was monitoring the events you have been part of, I thought he might benefit from joining me on a quick trip here."

"Which I appreciate greatly since you were always rather cryptic about what you were involved in during our last couple of phone conversations. I couldn't pass up the opportunity to hear the real story and see how you've been."

Kelly smiled and said, "I couldn't say anything because I really wasn't sure what we were getting into."

Once eveyone was settled in their chairs, the purpose of the meeting became clear. It was to celebrate their success and also update them on what occurred as a result of their actions.

"This success is not one we can celebrate publicly with medals," General Byrnes said. "There will be enough information out in the public about the Aum's atrocities to concern the citizens of Japan. If the public knew what we were involved in and what could have happened if you had not succeeded...well, we just can't let that happen."

All the officers nodded.

General Byrnes continued, "We've looked into the North Korean situation and found that unless we can prove a direct link to the Aum organization, we can't press the issue. Accusing them of planning to invade South Korea would not benefit anyone. In fact, it would hamper any further negotiations." Byrnes looked at Maddock to expand on his comment.

"Our main goal is to get them back to the negotiation table. We don't want to do anything that might hinder that," the ambassador said. He then added, "At least publically. Behind the scenes, we're making it clear to the North Korean leadership that we know they have been working with members of the Aum organization to further develop their atomic weapon systems. And while we could bring this to the public's attention, we've chosen not to in order to save them any greater disgrace. On the other hand, publicly, we'll refer to the misuse of their nuclear technology. That, combined with everyone's awareness that they've been testing their missile system, is enough to demonstrate further proliferation of their nuclear weapons program. We'll rely on the international community to put pressure on them to get back to the negotiations table." Murdock closed with, "That may be oversimplifying the situation, but that's how things stand for now." Murdock looked at General Byrnes.

"So we want to congratulate each of you on a job well done," Byrnes said, "and hope you understand why we cannot document any public recognition of your achievements."

"We've already had discussion about this, sir. I believe I speak for everyone when I say we understand and have no problem with that," Northrup said.

"Now that you're finished with this little escapade," General Byrnes said, "you'll be going back to your regular jobs, so I encourage you to take some time off."

"You've earned it," the ambassador added.

From this point in the meeting, discussions became more informal and relaxed.

Finally Onishi spoke up, "Since I first got Major Johnson involved during a dinner at my home, the least I could do is invite you all to a small family dinner this evening to honor his departure."

"Isn't that a bit of short notice for your wife?" Kelly asked.

"Actually, I've already discussed it with her. She thought it would be a great idea and has already begun making preparations. As it so happens, our children will be having a sleepover with some friends down the street. So you won't have to worry about them."

General Byrnes responded, "That sounds like a great plan. I'd like to join you, but I'm afraid Colonel Jackson, Major Walker, and I will have to forego your little celebration. We're all flying out to South Korea in two hours. We're briefing the commander of the Pacific Command at his headquarters in Seoul first thing in the morning. Kurt, you deserve a great send off. I appreciate all that you've done for us."

"Thank you, General. I'm glad I could help."

"Major Northrup and Captain Onishi, thank you for looking after my daughter," General Byrnes added with a smile and a wink directed toward Kelly.

Major Northrup quickly responded with, "I don't think she needs any looking after, General. She's as good as any seasoned soldier I've ever worked with. I'd feel fortunate to have her working on my team anytime, anywhere."

After allowing an appropriate pause in the conversation, Masa directed his next comment to the three other invitees and said,

"Dinner will be at six thirty p.m. If you'd like to come earlier to visit, you're more than welcome."

Northrup looked at Kurt and then back to Masa and said, "That sounds great to me. How about you, Kurt?"

"Since I'm taking the red-eye flight back to Seattle tonight, I've already checked out of my room back at Camp Zama. In fact, my bags are packed and in Major Northrup's car. He was nice enough to give me a ride here, and we were going out to dinner from here before the airport anyway, so that's fine with me," Kurt said.

"Then that's settled," Northrup confirmed.

Kurt decided to add, "I just need to make sure I'm at the airport by eleven p.m. A good meal will help me sleep through the long flight back."

Looking at Major Northrup, Kelly said, "I know the airport is the opposite direction for you, since you've got to get back to Camp Zama. I can give Kurt a ride to the airport after dinner. But if you can give him a ride to Masa's place, that will give me a chance to stop by my place for a change of clothes."

"Good. Seeing that you're all set for dinner and the trip home, it seems to me this meeting is over," General Byrnes said as he stood. Looking at Colonel Jackson, he added, "Well, Joe, I guess we've got a plane to catch as well."

This signaled everyone to stand. Before parting, Kelly said good-bye to her father and then turned to Carl. As she approached him, she noticed he had a big smile.

"What are you grinning about?" Kelly asked.

"I'm just glad to see that you've lost the starch. You've even got a certain glow about you, too. And I think I know where that came from." He looked toward Kurt, then smiled again.

Knowing what Carl was alluding to, Kelly could only smile in return.

An hour later the General, Colonel Jackson, and Major Walker were on their plane heading back to Korea while Northrup and Kurt joined Masa at his home.

Two hours later, Kurt was still sitting with Northrup and Masa, eating snacks, drinking, and making small talk, while awaiting Kelly's arrival. Kurt was beginning to wonder if she would make it at all. "Is Kelly often late?" he asked, looking at Masa.

"Don't worry, traffic is probably heavy." It was still fifteen minutes before dinner was scheduled. "I've never known Kelly to be late for anything."

A few moments later, there was a knock at the door.

Masa answered it, stepped back, and said, "Wow, Kelly, you look great." He led her back to the living room where the other two men rose. Northrup immediately responded with a similar compliment, while Kurt stood silently and stared.

Am I feeling the effects of the liquor or is it Kelly? Kurt thought.

"Hey, Kurt, are you going to say something, or are you just going to let Kelly stand there?"

Kelly wore a low-cut black dress, a simple gold chain with a diamond pendent, and matching diamond earrings. While Kurt had always thought she was attractive, tonight she looked stunning. "You look terrific, Kelly."

"Why thank you, Kurt," Kelly stated.

"You're just in time. Dinner is ready. Shall we move to the dining room?" Masa said.

Kurt thought he felt Kelly's hand brush his as she passed in front of him. *This could be an interesting evening*, he thought.

When it came time to leave, Kelly drove Kurt to the airport. Once they arrived, Kelly dropped him off in front of the check-in entrance and went to park the car. By the time she returned, Kurt had already checked his bag and was waiting near the counter.

Kurt didn't know how to handle his good-bye with Kelly. When she came up to him, the embrace and long kiss just seemed natural.

"You realize this makes my departure more difficult, don't you?"

"On the contrary, it will make the return easier."

EPILOGUE

Led by Chief Komatsu, the officers of the TMPD made up the special unit who took the lead in the investigation. With all that needed to be done, and with so many Aum members involved, it took some time to gather enough evidence to justify a raid. The charges against the Aum included kidnapping, illegal confinement, extortion, murder, forgery, and the production of firearms, biochemical agents, and explosives.

It wasn't until late into March that a search would be carried out on the pretext that the Aum had kidnapped a man who wanted to leave the group. Hundreds of police officers searched their facilities across the nation.

Like many of the Aum members, Haruka, Mori, and the guru were roused early at their compound. Thanks to intelligence provided by Kurt's initial visit, two other top lieutenants were found hiding in a secret basement of Satian 2.

Justice, in some cases, would take years, while Mori's demise was more immediate. One evening on the last full weekend of April, Hideo Mori was stabbed to death outside the Aum's Tokyo headquarters. The man found responsible for his death was originally thought to be a Japanese man named Kiroyuki Jo. Later, his true identity was established, he was a twenty-nine-year-old Korean named So Yu Haeng.

Only one important member was still missing following the long, arduous investigative efforts and massive roundup by the National Police Agency. Yasuo Higuchi remained at large and was last reported to be in Thailand. Otherwise, all the major players were accounted for.

Even after the raid, the Aum leaders continued to strike back. It was the last Sunday of March when an attempt was made on Chief Takaji Komatsu's life. Early in the morning, a chauffeur-driven car was sent to pick him up at home and then head to the National Police Agency. His aid greeted him in the lobby, held an umbrella for him, and they walked to the car. It was then that an unknown assailant shot Takaji four times, twice in the chest and once in the abdomen and leg. The chief survived, even more determined to bring the Aum to justice. Masa continued to visit his friend throughout this period.

Even as the police mustered for a massive assault of their own against the Aum Shrinrikyo, a retaliation was being planned. One that would never be forgotten—a sarin gas attack on Tokyo's subway system.

Almost a year after the sarin attack in Matsumoto, police absolved Yoshiyuki Kono, whom they had falsely accused of causing the gas incident. His wife remained in a coma for fourteen years before she died in August of 2008.

A month after Kurt went back to the states, he returned to Japan to fulfill his obligation to work in the exercise his orders were originally intended for. Kelly and Kurt saw a great deal of each other during that time.

As the trials progressed, Kurt received updates through regular correspondence from his newfound friends. He found it puzzling that such significant international events as he had witnessed had been buried in the local news by the capture and trial of O.J. Simpson.

28742407R00164

Made in the USA
Charleston, SC
18 April 2014